THE TRUTH

ABOUT
EVERYTHING

BRIDGET FARR

THE TRUTH ABOUT EVERYTHING

BRIDGET FARR

Mendota Heights, Minnesota

The Truth About Everything © 2022 by Bridget Farr. All rights reserved.
No part of this book may be used or reproduced in any manner
whatsoever, including internet usage, without written permission from
Flux, except in the case of brief quotations embodied in critical articles
and reviews.

First Edition
First Printing, 2022

Book design by Karli Kruse
Cover design by Maggie Villaume
Cover illustration by Millie Liu

Flux, an imprint of North Star Editions, Inc.

This is a work of fiction. Names, characters, places, and incidents are
either the product of the author's imagination or are used fictitiously,
and any resemblance to actual persons living or dead, business
establishments, events, or locales is entirely coincidental.

Library of Congress Cataloging-in-Publication Data
Names: Farr, Bridget, author.
Title: The truth about everything / Bridget Farr.
Description: First edition. | Mendota Heights, Minnesota : Flux, 2022. |
   Audience: Grades 10–12.
Identifiers: LCCN 2022017241 (print) | LCCN 2022017242 (ebook) | ISBN
   9781635830804 (hardcover) | ISBN 9781635830811 (ebook)
Subjects: CYAC: Schools--Fiction. | High schools--Fiction. | Belief and
   doubt--Fiction. | Survivalism--Fiction. | Family life--Montana--
   Fiction. | Montana--Fiction. | LCGFT: Novels.
Classification: LCC PZ7.1.F3678 Tr 2022 (print) | LCC PZ7.1.F3678
   (ebook) | DDC [Fic]--dc23
LC record available at https://lccn.loc.gov/2022017241
LC ebook record available at https://lccn.loc.gov/2022017242

Flux
North Star Editions, Inc.
2297 Waters Drive
Mendota Heights, MN 55120
www.fluxnow.com

Printed in the United States of America

This book is for anyone who has ever answered
one of my many questions,
and for me, who has never been afraid to ask.

BEFORE

Mom told me a story once about a man who built an enormous boat. And because he spoke another language, he called it an *ark*, but really it was just a boat. Apparently, god was so mad that he decided to make it rain and rain until the whole world was covered in water. Mom didn't know why, really, but she said probably murder. God's anger would send a flood to swell up over every piece of land.

Water and rain to wipe it all away.

But god loved one man so much he told him to prepare for the flood. The man was to build a boat (the ark) to save his family. But not just that. He had to take all of the animals in the whole world (except fish because of the water) and put them in the ark, as many as he could fit.

When the man started building this huge boat, bigger than anyone had ever imagined, people started to make fun of him. *What are you going to do with such a big boat?* They laughed, patting their murderous bellies and scratching their murderous chins. *There's no water near here! We live in a desert.*

They didn't know the rain was coming.

Just like all the people around here didn't know the danger. Still don't. Like the people in the story, they look up and see bright blue skies. They weren't ready for Y2K, and they weren't ready for the Great Recession. Now they still aren't prepared for earthquakes, asteroids, nuclear attacks, or the government takeover. They live like they can't see the clouds above.

But we do. Dad says religion is the opioid of the masses, but we aren't that different from the man with the ark. Like him, we prepare. Mom and I can and store apples and choke-cherries and even some peaches Dad buys in August from the Elks Lodge in town. We stew tomatoes and boil all the fresh corn, mixing it with salt and butter before sealing it up tight. I hardly get to taste the fresh bits of summer. Dad and I hunt year-round, carefully sneaking onto nearby land to bag the bucks we watch all season. He doesn't care about tags or Fish and Wildlife. They're all government, anyway. Each time Dad comes back from a trucking job, he brings more supplies to store in the cellar: kerosene, bandages, hunting knives, two used rifles, a scratched-up pistol, and a radio you power just by turning the crank. Last winter, Dad took down some of his books and lined them up in alphabetical order. He bought extra batteries for the flashlight. Instead of cramming the ark with lions and spiders, we fill up the cellar.

Grandma Betty thinks we're crazy. "Your dad should be worrying about feeding his family, not preparing for the apoc-alypse," she says, but Dad's friends on the internet believe him. They're building their own life-saving arks in their basements.

I believe Dad, too.

Most times.

After his flood, the man in the story got a new world. He parked the ark on a mountainside and let the animals out, back to find their homes in the prairie or a far-off jungle. Back to grazing and hunting and swatting the flies away because remember, he brought those, too.

The man got a dove and a rainbow as a reward for his preparation.

Dad got a cellar full of canned chokecherries and a couple of used rifles.

We're still waiting for the rain.

Homeschool versus Government School

Homeschool	Government School
Useful	Pointless information
Practical	Government propaganda
No teachers to hold me back	Holding tank
Independence	Rules to make me a sheep
My mind is my own	Unnecessary information
	Lazy teachers
	Boring
	Germ factory

CHAPTER 1

The fish in my hands is too small to eat, but I don't want to let it go. My fingers slide along its scales, gliding against the shine one direction, then scuffing against it on the other. Fish have gills—Dad told me that—to breathe instead of lungs, but what's inside those little flaps? I don't know. Does the air rush inside and mix around with their flesh and suddenly they're breathing? Is that why they jump from the water in the evening? They've been holding their breath the whole time?

This fish is too small to eat, so I have to let it go. I squeeze down behind its gills, watching out for the sharp ends of the fin. The hook is off to one side of its mouth, ripping a small hole in its skin. Under the pressure of my hand, I twist the hook loose, holding the metal tight so it doesn't swing in the breeze. I don't want to get caught on a hook again. I toss the fish back into the murky water; it pauses before swimming away.

"No luck?" Dad yells, and I turn to see him sitting ten yards from me along the dam. His camp chair is so close to the water I can just see his cap through the reeds. He's wearing his blue jacket, my favorite one with the soft lining. He's never too hot, even though it's almost ninety degrees out here. His feet are in the water, his boots and wool socks somewhere on the shore beside him. Dad leans back in his chair so he can see me.

"You wanna stay here for a while or go with me down to Mike's?"

I rest my pole against the dirt, its skinny line getting mixed up with the reeds that are almost taller than my head. Another pain ripples across my stomach. It feels tight, full, even though I'm not. I never am.

"Why are we going to Mike's?" I ask, making my way toward Dad and the coolers.

"Mike's got an old generator he's going to let me boost some parts from." Our backup generator has been down for a few months. Dad smiles. "And he wants to show me this new hunting rifle he got. Idiot bought it at Cabela's, so now he's in the system—they always get you with Form 4473—but it still sounds pretty sweet."

Of course Mike did. He still gets deer and elk tags from Fish and Wildlife. He doesn't know that any act that *could* lead to confiscation of his guns *will* lead to confiscation. I shake my head.

When I reach Dad, I open the top of his small Styrofoam cooler. Two fish lie side by side in the water. He did better than me. One's a northern pike, almost a foot long, but I don't recognize the other.

"What's that one?"

Dad leans over to look. He shrugs. "Not sure."

Dad is not sure about some things and one hundred percent sure about everything else. I used to ask him all my questions: Do bees eat their honey? How does power become light inside a bulb? Why is there a positive and negative terminal inside the motorcycle battery and what's a volt? Dad is my teacher. Him and the mail-order packets. Or, they used to be. When school was actually hours marked in the day.

But Dad doesn't always know what he thinks he knows. So I don't ask anymore.

I dig in the plastic cooler, but all that's left are Snickers wrappers. I wanted to try one.

"You ate them all?"

"You know those ain't for you."

Yes, I know. No processed sugar for me because my body is still pure. I've only ever eaten food from the earth, from our harvest. Or Shake 'N Bake from Grandma Betty, but Dad doesn't know about that.

"You want some jerky? There's a bag in the truck."

I don't. I tell him so. I'll ignore the ache until we get home. Hope it doesn't get worse. If so, a tablespoon of apple cider vinegar might help. Or a cup of mint tea.

"Go get your poles, then, so we can head down to Mike's quick. I want to get home and try and fix that generator before I leave tomorrow."

"Where you going this week?" I ask, though I don't really know the places he goes anyway. Casper. Steamboat Springs. Ponca. Ponca City. Lincoln. Tulsa. We have a map that Mom and I use to track the roads Dad travels, the places he gets to see. Routes become a blue river, the same lines going back and forth with a few stretches to the sides, like Mom waking up in the morning, her arms and legs extending.

"West Coast," he says, gesturing with his hand like he's swatting a fly. "Bellevue. Means 'beautiful view' in French, but I'm sure whoever named it hasn't been there."

Dad took French in high school. He went to high school. Well, sometimes. Most times. When he wanted to. I don't know if Bellevue actually means "beautiful view," but it sounds like it could.

"I'll go get my stuff."

My boots slip in the green algae on the shore. That's why I don't swim in the dam much anymore. I hate the way it slides over my body, clinging to my hair. I pick up my Tractor Supply hat, my pole, the mason jar of dirt and worms Mom packed yesterday. Dad's already throwing his chair in the back of Big Green, the old Ford truck that used to be Uncle Charles's before he stopped being able to drive. I lay my pole down in the back on top of the metal rods and firewood and some orange extension cords. I really like this pole and don't want it to break.

"You drive," Dad says with a yawn, and we cross behind the truck, our arms brushing as we pass. Dad whistles as he hops in, slamming the truck door since it doesn't close good on that side. He'll be asleep in minutes.

I clunk off the mud on my boots on the edge of the truck before hopping in. I inhale the mix of diesel and the scratchy fabric seats woven in shades of green. I've been driving since I was nine, and it's never gotten old. Not like feeding the chickens or weeding the garden. This responsibility feels like freedom. I grab the keys out of the ash tray. My foot presses down the clutch all the way to the dusty floor, trapping a few pieces of grass.

"You can hang with Alex when we get there," Dad says, his head tilted against the glass like he might fall asleep any minute.

I know. That's why I'm going.

CHAPTER 2

Big Green bounces over the dried mud ridges in Mike's driveway. We pull up next to the gas tank and the enormous satellite. I don't know what they use it for. Across the dirt lot, Mike's grandson, Alex, is shooting hoops at the rim attached to the barn. Each time the ball bounces off the wall, red paint chips shower the ground. The whole barn sags to one side, like the wind is slowly blowing it over or the world got too heavy to carry on its aluminum roof. I tap Dad's knee since he's still snoring lightly. He fell asleep halfway here. The bumps in the dirt road make Mom carsick. They put Dad to sleep.

"Shouldn't take longer than twenty minutes," Dad says, as he jumps out the side of the truck. "You go play with Alex."

I sit in the hot truck with my hands pressed to my stomach, watching Dad cross to the yellow-and-white garage next to the house. Just like the barn, the paint on the garage is chipping off, and the wood is scuffed at the bottom of the open garage door. Inside is a maze of tools and old tractor parts. In November, Mike might even have a deer carcass hanging from the rafters. Mike is the only person Dad really spends time with except for me and Mom. They're not really friends—I'm not sure Dad has friends anymore—but Mike helped Dad a lot when he and Mom first moved out to the farm. He thought Dad was a little kooky for wanting to live off-grid, making all our food and not paying taxes. Mike's been a farmer and rancher his whole life, but he doesn't hate the government. At least not as much as Dad. Mike even has some fields in CRP, Conservation Reserve Program, which Dad says is just another step in the government takeover. Mike calls it money.

The basketball bangs against the front of the truck. I open my door.

"Hey! Knock that off!"

Alex smiles as he scoops up the ball. He's still wearing clothes from football practice in town, sweat ringing the edge of his tank top. Alex goes to public school on the reservation in Wolf Point, where I would go if I went to school, even though I'm not part Native American like him. His brown skin is darkened tan from a summer helping his grandpa, and wet strands of his long hair cling to his temples. I look away as he pulls his shirt up to wipe his face.

Alex has lived at Mike's place off and on since he was little. Back then, his mom was trying to work three jobs and take care of a baby while his dad, Mike's son, was causing her trouble with all the drugs he was into. Meth, mostly. His grandma in town's sick a lot—cancer, maybe, or something with her lungs—so it was easier for Mike to watch Alex. Mike likes kids, he says. Even though his own son didn't really turn out.

Alex lives with his mom now, so I don't see him as often as I used to. Last summer, I helped him fix up an old truck of Mike's, but then he didn't come back much once school started. I'm grateful for the summers, when he helps Mike with harvest and asks me to play basketball.

I ignore the pain spreading from my stomach to my head and get out of the truck. Alex shoots—a swish if there was a net hanging. Instead, the ball clangs through the metal circle and down against the barn door before rolling out to me. I pick it up.

"Let's see what you got, Home School." Alex wipes sweat off his forehead with the back of his hand. My own sweat collects under my arms, my thighs.

"I don't play."

"You said that last time. Then you played."

I take a step forward, my boot rocking in the mud rut. Hard to get footing in this mess.

"You can always shoot it granny-style," Alex says, motioning with his hands between his legs as he pretends to arch a basketball up toward the rim.

I rest the ball in my right hand, up next to my shoulder like I've watched Alex do a hundred times. I bend my knees and then push. The ball arches and bangs off the barn nowhere near the rim. Dust coats my fingers, and I brush them off onto my jeans.

"Want to play Horse?" Alex asks, running up to shoot a layup.

"Fine." He'll win. I'll lose. It's still fun. "When do you start school again?"

"Next week," Alex says as he paces out so far from the rim, he's almost at the gas tank. He takes a quick run before his arms shoot into the sky. The ball bangs off the rim. Thankfully. I'd never make that shot.

"And now you're . . . a what?"

"A junior."

"Your last year?"

"No. One more after this."

Alex bounces me the ball. It swerves off another rut, and I

have to jump to grab it. I walk as close to the basket as possible. A sharp pain pulses in my stomach again.

"Do you like school?" I ask.

"I like basketball. And my computer classes."

I send the ball up and it bangs off the backboard and into the hoop. *Yes!*

Alex grins. "You're getting better." He takes the ball from me and pushes me aside with his hip so he can stand exactly where I was when I made my shot. A familiar tingle runs through me. Alex launches the ball, his muscles flexing as he releases. Of course it goes in.

I move a few feet back, but stay on the same side. I throw the ball up and it bounces off the rim. Alex grabs it on the run and dribbles up toward the right side of the hoop, lifting up into the air as he shoots with his right hand.

"Do you wish you could go to real school?" he asks after rebounding his own shot. "Or is homeschool awesome?"

Homeschool *might* be awesome, but I don't do the school part much anymore. It's just home. And chores. Mom taught me the basics—letters and numbers and songs that some-times still pop into my head. *The ants go marching two by two, hurrah, hurrah.* Dad used to order packets from a homeschool website. My favorite was the history one. There were lots of pictures, and in my favorite section, a part about a king who put all these warriors in his grave. Horses, too. On days Mom couldn't get out of bed, she'd tell me to go ahead and read the stories to myself. Reading was hard. Still is. Most days I skipped it, and she never asked.

When it rained and Dad couldn't work in the fields, he'd take over, read to me, tell me about the Founding Fathers, the heroes of Justus Township, a scientist named Albert Einstein. One time he put baking soda and vinegar in a jar that spewed all over the counter. A volcano. An experiment. I still don't really know about either.

Eventually, money got tight. Wheat prices were too low. The garden didn't produce. Dad got the rig and went back to driving truck. Mom spent more time in her room. Some weeks, there was no fuel for the generator. Not enough meat in the fridge.

The packets had to go. They were crap anyway, Dad said. Just a way for the companies to rip us off. I could learn without them.

I didn't.

I've asked him a few times since if we could get more packets. He laughed—what kid wants more homework?—and handed me a book instead. *Read this.* I would if I could.

But I can't.

Alex throws me the ball so hard it bounces against my chest. I grab it and move over to that side of our dirt court. I look at the hay-covered ground, wondering how I'll ever be able to dribble when the ground is so uneven. I keep my eyes down as I dribble the ball so slowly Alex starts laughing behind me. It doesn't bounce high enough for me to keep going, so I grab it and shoot from where I am, trying to stretch my body the way Alex does, wondering if I'll ever be able to arch and curve like him. The ball doesn't make it to the hoop.

"You've got an H now."

"I know."

"So, is it sweet? Not having to go to school? Get to do whatever you want."

"I don't get to do whatever I want."

Alex moves even farther back this time, his feet covered in the weeds that surround the base of the gas tank. "I have chores, too, at my mom's and sometimes here. Still beats going to school."

I don't know if that's true. Maybe my life really is better. Dad thinks so. Mom doesn't think much of anything anymore. I don't mind chores. I don't often get that burst of energy in my chest like when I'm riding the motorcycle or looking at the clouds before a storm. Mostly, it's just quiet. A quiet that makes me wonder what else could be going on inside my brain if I went to school.

The ball swoops into the rim. "What do you learn at school this year?" I ask.

Alex smiles a wide grin, his front chipped tooth showing though he normally likes to hide it.

"I don't know," he says, grabbing the ball and handing it to me. "Back up."

I take a few steps backward with the ball. Alex steps closer, moving me with his body. I smell the tang of his sweat. I wonder if he can smell mine. "Keep going. Keep going."

My back is almost pressed to the gas tank. "You didn't go back this far."

"Fine, you can scoot forward a few steps. Stop!"

"But you get to play basketball, right? If you go to school."

Alex nods. "All sports, but stop stalling and shoot."

My arms should be pretty strong from all the stuff I haul for Dad. I bend my legs, ready to run. I take a breath, smelling the alfalfa from the pony pen to our right. I run a few steps and lunge my body and the ball forward. It sails up in an arc and through the hoop.

"Yes!" I shout, twirling with my hands outstretched.

"Whoa," Alex says, his face distorted. "Um, Lark, you've got . . . stuff on your . . . you know, pants."

I look down at my jeans but see nothing but some mud from the dam and the damp hems.

"What?" I ask. He can't be talking about mud.

He shakes his head, his cheeks turning red. "No . . . on the back. You can use the bathroom in the house. Just leave your boots on the cardboard in the garage."

I reach a hand back and feel wet. I pull my hand forward to see the tips of my fingers covered in red. I know what this is.

I lost a baby.

Babies

What I Know	**What I Don't**
Small	Why they die
Fragile	What their cry sounds like
Gift from god (according to Mom)	When they can walk
Bundle of cells (according to Dad)	What a baby head smells like
Precious	How I got one
Animals mate to make babies; Humans love	
Should take 280 days (roughly the same as a calf)	
Getting them out is blood and pain	
Head smells good (people say)	

CHAPTER 3

'm an only child, but I share a room. The crib has been here longer than I've been in the world as a plan or even a thought. It sits across the room from my twin bed, both of us pressed next to the pale blue walls, a window for each of us where the light streams in so bright in the mornings I never need Dad to wake me. We both have quilts; mine even has some of the same fabric, a puzzle piece of connection from across the room. But that quilt came before me, just like the crib and the single baby dress Mom sewed before she gave up. She wanted to make all of the clothes for her babies. Wanted to make her own clothes, too, but apparently, it's a lot harder to sew pants and skirts and make your own bras. Seams, wires, buttons, all that. Now the sewing machine sits in the corner of her and Dad's room, a backup clothes rack to hold her clothes.

I'm an only child, but I'm not the oldest. Before me was Augustine, who was old enough for Mom and Dad to know he was a boy. He died at twenty-four weeks. Then came Ashton and Aspen, both gone before the doctors could tell. Mom loves to talk about my siblings. She tells me stories about how she picked their names, what our family would be like if we were more than double in size. I think about all my invisible siblings whenever I'm hoeing in the garden or canning with Mom. Not because it would be less work, but maybe it would be more fun. It would be nice to have a friend who wasn't also my mother. Above the crib is a shelf with three picture frames of six tiny feet, their names and dates printed in Mom's crooked handwriting.

After the first babies, Mom and Dad moved here to the farm. Mom stopped being a CNA at the nursing home, and Dad left his job as a truck driver for the oil companies. They came here, away, to Uncle Charles's farm now that Uncle Charles was living in Wolf Point at the same nursing home Mom just left. Dad read about it on the internet, information zinging to him from the sky: people who left the city to grow their own food and raise their own animals and live off the land and suddenly they had babies. Babies were waiting for you in the country. They couldn't be born in town with all the pollution and politics and doctors who think they know everything just because they went to a fancy college. They don't know any better than us, Dad always says.

And I'm proof.

A year after Mom and Dad moved into the yellow house and planted a garden and bought some chickens, Mom had me.

Eventually, Dad gave up on farming and went back to driving truck, but we still grow all our own food, burn our own firewood that Dad cuts down at the coulee over by Mike's. But even with the homegrown food and chemical-free air and the homemade soap, Mom started losing the babies again. There's six of us now. Avery came and left when I was five. Ave went last spring. A few others came and went, not here long enough to know if they really even existed.

I'm the only child who walks in the house, but not the only one who lives here.

CHAPTER 4

In minutes, Dad joins me in the truck.

"You okay, Larkie-Loo?" he asks, and I nod but can't speak. I lean forward, trying not to sit too heavy so I don't get blood on the seat. I press my arms against my stomach, hoping the pressure will ease some of the pain. And the bleeding.

"I'll get you home," Dad says as he starts the engine. Out the side window, Alex is standing next to Mike, the basketball on his hip. They don't wave like they normally do when we pull out of their driveway. I rest my head against the dashboard, feeling the grime pressing a line across my forehead.

The bumps on the dirt road are making me sick. I roll down the window, letting dusty air in to cover my hair and fill my lungs. Dad chomps on another Snickers bar—where did he get that?—bits of chocolate spraying as he whistles an unfamiliar song. What did Alex tell him? He doesn't seem worried. Does he not know about the baby? A pain surges in my stomach, lower, underneath my belly button. I press a hand against my body. Mom talked about this part. Your body getting the baby out.

But how?

Mom says babies are a gift from god, which is why he wants them back. She says babies are made of love, a touch, some sounds I've heard at night, I'll-know-when-I'm-older. Human babies are made with hope, not like the climbing, thrusting rush of animals.

Babies are a gift from god, but I didn't ask for one.

My body curls as I almost throw up. I don't. Just choke out a cough. I'm scared but I don't want to be.

"Almost there, Larkie," Dad says, stuffing his wrapper into the ashtray. It's so full of other wrappers that it doesn't close all the way. I crunch a few more beneath my feet.

Finally, I can see our trees and sit back, my hand on the door handle so I can bolt from this truck the minute it stops. We pull up next to the house, and I jump out before we've parked.

"Hey! We gotta bring in these fish!" Dad calls, but I keep running.

On the porch, I press one foot to the heel of my boot to free it and use my toes to dig myself out of the other. The house is hot and dark, Mom's blankets still covering the windows until the night breeze comes. I race to the bathroom, slamming the door closed behind me. Inside, I grab a brown towel and lay it on the floor. I pull off my pants, noticing the red circle that is the size of my palm. I take off my underwear. The center strip is red, too. It'll stain brown, just like the pairs I've washed of Mom's and hung on the line to dry. Mom says the sun will bleach it out. It never does. Rolling them into a ball, I lay them on the corner of the towel. I sit down in the center to wait for what comes next.

I hope it doesn't hurt too bad.

A hand slaps onto the door. "Open up," Mom calls, her voice deep like she's barely awake. She probably just got out of bed. The handle turns and Mom's head appears in the open door. Her hair falls down the side of her face, the curls knotting together. Her eyelids droop as she looks me over.

"What's wrong, baby? Daddy says you got sick."

"I..."

She reaches down and grabs my pile of clothes with the tips of her fingers, lifting up my pants by the leg.

"Oh, Lark," she sighs, dropping the pants down onto the floor.

"I don't know how it happened."

Mom leans her head against the door. "You're just that age."

I didn't know age mattered. Babies coming and going like getting taller or snow in the winter.

"How long will it take?" I ask, but I know. I remember Mom and the babies: a few days of bleeding, a few months of tears.

"Not long," she says. "Maybe a week." That sounds right. I wince, another stab of pain bending me over. "Cramps? I'll get you a castor oil pack and make some willow bark tea."

Mom reaches out, rubbing her hand in circles on my back. A flutter in my chest joins the pain in my stomach.

"I don't have a name yet," I whisper.

Mom tilts her head. "What?"

"I didn't know so I didn't think of a name. I don't have any names."

Augustine. Ashton. Aspen. Avery. Ave. Everyone has a name.

Mom pushes into the room so I have to slide back, trying to drag the towel with me.

"A name for what?"

"The baby." The words are squeezed out of me as another wave of pain crushes my stomach.

"A baby? Did you ... ?" Mom's eyes are huge and she shakes her head. "With who? Alex? When are you even alone?"

"We're not! We just play basketball."

Mom crouches down so she's staring right into my eyes.

"Have you and Alex ever been alone together? Be honest with me."

"No."

"And do you and Alex ever do anything besides play basketball?"

"No. Not really."

"Not really?"

"No!"

"And when you're together, you never . . . take your clothes off?"

I pull back. "No!"

"Not even once?"

I shake my head. Why is she asking me all this?

Suddenly, Mom smiles, the corners of her lips pulling up to show her crooked teeth, and now she's laughing. Laughing so hard she falls back against the door, stretching her legs out over my towel and the pile of clothes. The sound echoes in the bathroom. She's never laughed like this with the others. She cried. Or was quiet. But never laughing.

"Oh, Lark," she finally says when she gulps a breath. "You're not pregnant. It's just your period."

She laughs again, this time bending at her waist, her hair flopping onto the floor. She looks up and tears are in her eyes, but she's still smiling.

"You have to have . . . well, you just, you know. It's not a baby. This is just what your body does."

This isn't funny.

She wipes her eyes with the back of her hand. "I guess I should have told you, but I can't believe you're that age already.

Honestly, you should have gotten it sooner. Fifteen is pretty old, but I don't know. Maybe 'cause you're so thin?"

"So, it's not a baby?"

"No, baby," she says, reaching forward to touch my face. "Remember, babies come from god and god didn't give you a baby. This is just your body preparing to have a child. Someday. When god wants it."

"Is it supposed to hurt this much?"

Mom shrugs. "Sometimes. Mine have never been that bad. I didn't get my period for years in high school. Cysts or something. Hasn't been regular since. Go ahead and wash up, and I'll bring you some cloths."

She drags herself off the floor, clinging to the door like she doesn't have the strength. It clicks shut, and all I can hear is my pounding heart.

I guess I should have told you.

The pain in my stomach meets a new burning in my chest.

I guess I should have told you.

What else don't I know? What else aren't they telling me?

CHAPTER 5

'm sitting on the front step when Alex pulls up on his four-wheeler. He yanks off the turquoise glitter helmet his grandpa makes him wear, placing it on the back rack. I take off my right boot, dumping out the bits of straw and dirt before standing up and grabbing the basket for eggs. I wonder if he notices the lump underneath my clothes. Mom helped me fold some old towels into rectangles to stick inside my underwear. They feel too full now, like I have to lift myself higher to keep from touching the damp. I press the back of my hand to my face to cool my cheeks.

Alex turns off the four-wheeler and the quiet blankets us both. A killdeer runs across the drive.

"You okay?" Alex asks, rubbing the dirt from his eyes.

"Yes."

I start walking toward the chicken coop, and he hops off to follow me.

"You seemed really upset."

"I'm fine."

"You don't have to be embarrassed."

I keep marching. The sun's already setting behind the shelterbelt.

"Seriously, Lark, it's not a big deal."

"How do you know?" I say, stopping at the fence, my hands struggling to unlatch the wire that I unhook every day.

Alex tilts his head, a smile slipping across his face. "It's not a mystery."

He follows me through the gate. The chickens scatter as we walk, running away before looping back, too stupid to tell the difference between the egg basket and the bucket carrying their food.

"I mean, I've picked up stuff for my mom before. At the grocery store. Or the Conoco. It doesn't weird me out. Here." Out of his pockets, he pulls three squares—one yellow, one red, and one black. "This isn't great chocolate, but it should do the trick."

"What's it supposed to do?"

Alex shrugs, dropping the chocolate in my open hand. "Not sure, exactly, but my mom always craves chocolate when it's that time of the month."

It's monthly? Mom didn't mention that. Another something I should know.

Alex continues as I unlatch the coop door. "Apparently, there's a study about it, too. I know normally you don't eat this stuff, but I thought maybe today you'd want to."

"Thanks." I shove the chocolates in my pocket. No one ever mentioned anything good about sugar. Another thing they should have told me. "I didn't know that."

"The best kind is the yellow one. It has peanuts."

"Your mom told you about it?" I ask as I grab three eggs under Hazel, my favorite hen. She's never pecked me, and she even lifts up her body as I begin to reach my hand underneath her red feathers.

"About periods? A little, yeah, but we learned in middle school. The boys went to one room and the girls to the other, but we all got the same talk: puberty, testosterone, body hair, girls getting their period. No sex ed, though. Abstinence only."

So many words I don't know.

"You learned all that at school?"

Alex shrugs. "Yeah, and kids talk."

I don't have school and I don't have kids and I don't know the words that fill Alex's head. I grab the last few eggs and head to the door. Alex steps back as I pull it closed, securing it with the nail. I open the small entrance so the rest can come home to roost. I'll come close it before I go to bed. I know how to do this. I know about chickens and eggs.

But I don't know about me.

"Would you try asking your parents again if you could go to school?" Alex asks, leaning against the worn wood of the coop.

"He'd never say yes." I tried to ask for what I wanted—time in the day for lessons, books I could understand, something I knew I was missing but couldn't quite describe—but they always had excuses. We'd have money for more once Dad dropped off this load. Mom would read with me just as soon as she felt better. It never happened. And it got easier to pretend I'd never asked, didn't even want it.

"And what your dad says goes?"

"Not always."

Alex laughs. "Those chocolates are still in your pocket even though I saw you eyeing them. You want to eat them, but you won't. Because your dad said no."

I grab one of the candies out of my pocket. The yellow one. The best one. Without thinking, I unwrap it and pop it into my mouth, my tongue exploding with the intensity of the sweet. Like honey, but brighter, a smooth film coating my mouth. Bits of sweet stick in my teeth. I let it swirl around my tongue while Alex applauds.

"Way to go, Home School! Look at you breaking the rules."

I smile. That was better than I imagined.

"Next thing you know you'll tell your dad 'Screw this,' hop on your motorcycle, and head to school."

Alex laughs again, his head tilted back, his hair swinging in the wind. And suddenly, I realize he's partially right. I would never swear like that but I might be able to go to a school. I never saw the option until just now. A new fork in a familiar road. I couldn't attend—they'd never let me—but maybe if I just went, I could see what I might be missing.

But should I? Do I really want to know?

I unwrap the red chocolate and take a bite.

Babies

What I Know	What I Don't
Small	Why they die
Fragile	What their cry sounds like
Gift from god (according to Mom)	When they can walk
Bundle of cells (according to Dad)	What a baby head smells like
Precious	~~How I got one~~
Animals mate to make babies; Humans love	Puberty
Should take 280 days (roughly the same as a calf)	Abstinence
Getting them out is blood and pain	How exactly I'll get one . . . if I even want it
Head smells good (people say)	

CHAPTER 6

The next morning, our red Honda motorcycle bumps along the cow paths as I cross through the Johnson property. It's hot, and the dust kicking up in swirls around me dries out my eyes even more than the sun. The bottoms of my flannel shirt flap at my sides. I forgot this shirt was missing that button. Up ahead, I can see the highway, the flat black line that will lead me to the school I've heard about, driven by, but never visited. Willow Creek Christian School.

Dad hates anything Christian: the judgment, the hypocrisy, all the singing. There's no evidence of god, he says, and Dad only believes in things with reliable evidence. Proof. That one word—Christian—in this school's name means I'll never get to go even though it's less than twelve miles away (if I calculated right). Well, Dad won't take me. But twelve miles isn't too far on my own.

Harvesting wild echinacea for pain relief. That's what I told Dad I was doing today. Because of the cramps. He doesn't know about the bundle I dug up last week while he was gone that will pose for fresh-picked today. I have about two hours before he'll begin to wonder, before I need more flowers in my pile to make up for the time gone.

It's faster to cut across this field, so I pull off the path and navigate the bike through the tufts of large grass, my body shaking as the bike jostles over each bump. My palms ache from holding tight, but I see a truck whiz ahead on the road and know I'm close.

When I get to the barbed wire fence, I turn the bike off, kicking the kickstand three, four times until it sticks in the hard dirt. I dust off my pants before examining the fence. If it was me and Mom, she'd put her foot on the bottom wire and pull up on the top, creating a diamond-shaped space for me to crawl through. "Duck your head," she'd remind me so my hair didn't end up tangled on a line. If it was just me, I'd attempt the same move, holding one section down with a foot and lifting the top wire with my hand, knowing for certain I'd snag my shoulder or the back of my hair. But now I've got a motorcycle to get through.

Finding space between the barbs, I press my hand along the wire, testing its firmness. It pushes far down, not tight at all. Dad hasn't redone this wire in years, but I guess we haven't had cattle over in this pasture for a long time. I yank up on the bottom wire to see if I can slide the motorcycle under on its side. It's dirty anyway, so Dad won't notice. I roll the bike closer, but it won't fit. I can tell from here. I roll the bike as close to the fence as possible, then press down on the bottom wire so hard it meets the ground and lift with my other hand. It's going to scrape the handlebars, but I can get it through. I slowly move the bike underneath, shifting my feet and my hands as I move the bike through the diamond, making sure none of the barbs puncture the tires. One barb catches on the leather of the seat, deepening a crack that already existed from years in the sun. When it's finally through, I roll it down the drainage ditch, not wanting to risk the rocks or logs hiding beneath the overgrown grass.

Up on the side of the road, the riding feels exactly like I always want it to. Smooth, a cool breeze blasting my cheeks, the power of being able to enjoy the ride instead of handling the bike. In the distance, four large pine trees hide a white building. On either side of the school are regular fields, but the lawn in front is bright green. They must be irrigating. That's a lot of water. More than what we catch in our rain barrel. Large blue letters on the white walls poke out from behind the trees. Wi. Cr. Ool. I park the bike in the lot next to the few trucks and cars and walk toward the main door.

The front office is filled with quilts. A large quilt in shades of blue hangs behind the enormous counter just past the door. Another multicolored table runner lies across the counter along with trays of paperwork on both sides and a cup full of black pens. At identical desks on opposite sides of the room sit two nearly identical women, both slightly younger than my Grandma Betty. Both have the same older lady hairstyle, combed into a round ball. Each has a wrinkled face with a big smile. They're laughing about something before they notice me.

"Hello there," the brown-haired one says, swiveling in her chair to face me. "Welcome to Willow Creek Christian School. I'm Ms. Frandsen. How can we help you on this fine Friday morning?"

I didn't realize it was Friday. Didn't think about it all.

"I want to see about going to school here."

The white-haired one tilts her head. "Where do you go to school now?"

"Homeschool."

They nod, smiling, approving, not like the way Grandma

Betty does anytime she brings up my education. She thinks Mom and Dad are idiots for homeschooling me. *Neither of you are smart enough to be teaching anybody.*

"And what grade are you working on at home? You look pretty young to be in high school, but that's the benefit of homeschool. You're not stuck at the pace of those public schools," Ms. Frandsen says with a wink. She gets out of her rolling chair and crosses over to me at the counter. She looks at me, waiting for me to answer, but I don't know what to say. Alex is a junior and he's two years older than me. I never asked what to call my age in school.

"I'm not exactly sure," I finally say because it's the truth.

"Don't worry. We can figure that all out. Did you come here by yourself?"

I nod.

"Well, we're gonna need your mom or dad to come fill out the application."

"Can I take it with me?"

"You can fill it out online; it's on our website." She smiles. "That's right. We're high-tech now."

The two women laugh.

"Do you have a paper copy I can take?"

Ms. Frandsen purses her lips. "Did we print any this year?"

I don't think she's asking me. The white-haired woman shakes her head before rifling through the folders on her desk. She shakes her head again. "I have this one from last year. It'll work."

She grabs a pen and scratches something out. When she hands it to me, I notice she's changed the year. I flip through the pages and then see the word. *Payments.* I didn't think about that. "Excuse me, but how much does it cost to go here?"

Ms. Frandsen smiles, points. So many zeros. "The range depends on some of the services you choose. Plus a $250 annual registration fee."

A sinking. We don't have that.

Ms. Frandsen reaches across the counter to pat my hand. "But we don't want finances to get in the way of anyone's education. Blessed are the poor and blessed are the donors! Hand me one of those scholarship applications, Janine."

Ms. Frandsen slips a light blue paper into the back of my application. "We've got some generous folks at the church who are thrilled to support our students. Enrollment's been low, so we actually have some available funds even though the school year has started. Might not cover full tuition, but it'd be something."

She winks, squeezing my hand one more time.

"Just fill this out and bring it back at your earliest convenience. We'll also need a copy of your ID and your immunization record."

"My what?"

"Your shot records. Vaccinations."

I don't have any of the vaccines. And won't. Dad says vaccines are meant to cure diseases that aren't even that bad, but when I asked him, he said he never had measles, so I'm not sure he actually knows how bad they can be. Vaccines are an attack on my personal freedom, Dad says, but now not having them might prevent me from the one thing I want.

"What if I don't have a shot record?"

Ms. Frandsen purses her lips. "Well, then, you'll need this religious exemption. A couple families have it here."

"And what if I don't have an ID?"

"If you don't have your driver's license yet, just bring a copy of your birth certificate. Or if you bring the original, we can make a copy here."

"I don't think I have a birth certificate." I *know* I don't.

"No problem. We can take your social security card or a passport . . ."

I shake my head. Ms. Frandsen purses her wrinkled lips.

"Oh . . . well . . . I guess any form of picture ID or even your name in a family Bible?"

"I have that." I take the vaccination form, grateful there's still a chance, though I'm not sure what "religious exemption" means. Ms. Frandsen flips to the back page of the packet. "Be sure to sign this page, too. It's the covenant form. Part of the applicant criteria."

I scan the words for ones I understand: *Willow Creek Christian School . . . prayers and the* something *gifts of our* I don't know, *and . . .* skip it . . . *before God and community to follow Jesus's teachings, I will not:*

1. *Use tobacco, alcoholic bev . . . or drugs,*

2. *Frequent some kinds of places in person or on the internet,*

3. *Act in any way as to bring dishonor or shame to God, my family, church, or community.*

I can't sign this. I don't know what I think about god and I don't have a church to bring dishonor upon. Mom says god doesn't care about our homemade Catholic mass, but this, coming to school, brings dishonor and shame on my father.

Signing the paper would automatically disqualify me from attending.

"Nothing to be scared about," the white-haired grandma says as she pats my hand. "Just what any good Christian student would do."

I'm not a good Christian.

I'm not a good student.

I grab the paper and walk back out the door to the motorcycle and a field and place where I am good just being me.

CHAPTER 7

My foot catches in the loose seam of my quilt, the sound of Dad boiling water for coffee waking me up before the sun. A breeze blows in my window, bringing the smell of dust and hay. I untangle my toes, curling them under to stretch my legs as I listen to Dad's morning sounds. Mom will be silent for another few hours.

"It's boiling," I tell Dad when I enter the kitchen, the steam from the kettle already reaching up toward the stained ceiling tiles. He's stretched out at the wooden dining room table, one foot propped up on a chair and the other bouncing on the floor. Bread crumbs dust his arms, his mustache, the table, and he wipes a slip of my chokecherry jelly off the table with his thumb and into his mouth. In his other hand is a thick book with a cover I don't recognize.

I pour him a cup of coffee and bring it to the table, then take his empty plate and drop it in the sink. I'll wash these later. I head toward the coat closet when Dad stops me.

"I already let out the chickens."

"Thanks," I say, grateful again that when Dad's home my chores are cut in half. When he leaves, it will be another four to six weeks of doing it all on my own.

"I told Mike you'd meet him over at Myron's. He wants to finish cutting the south field today. Supposed to be hail tomorrow afternoon."

I roll my eyes. Mike always says there is supposed to be

hail. He's always fretting about the weather, seeing storms in plain summer-day clouds.

"Can I take the truck?" I ask, pouring the leftover water into a glass for tea now that I have a few minutes. "The Honda's been acting up."

Dad shakes his head. "No, I need to run to town to grab some parts before I head out tomorrow. That piece of shit rig already lost me a day."

I spread the thinnest smear of jelly along my bread, so little it barely registers as red. I have to make up for Dad's heaping spoonful, the traces he left on the spoon enough to be bait for the flies. I won't touch it now that they have.

"I'm going to finish this book before I go and then it can be your next study." Dad holds the book up to me, *Undaunted Courage*, and I cringe at the letters, certain I don't know what the first word means or even how to say it. "It's dense, full of our history, but for a genius like you—it'll be a fast read."

A fast read for Dad means weeks of secret struggle for me. When he's gone, I don't have time to read the stack of books he's left, but it's also hard to just figure out the words. Dad holds books below his eyes, flipping pages with his thumb, able to eat and scratch and still take in the information. It's not like that for me. I stare at the tiny curved lines, the pages and pages of words unlocking the world my dad wants to show me. But it's often blurry, like a shape on the horizon when you can't tell if it's a cow or a deer.

Dad lays the book open on the table, revealing glimpses of bent corners and black scribbles on the edges. "This is how government could be. I mean, can you imagine, Larkie? They sent thirty men out to explore the uncharted wilderness at a time when Jefferson still thought they'd find a woolly mammoth, and only one man died. They crossed the Rockies with zero machinery and were friendly ambassadors to all the tribes—except the Blackfeet, but that's expected."

Dad folds the corner of his page before tossing the book to the center of the table and brushing his hands off on his dirty pants.

"Do you think our government today could handle something as massive as that? Hell, no. We spend all our time dropping bombs with drones and filling people with expensive prescriptions they don't need. Know what we could be doing?"

He looks at me, but he won't wait for me to answer.

"We could be exploring Mars! The whole damn galaxy! We have the technology if we wanted to use it. I mean, the solar system is our Louisiana Purchase!"

"Dad, I got to head out."

He pauses, nods. "Right, right, yeah."

He stretches his arms above his head before pushing himself out of the chair with enough force that it tips back against the wall. He leans over to close the window, pulling down the blanket to block out the morning light.

"It's already getting hot," he says as he pulls me into a hug. He kisses the top of my head, and I relax into him, grateful that his hugs feel like they're for me. "See you later, Larkie. Take care of your mom."

I do. Every day.

I brush the crumbs off Dad's chair into my palm as he walks out the door.

It's sunset, and the Honda still won't start, so Alex gives me a ride home. When we come down the hill, a red truck I don't recognize is parked by the shop. North Dakota plates. Two rifles on the rack in the rear window. The back bumper and tailgate are covered in stickers, some fresh, others peeling. An "A2" in stars and stripes covered by an AK-47. *US Army Veteran. Tyranny will be met with force.* A skull with three lines. Lots of skulls, really.

Alex pulls the four-wheeler up to the steps.

"Whose truck?" he asks. I don't know. I bite my lower lip, running through the visitors that have ever come to the house. Uncle Charles before his eyes got too bad. A man to fix the well when Dad couldn't. Some hunters wanting to hunt on the south field (Hell, no. Those bucks are ours). A cousin of mom's who drank all the sun tea.

Whoever it is, they're not from the county. Or the Feds. The "Love my country. Fear my government" bumper sticker says enough.

Unless it's a fake. A government agent in sheep's clothing.

"Larkie!" Dad calls, poking his head out the shop door. "Come here! And bring that Mountain Dew off the rail."

"You can go if you want to," I tell Alex, but he shrugs.

"I'm in no rush."

I grab the dripping can off the steps, and we walk to the shed.

A man's voice booms through the room as if Dad wasn't standing a few feet away from him, leaned up against the work counter.

"Nah, nah, nah!" he says. "I know you think it's a great idea—living out here away from it all—but that's not going to be enough when martial law hits. They're going to find you and then what? Your plants going to save you? You going to take down the agents with some corn?"

The man laughs, his head thrown back. His entire body is covered with freckles. He's young, though his hands are calloused and darkened with oil. He's wearing a T-shirt with the same skull from his truck and an Army baseball cap pulled over shaved red hair. "Beat 'em back with a bunch of carrots? No, you gotta be ready to fight back!"

Dad shakes his head, a smile creeping across his face. "I've got enough guns to hold my own."

"But it's not going to be just holding your own! You've got to be proactive. Preempt their force with even more force."

"Hold on, hold on. I want you to meet my girl." Dad waves me forward. "Sam, this is my daughter, Lark. You ever get that Chevy off the blocks, she'll have it running in two weeks flat."

Sam smiles at me with perfectly straight teeth. "She good with a gun?"

"Try to take it and see."

I hand Dad his pop and wipe my hands on my pants. He sips it with one hand while resting the other on my shoulder. I still don't know who Sam is. Dad doesn't have friends. Except me. And Mom. Sorta Mike. Unless Sam's one of his friends from the internet. But they've never come to the house.

I turn to see Alex leaning against the shop door. He smiles, widening his eyes before shaking his head. Not sure why.

"Oh, hey, Alex," Dad says after a few big swallows of Mountain Dew. "Sam, this is Alex. He and his grandad live just down the hill. They farm our fields now that I'm on the road."

Sam looks at Alex. Barely nods. Alex lifts a hand in greeting.

"So, when you going to take me to see this perfect bug out?" Sam asks. "I can't be here forever. I still gotta drive back to Minot tonight."

Dad's taking him to the bug out? No way.

"Don't look like that, Larkie," Dad says with a laugh. "He's not getting to see the bug out, despite what he thinks." Sam groans—*come on, man.* "He's just here to buy the old trailer."

Ah. Okay. Makes more sense. Dad's been selling off Uncle Charles's old farm tools every couple of months. Usually, he just takes them in the truck with him, dropping them off along his route.

"You've been posting about the bug out for months, and now that I'm here you're not going to show me?" Sam shifts back and forth like he's gotta take a leak. "I need to be ready. You know it's going to happen this year. Martial law. For sure. With that shithead in the White House and all these liberals and minorities trying to turn us all into commies."

Alex frowns, kicks a piece of straw with his boot. Sam keeps going.

"Like any of them have brains enough to run anything. Has anybody seen the shithole that is Cuba? Mexico? No wonder they're all crawling over the borders."

Dad shifts behind me, his hand tightening on my shoulder. Something's off, but I can't tell what. I know the dangers of *martial law* and *commies*, but *minorities*? And these places: Cuba and Mexico and their borders?

"Those are government problems, not people problems," Dad says.

"Yeah, maybe," Sam says. "But—I know this isn't PC and all—but like, minorities just aren't capable of running good systems. Look at the inner cities. Hell, look at the reservation down the road. No offense—"

We all look at Alex. A darkness edges his eyes.

"Offense taken," Alex mutters, before turning to me. "I'm gonna head out."

"I'll go with you."

I pull from Dad's hand and follow Alex toward the door.

"Hey, lay off talk like that," Dad says as we're leaving. "It's not about skin color. It's about free thinking. I know plenty of white guys who—"

Alex sends a dirt clod sailing as he marches toward the four-wheeler.

"I'm sorry," I say as I catch up to him. "I don't know why he would say that."

Alex scoffs. "I do. He's racist."

Racist. Alex says it the way Sam said *minorities, commies, reservation.*

"Dad shouldn't have let him come here."

Alex hops on the four-wheeler, his face still clouded. "It doesn't matter."

He says that, but I know it does. We both do.

Later that night, when Sam is back on the road and a patch of brown grass marks the trailer's old space on the junk hill, I ask Dad about him.

"Sam's an idiot," Dad says as he counts the envelope full of cash a third time. "Just some guy I met on a forum."

"Then why did you invite him here?"

"I wanted to sell the trailer. He had the cash to buy one."

"He knows where we live now."

"He's fine, Lark."

"But what about what he said about the reservation? And . . ." I try to remember the names and places he mentioned, the ones I might actually learn about in school. Dad wants me to be smart, to use my brain. Maybe he just doesn't want a school like the one he grew up in. "You don't talk like that."

"Well, no," Dad says. "I believe all men are created equal—"

"And women."

He smiles. "Yeah, Larkie, and women. It's in the Constitution."

"I know. But Sam doesn't."

Dad laughs as he puts the cash in the lockbox and hangs the key on the hidden hook. "Some people still hold those old ideas. Sam's got a lot of the right beliefs when it comes to the government and the collapse. He's just uneducated. Doesn't get how much we have to learn, how much the Indians know about the land, all the things they could teach us. But he's a patriot."

A patriot and a racist? Doesn't seem like a person could be both.

Sam has lots to learn. He's uneducated.

. . . Like me.

CHAPTER 8

Three slams on the horn. A pause. Two more.

She better not make me come in there and get her.

I want a pork chop, Mom said. That's how this all started, almost a year ago now, when Dad was gone and the cellar was bare and all Mom wanted was a pork chop. Now we go every weekend Dad is gone.

And he just left an hour ago.

I blast the horn again, but it only startles our black Lab, Gizmo, who runs back and forth in front of the truck, his tail waving. No movement behind the picture window. "Come on."

I slam the truck door, taking the steps two at a time, letting the screen door slam behind me. I don't bother to take off my boots. Mom and Dad's room is dark, the blinds closed, and Mom's hidden under a mass of quilts and unfolded clothes.

"Mom," I call from the door. "Let's go."

She groans, rolling over under the covers. Only a few of her brown curls show out the top of the sheet. One of her bad days again. I grab a pair of jeans off the floor. She hates this pair, but her others are still drying on the clothesline. I push her shoulder with my hand, pulling the quilt down with the other.

"Mom, we have to hurry. She doesn't like it when we're late."

Dinner is served at one. The roast will be dry if she has to keep it warm in the oven.

"Mom, please."

She sighs, flapping back the quilt and holding out her hand. I pass her the pants, and then get her green sweater off the chair by the bathroom. I pick off a hair ball before handing it to her. She yawns as she slides her arms into each sleeve.

"Let's go."

"Don't rush me," Mom snaps, pulling the sweater over her head.

"I'll wait for you outside," I say, hoping I don't have to come back in here. From the truck, I survey the edges of our garden: 1,400 square feet of plantable area. Should be enough to feed a family of three. Dad read that on the internet.

It's not.

Zone 4A. Three to four months to grow what we need for the year. I did it all, just like Dad said: tilled in May, planted after the last frost, spaced and weeded and waited for the rain. Not enough of that this year. I amended the soil, a combination of our compost and manure I trucked over from Mike's. We've got zucchinis—some monsters I missed behind the leaves—and the beans turned out better this year than last. I pulled off the orange potato beetles with their black and white stripes and the tomatoes are fine—thank god—but something's wrong with the corn. Not enough drainage, maybe. Or not enough water.

It's not enough.

1,400 square feet of plantable area turned into 1,000 square feet of edible food into 300 cans if we're lucky. Not even one a day.

I really need to eat.

I'm about to lay on the horn again when the front door opens and Mom slinks down the steps, her curls blowing in the wind. Mom hops in the front seat, tossing three canvas bags on the seat beside her. She grabs a handful of sunflower seeds from the jar between us and shakes a bunch into her hand.

"You should have added cayenne pepper," she says, popping a few into her mouth. "Made them spicy."

"Next time," I say, ignoring the fact we don't have any cayenne pepper. I put the truck in reverse, turn up the radio, and head toward the highway to take us into town.

Thirty-five minutes later, we pull up to Grandma Betty's house. Mom's head is slumped against the window, but I don't know if she's asleep or just closing her eyes. Grandma Betty's house is the town version of ours. Fancier, cleaner, no dust covering the windowsills or bugs in the flytraps. The grass is cut, and the paint on the porch is a fresh rust color. No dandelions poking their yellow heads between the rocks in her flower beds. Houses in town are like people in town: cleaner, softer, not weathered by the wind and dirt. I don't want to be a town kid, Mom says. Town kids are weak.

We head around the side of the house to the back porch. Mom doesn't knock, just takes her shoes off on the welcome mat and pushes in.

"Mom! We're here," she calls, even though Grandma knows already. She spends her days watching out her picture window. I hear her slippers shuffling on the linoleum. Mom's already grabbing a glass out of the cupboard and heading toward the fridge.

"Hi, Grandma," I say when she comes around the corner.

Grandma doesn't smile. She never really smiles when we're here. She just starts cooking.

"You could have called," Grandma says as she squeezes my arm. She says that every time even though she knows we don't have a phone. She pulls a tissue out of the front pocket of her floral house apron and rubs it underneath her nose. "Good thing I bought the four-pack of chops. What can I get you to drink?" Grandma asks me, seeing Mom is already filling herself a glass of orange juice.

"Lark can't have any of this," Mom says as she gulps down half her glass. "Too much sugar and preservatives."

"Didn't hurt you any."

"So you think. You know I've got bad joints. Besides, we want different for Lark."

"Well, I got milk and some tea and cranberry juice," Grandma says, resting her hand on the open fridge door. "We also got pop downstairs: Mountain Dew, Pepsi—"

"Pop is worse than juice," Mom says from the kitchen table.

"I'll have some milk, Grandma."

Grandma takes out the gallon jug and plops it down on the orange countertop as if it's the heaviest thing she's carried all day. Grandma's whole kitchen is orange. Different shades of it—orange tile, orange counters, even a curtain with little orange slices sewn on the bottom. I've only eaten a fresh orange one time; the rest was the tiny oranges in a can.

"I'll get a package of rolls from the freezer and then you can help me mash the potatoes, Lark."

My stomach grumbles as I wonder what else we'll get to eat.

Dad says grocery store meat has to be washed in bleach to kill the germs that come from big farms. And sometimes the government puts in other chemicals they say are vitamins but are really poison to keep down the masses. I'm not the masses, not yet, but Grandma must be. With each bite of grocery store pork, the chemicals slip into her mouth and through her stomach and into her blood, turning it cloudy brown like pond water after your foot crashes into it.

I take another bite of my pork chop, letting the poison slide down my throat, though I don't feel any different. Just less hungry. We've been eating at Grandma's whenever we can, and if my body was really being destroyed by all the chemicals, I would feel different, wouldn't I? Look different? But I don't. Mom's already finished her first pork chop and moved on to a second. It all tastes so good, but Dad says the government made it that way. To fool the masses.

I take another bite.

Mom sits across the table from me, her feet propped up on the empty chair at the end of the table where Poppa used to sit. She takes another swig of her Mountain Dew. So much sugar could cause cancer, Dad says. Mom says she misses the caffeine. She's willing to take the risk.

"So, when does he get back?" Grandma asks as she carefully cuts around the circle part of her pork chop. Grandma's plate is organized with each ingredient in its own corral.

"Not for a month," Mom says, and I wonder if she worries, too, that Dad might show up and we won't be home. We'll be here, at Grandma's, eating chemicals and watching TV that will rot my mind.

"And he's making enough now driving truck?"

Mom drops her feet to the floor as she reaches for one of Grandma's buns. She scoops some bright yellow margarine out of the tub and slathers it over both sides. It's not real butter, just yellow plastic, but she closes her eyes when she takes a bite.

Grandma continues asking questions. "Can he provide for his family now? Instead of leaving you two to starve?"

I didn't realize I was starving, but maybe that's what this is: the hurt in my stomach plus the shape of my bones. Maybe that makes me more than hungry. *Starving.* I poke a green bean that used to be frozen until Grandma heated it up in the microwave. I don't know what makes microwaves so dangerous, but I'm sure there's something since we don't have one. I'd like to see inside one, take it apart.

"He just got started. It'll take time to get his savings."

"And how long will that take?"

"I don't know," Mom sighs as she pops the tab on another can of pop, this time A&W Root Beer.

"School starts next week," Grandma says. "They've got backpacks now at Miller's Corner. You still going to keep her out of school?"

I think about the application hidden underneath my bed. Grandma would approve. Probably. It's hard to tell what she's thinking most times.

"We homeschool," Mom says, and Grandma snorts.

"Even if that were true, you can't teach her high school level classes. Chemistry? Calculus? You didn't pass those when you were in school."

"Lark's brilliant. She'd be bored in regular school. I know I was."

"Your boredom had nothing to do with brilliance," Grandma mutters.

"We don't have to come, you know," Mom says, setting down her silverware. "I thought you wanted to see your granddaughter."

Grandma looks at me, but I can't speak since my mouth is full of mashed potatoes and gravy made with the extra Shake 'N Bake sauce and pork chop fat.

"I'm just asking," Grandma says. "Someone's got to think about her future. What's she going to do when she turns eighteen, and she's barely been off that damn farm?"

"I do! She's my kid."

"I'm right here," I say, and they turn. Grandma takes a bite of her pork chop.

"What's your plan? You think you're ready to live on your own when you turn eighteen?"

I didn't realize that was the date I was waiting for, an age that meant anything at all. I hadn't thought about a time that isn't me on the farm with Mom and Dad and the babies. I belong there. I was born there—the sky, the hills, they're under my nails, in my bones. Would I even be able to leave if I wanted?

"I don't know."

"See?" Grandma throws up her hands, one still holding the bone of her chop.

"We don't have to come if you don't want us to," Mom says, and I hold my breath. Even if it's full of poisons, my plate isn't empty yet. I'm not ready to stop eating.

"Don't be so dramatic. I want you to come." Grandma scoops green beans onto her plate, a drip of light green water landing on her lace tablecloth. Mom takes another bite of her bun. "Save room for dessert."

On the counter sits a silver cake pan full of raspberry dessert. A layer of pretzels. A layer of raspberry jam Grandma made by boiling frozen raspberries, some boxed Jell-O, and more sugar. Then Cool Whip mixed with cream cheese.

It might kill me, but I'll eat every bite.

CHAPTER 9

I t's a Sunday we're Catholic because Dad is in Walla Walla. Mom woke up before me, even had our homemade hosts pressed and laid out on a plate when I walked into the kitchen. Without Dad around, she's been singing hymns, some just a hum, others a full-voice belt as if she's in front of a huge congregation and not just me and the flies on a hot summer day.

"Peace be with you," Mom say as she pumps my arm like I'm the old well, her damp hands clasped around mine. "Peace be with you."

She pulls me into a hug and then kisses my forehead. She rushes to the front door, letting in a blast of hot, dry air as she yanks it open to call "Peace be with you!" to the world outside. Gizmo waits at the door, his tongue dangling, his tail whipping back and forth.

"Peace be with you, too," Mom says, grabbing Gizmo's paw and shaking it with the same force as mine. "Come give the sign of peace to Gizmo and the birds."

I shake my head. Every day Gizmo lounges in the driveway, casually chasing the barn cats if they come too close. He's already at peace. I'm sure the birds are, too.

"Come on, Lark!"

"You're letting all the cool air out."

The room is dark, the blankets already pulled heavy over the windows, the blinds closed since early this morning. There never really was a cool enough breeze.

"Fine," Mom says, pushing Gizmo's shoulder so she can close the door. She begins singing "Lamb of God" as she crosses the living room to grab the plate of hosts and the cup of mint tea. We don't have any juice. We never have any wine. She holds them up over her head, singing loudly again, before setting them down on the cold wood-burning stove.

"Come here, Lark," Mom says. "I'll serve you."

I take a step forward, clasping my hands in front of me the way she taught me last year when Dad started driving truck and we started being Catholic. Someday she'll baptize me, but I don't know when. This all should have happened when I was small, but better late than never, Mom says. I'm not sure she knows if that's true.

None of this means anything to me yet—the singing, the communion. Not like it does for her. Do I believe in god? Do I want to? I don't know. But I'm happy to play along with Mom while I figure that out.

Mom grabs a pressed circle of bread off the plate and presses it into my palm. "Body of Christ," she says, and I wonder why she skipped the prayer this time. Sometimes we kneel before this part. Sometimes, she tells the story of Jesus and the disciples and the Last Supper.

"Do you think I should learn more about god?" I ask, as I hand Mom the cup of tea. She takes a sip, before she traces a cross from her forehead to her chest, then shoulder to shoulder.

"You know about god."

"A little bit. But not very much."

Mom frowns. "There's not really that much to know."

She holds the cup up toward me, and I take a sip, wishing she hadn't added so much honey.

"Could I read the Bible?" I ask.

Mom's eyebrows scrunch, and she pushes a loose curl behind her ear. "It's not that good of a book."

"I still want to read it. You wouldn't be mad, would you?"

"No, why would I be mad?"

Because Dad would be. He'd be furious with all of this, but what he doesn't know can't hurt him. How much harm can some flat bread and a cup of mint tea cause, anyway?

"You said there were important stories in there, things I could learn. About heaven or that man with the boat. The ark. People do study the Bible, like at that Christian school down the road. Willow Creek."

Mom shakes her head, flopping back onto the couch and tucking her legs up beneath her night dress. "Do you really want to read the Bible?"

She reaches out an arm, gesturing for me to come sit with her. I sit on the floor in front of her instead, and she begins to play with my hair, stretching out pieces and then beginning to braid.

"I went there, the other day. To the school."

Mom's hand stops. "Why would you do that?"

"I've been thinking maybe I could go. To school. It's not a government school. And it's only a few kids. All farm kids."

I turn to look at Mom, resting my arm on the cushion behind me.

"I don't think that's a good idea. You know what your dad thinks about all Christians. Besides, he's in charge of your education."

"I know, but he's been gone more now, and he doesn't always have time." I wonder what his excuse has been for all the years before he started driving truck, when school was something I knew existed for everyone but me. "You heard what Grandma Betty said. What happens when I turn eighteen?"

Mom scoffs. "Nothing. You'll still be here with me and your dad."

That's what I always expected to happen, too, but now, I'm beginning to wonder if I'll still want to stay if I have no other choice.

"Please, Mom. It's not far from here. I could go and take classes and still be able to do all my chores."

"I don't know," Mom says, biting her bottom lip. "I'll have to talk to your dad, but I don't think he's going to like it."

"We wouldn't have to tell him."

Mom frowns. "I'm not going to lie to your father."

"What about church?" I ask, gesturing to the plate, the cup, the dog outside who's been offered peace. "We never do church when Dad is here."

"That's different."

"What about Grandma Betty's? Dad doesn't know about that."

"Grandma Betty is my mom and your grandmother. And being Catholic is just . . . it's just church. It's not like school. That would change you."

I imagine myself growing wings.

Maybe I want to change.

I get up from the floor, knowing I'm late to let out the chickens, who will start pecking each other soon. "Don't tell Dad I asked. It was stupid. I don't want to hurt his feelings."

"Go in peace, Larkie," Mom says, her eyes already starting

to drift closed as she nestles into the couch. "To love and serve the Lord."

Down in Mike's utility room, I stand in front of the fridge with the door open, the cool air chilling the sweat that clings to my hairline. The inside of the fridge is packed with all different kinds of pop: Mountain Dew, Pepsi, Diet Pepsi, A&W Root Beer, Sprite, Squirt. Inside the small top drawer is a bunch of green glass bottles, labeled with names I don't recognize. Antibiotics for his animals probably. Mike doesn't care what those do to the cows, to him.

I grab a yellow can of Country Time lemonade. It has fruit on it, and it's a good source of Vitamin C. It says that. *Natural lemon flavor drink with other natural flavors.*

Natural. Unlike antibiotics. And taxes.

I've had tea with lemon. Lemon throat drops.

It would be nice to have something this cold to drink.

"The really good stuff is in the other one."

I jump, hitting my head on the freezer section before I see Alex laughing in the doorway.

"I didn't think you were allowed to have that kind of stuff," he says.

"It says it's natural."

Alex snorts. "Natural lemon flavor. That just means it tastes like something that's real—a lemon—and not like Mountain Dew. No fruit's that green."

I set the can back on the shelf.

"Do you know how much sugar is in that?" he asks. "Way more than that little chocolate."

"I didn't drink it."

"You could. I won't say anything." Alex smiles, stepping over to the other freezer. "But if you're going to go hard with sugar, you might as well go all the way."

Stacked on the frost-covered shelves are different sized white boxes and several white plastic tubs. Alex reaches his hand into the torn ends and pulls out a variety of paper-covered shapes.

"If you want to go with 'fruitlike' you could do a Twin Pop. Best flavor is orange, but if you want to try more than one flavor we can split and trade. Or a Drumstick."

"Like a chicken leg."

"Same name. Different experience. Grandpa has these boring chocolate-covered bars, or you could have"—his hand comes out this time holding a shiny, golden wrapper—"the holy grail of all desserts. Ice cream perfection. The Gold 'N' Nugit."

He waves it in front of my nose.

"No, thanks."

"Let yourself be seduced by the chocolate coating, the peanuts drenched in caramel tucked in a creamy layer of premium vanilla ice cream."

"I don't want any."

"You do," Alex says with a smile.

"Fine. I'll have it."

"There we go, Home School!" Alex high-fives me before grabbing another golden wrapper from the freezer and dropping it into my hand. It's cold against my palm. I almost press it to my neck. "What are you doing here, anyway?"

"Part broke down. I'm waiting for Mike to find the replacement. He said there was cold water in the basement."

"Wrong fridge," Alex says, walking over to the third fridge and pulling out a jug. "Glasses are upstairs."

I follow him up to the kitchen. He's already eaten one ice cream bar before we get back, and he downs another one while pouring us two glasses of water. I glance out the kitchen window, the ice cream softening in my hand. Mike must still be in the shop. I unwrap the end and take a bite. Sweet and a little bit salty with the peanuts. I get why it's Alex's favorite.

"I went to the Christian school. Willow Creek. Last week."

Alex raises an eyebrow as he chugs half a glass of water. "Aren't you atheist?"

"Dad is." A few more bites of ice cream. "I don't know what I am."

"And he's letting you go to a Christian school?"

"I didn't tell him."

Alex starts to clap his hands together really slow as he nods up and down. "I'm impressed. Two weeks ago, you would barely eat a piece of chocolate, and now you snuck off to school."

I shake my head. "I didn't actually go. I mean, I didn't take classes."

"Obviously, that's not how school works. You don't just show up."

I don't know how school works. Alex does.

"They gave me an application, but I need my parents to sign it."

"Why?"

"Why what?"

"Why do you need your parents to sign it?"

"Because the school said so?"

Alex sighs. "Yes, the school needs your parent or guardian's signature to enroll you, but why don't you just sign it yourself?"

I didn't realize that was an option. "She said it had to be my parent. I asked my mom and she said no."

Alex groans. "Lark, seriously? You take everything so literally. If your parents won't let you go, just forge it."

My cheeks are hot and I can feel stinging at the back of my eyes. I don't know what forging is. And why is it wrong to assume that when someone says I need my parents to sign something, they mean my parents themselves need to sign it?

"Hey, I'm sorry. Don't be upset," Alex says, coming around the counter. He stands so close I can smell the mix of his body and the sweet ice cream. "You still surprise me sometimes, but I shouldn't have been a jerk about it. I'm just saying: Your dad is gone all the time, right? That's why you were able to sneak off to the school?"

I nod, my eyes locked on the counter. He drops his hands.

"If you want to go to school, just sign the form with your mom's name. If they ask for a phone number, just put down a wrong number or tell them your service is down. I don't know how long you can actually pull this off, but maybe you can do this long enough to figure out if it's something you even want."

I do want it. I just didn't realize it could really be my choice.

"We can look over the application together before you take it over. Do you have a copy?"

"It's at the house."

Alex frowns.

"But they said it was online."

"Perfect."

CHAPTER 10

lex says on the first day of school you wear new clothes. This shirt is old.

Alex says on the first day of school you get to see all the friends you haven't seen all summer and even the kids you don't really know but who fill up your classes and change the scenery.

I don't have any friends here to see or even familiar faces to recognize.

Alex says the first day of school isn't really that scary if you just relax and enjoy it.

I am not afraid.

"Well, hello there, welcome back," says the older woman with the brown curls. Ms. Frandsen, I think. "We are so excited to have you here as a student at Willow Creek!"

She sets her palms on the desk and leans toward me. "Do you have all your paperwork?"

I dig in my canvas bag and pull out the application Alex printed, along with the scholarship application, the religious exemption saying my parents oppose vaccines because of god and not fear of the government, the birthday card I got two years ago from Grandma Betty—the only thing with my name and address on it—and the $250 in cash I took from the cellar. I slide it all across the counter. She frowns at the cash.

"Is a parent here with you today?"

I shake my head. "They couldn't make it."

"We're going to need to talk to them soon. Can they come tomorrow?"

"Maybe," I say. "My mom's been feeling pretty sick."

"Well, I hate to hear that."

I hold my breath as she flips through the pages. She doesn't hesitate when she gets to Mom's signature. My signature.

"And your identification? Did you find your birth certificate?"

"No, but I have this."

A white Bible with gold letters and a golden edge to each page. I wiped the dust off before I brought it. Its weight was heavy on my back as I rode. I turn to the second page: *Family.*

"That's me." I point to my name—Lark Justus Herbst—on the second row. Mom's smooth cursive noting my name and birth date: April 19.

Ms. Frandsen smiles, reading the rest of the names. "And where do your siblings go to school? Still homeschooled?"

Augustine. Ashton. Aspen. Avery. Ave.

"No."

I leave it at that. Her eyes hold the questions she doesn't ask.

"So, Lark Justus? That's a unique name. Very American."

Not really. Not the kind of American she's thinking. I'm named for the Justus Township, the land of the Montana Freemen, patriots outside the authority of any government. Her government.

She shoves my application and the cash into the folder. "It'll take me a few minutes to get this uploaded into our system, but in the meantime, I'll get Ms. Schmidt to talk to you about your class schedule."

"And who's this?" A tall man, taller than Dad, stands in the back office doorway with his arms crossed, staring at me.

"This is Lark Justus Herbst. She's enrolling today!"

"Just Lark is fine."

His giant hand reaches for mine and pumps my arm up and down a few times. "Well, welcome, Lark. We're glad to have you. I'm Mr. Leibach, the school principal. Your family just move in?"

"No."

"Homeschool," Ms. Frandsen says.

"That's great! So much freedom in homeschool, but most of our students find that our classes lend themselves to that sort of independent learning while still offering you the benefits of community and fellowship. Can I say a prayer with you, Lark?"

Both their heads are bowed, so I dip mine, too, but his words are like a train I missed and so I just keep staring at the floor. At the end, I cross myself, my middle finger dashing from my forehead to my heart, shoulder to shoulder.

"You're Catholic?" Ms. Frandsen looks at me like I'm spoiled milk.

"My mom is."

They share a glance. "But your Dad's not Catholic?"

"No." He's not Christian either, but I don't mention that.

"It's almost lunch already, so let's get you started. I'll get your paperwork going, and Ms. Schmidt—"

"Ms. Schmidt is meeting with a student." Mr. Leibach

THE TRUTH ABOUT EVERYTHING

mouths the word "divorce" and Ms. Frandsen nods, pursing her lips. "What do you need me to do?"

"Well, Lark's been homeschooled since . . ."

"My whole life."

"Got it," Mr. Leibach says. "Follow me."

Mr. Leibach sits me down in a back room of the office where the lights are just as bright. The shelves are stacked with different colors of paper, colors I didn't know existed in paper or in life. I want to touch them, hold them close to my eyes. I knew school would be different, but I thought colors were certain as snow in November. There are big machines behind me and even a few computers, though they look different than ours. Mr. Leibach pulls out a plastic blue chair, clearing the papers on the table in front of me with his hand. His hair is a mix of red and blond that I don't know which color it really is. Another new color in this room full of them.

He gestures toward the seat with his freckled arm.

"These packets range from a high school senior all the way down to sixth grade. This doesn't mean you would actually go into that grade—homeschool kids often skip grades—but we wouldn't put you back with the sixth graders. These tests will just give us a better sense of what you know. Look them over and decide where you want to start. If a test is too easy, you can stop where you are and pick up the harder test."

In front of me are two sets of papers in six piles, some tilted over boxes or metal machines.

"If a test is too difficult, don't feel bad about putting it down and taking an easier one. You can start where you want." He reaches for the stack right in front of me. "But I would start here."

Expressions and Equations: Grade 8. Mr. Leibach sets down three sharpened yellow pencils and a small blue calculator. The buttons are big and soft like tiny pillows for my fingers. I haven't ever really done math. Just basic adding and subtracting when we're measuring feed or mixing bread. I can do those numbers. Mostly. Maybe I just made them up. No one corrected me, but that doesn't mean I wasn't wrong.

"You can get started whenever you want," Mr. Leibach says. He smiles at me so large it's stretching his lips at the corners. He's waiting for me. I grab a pencil, rolling it in my fingers.

"You can put your name here," he says, pointing to a line across the top of the page.

This I know.

"I'll check back in a few minutes." He pats the back of my chair twice before walking toward the door. "You'll do great."

One. $32 \times 3\text{-}5 =$

Why are some numbers big and some small? I skip it.

Two. *Write this number in scientific notation: 312,000,000,000*

I didn't know numbers could have so many zeros. Scientific? Science. Are science numbers different than math numbers? I grab the calculator and press the buttons until the top screen shows 312,000,000,000. What could make this a scientific number? I press "C" and the number disappears. I skip it.

Three, four, five. Skip, skip, skip.

I put the paper back in the pile, wishing my name hadn't already stained it. He'll know it's mine, this blank paper without any sense.

Ratios and Proportional Relationships: Grade 7.

I can read, but I don't know those words. Only relationships.

Those I know about: relationships between the rain and the harvest, the relationship between Mom and Dad. I don't know about relationships in math. I grab the next paper.

The Number System: Grade 6.

One. *How many 3/4-cup servings are in 2/3 of a cup of yogurt?*

Yogurt. I know that. I know cup. 3/4 cup. 2/3 cup. I see those numbers pressed into the metal of our measuring cups. I can add them: 1 cup plus a little less than half of another. But the question isn't asking that. I type the numbers into the calculator, but there isn't a small line to separate them. 3,423 it tells me. I add the top and the bottom numbers and draw a line between. 5/7 cup of yogurt. At least I wrote something.

A couple hours later, I follow a girl in a flower-print dress—Jessica, she said—down the stairs to the basement, my new schedule in one hand, the brown bag lunch the counselor forced me to take in the other. Mr. Leibach didn't give away much when he looked at my test. Poker face, Mike calls it. Liar, Dad says. He took the two tests, both the easiest he could offer and yet both so difficult I almost got up and walked out of the room. I didn't. He mentioned words like "remedial" and "tutoring," but he didn't say I had to leave, and so now I'm headed to Spanish class. For freshmen. Like me.

"Okay," Jessica says when we arrive at a door covered in brightly colored paper flowers. "The period already started, but you should be able to slip in. I'll let Ms. Bamford know you're new. She's really nice."

My stomach clenches as Jessica reaches for the door. She pauses. Looks back at me.

"Do you have a backpack or anything?"

I shake my head. I didn't know what to bring, so I just came.

"That's fine. All of the teachers have journals you can use for today."

For today, but what about tomorrow? Where will I get journals or whatever else I need for school? Maybe Alex has extras. Or I could ask Grandma. She might give them to me without telling Mom. Maybe. As much as she hates my home-schooling, I'm not convinced she'd help me lie to my parents.

"Ready?" Jessica asks, opening the door before I can answer. A video plays on the whiteboard, and the teacher, Ms. Bamford, who was standing by the window, crosses to us. "This is Lark. She's new," Jessica says in a low voice, and Ms. Bamford smiles.

"Hola, Lark. Bienvenidos a mi clase."

I wait.

"Ven, puedes sentarte aquí, en esta silla libre."

She twinkles her fingers at Jessica, who backs out the door, before resting her hand on the empty chair. Silla? I sit down, a mini table wrapping around to protect my front like a seat belt. The video stops. The lights flick back on. A few students glance at me, but then Ms. Bamford is clapping her hands and speaking in Spanish, and soon she's lifting up items—an apple, a bar of chocolate, a book, a shiny round circle—and the students repeat after her.

"Me gusta," she says, staring at me. "I like. Me gusta . . ."

She waits. Stares.

"Me gusta." The words feel comfortable in my mouth. Smooth.

She lifts the book. "¿Te gusta leer?"

I repeat and she shakes her head. She says the line again, this time pointing at me and then the book.

"¿Te gusta leer?"

Oh. *Do I like to read?*

"No."

She nods. "¿No te gusta leer?"

"No te gusta leer."

Another shake. "No *me* gusta leer."

"No me gusta leer."

Clapping. I smile so big it hurts my cheeks. "¡Muy bien hecho, Lark! Fabulosa!"

No me gusta leer, but yes, maybe, me gusta school.

"So how was it?" Alex asks that night as he joins me to shut the chickens. "Your first day of real school."

"Me gusta la escuela."

"What?"

"It's Spanish."

"Yeah, I know. Your first day of school in fifteen years and you learned Spanish?"

I yank on the door, kicking away a clod of mud that's blocking it.

"Spanish and world history today. Tomorrow I'll have all my classes. I got there late."

"They don't like when you're late. You'll get a tardy."

I know. I'll have to figure that out later. Alex holds the bucket of eggs for me while I use both hands to bend the nail around the closed door edge.

"And so you liked it?"

"That's what I said. Me gusta la escuela."

Alex rolls his eyes. "Maybe it's a good thing you waited so long to go to school. Most kids complain about going, but now you're speaking Spanish on your first day. Did you meet anyone?"

"Yeah, the front office staff and Mr. Leibach, the principal, and Ms. Bamford—"

"No, not adults. Other kids."

I shake my head. "I didn't talk to anyone."

"Seriously? Lark, friends are the best part of school."

I hadn't thought about that. I thought school was the best part of school.

Alex grabs my shoulders, dipping down so he can look me in the eyes. "Promise me that tomorrow you'll talk to some people. Just chat. Get to know them."

I shrug and kick one leg over the fence, the bucket swinging on my arm.

"I will."

As we walk back toward the house, Alex's arm brushes against mine.

"I was thinking," he says. "I could come over on the nights I don't have practice and help with your homework. If you need it. Just because this is your first time in real school."

"Okay." I can't look at him or he'll see my cheeks have turned the color of tonight's sunset. Maybe he can feel their warmth anyway, the heat in my entire body. "But not when my dad's home."

"Of course. That won't be tough. His rig isn't hard to spot."

"So, when? Tomorrow?"

Alex smiles. "I have practice tomorrow. I can't come this

Wednesday, either, because Mike has me helping with some project in his basement. But I'll come next week." He pauses at his truck door. "I'll need a new name for you since I can't call you 'Home School' anymore."

"You could just call me Lark."

He laughs, wraps an arm around my shoulder, rests his chin on my head. "Have fun tomorrow. Try to meet some people."

Maybe I will. Maybe I'll talk to friends and take a test. I'll do school with a bell and assignments and more than one teacher. I push aside memories of the packets, the questions unanswered, and remember "Fabulosa, Lark."

Me gusta la escuela.

CHAPTER 11

few days later, my finger skips along the ragged black truck route, this line darker and thicker than the rest. Underneath the ink, the printed pink highway peeps out from the places where Dad's marker was unsteady. On the map, I pass small dot cities and gray roads and dashed curves bluer than the brown rivers they represent. Vida, Circle, Glendive. Then I-94 all the way across North Dakota and Minnesota before heading down into Wisconsin to Madison. He should get there tonight. I know this route now, how far he'll go in a day, those cities circled in red, but if I didn't, I could count the miles with my thumb the way Dad taught me. One day is twenty thumbnails for me, fourteen for him, if the weather's good and the truck holds up. He's twenty-eight thumbnails away today but has miles to go. He'll be back in three weeks.

Three more weeks of school. Almost a month total before I'll have to stop. Hopefully, just till he's gone again. But if not, how much information can I cram into three weeks? Enough?

I grab my bag off the counter, gently sliding the two books inside before nestling in a jar of water and some slices of bread and honey I wrapped in beeswax. I grab the coffee can full of scraps from under the sink, knowing I'll have only a few minutes to feed the cats if I want to be on time. At school they really care about time, down to the minute, everything marked by a bell and not by the shadows. Punctuality—it's a virtue, a value they all share, but it's not mine.

Still, I don't want to be late.

"Where you headed?" Mom says, and I jump. I didn't hear her get up. I grab the can, closing the cupboard with my foot.

"Bloom's."

Mom leans her head against the doorframe, a loose curl covering her eye. She blows it up with a puff of air, but it falls back down on her cheek. "Why?"

"I'm fixing the fence. About a half mile is down."

"Your dad's been wanting to fix that forever. He'll be happy it's done."

It won't be done. Not by me. Not for three more weeks. Hopefully Mom forgets I mentioned it before he gets home. She doesn't normally care what I'm working on as long as I feed the cats. They howl outside the door when they're hungry. The cats she notices. She's never even seen this fence.

"Why do you keep packing a lunch?" she says, pointing at my bag. "Just come home. I'll make you something."

"I want to get done before it's too hot."

Mom crosses toward me, pulling her thin floral robe tighter around her waist.

"Whaddya even pack yourself?"

She reaches for the bag and I pull it back.

"Nothing much."

"Do you have any protein? Almonds? Some dried apple slices?"

She reaches again, and I clutch the bag under my arm.

"What you got in there? A pop? Did you sneak one from Mike?" She laughs, reaching again for the bag.

Mom frowns as I back toward the door. "I got to go. I'll be back this afternoon."

"You know you're not supposed to drink that stuff. The sugar is like poison."

"I know."

I wonder if these books are poison, too.

Without saying goodbye, I back out the door.

A large chunk of words and then it will be my turn again. My eyes dart over the browned page, the tiny letters, the halting voice of the boy four desks away, leaving my mind unable to grab hold of the ideas. Instead, they dart around like new lambs in the pasture. I scan the words while I listen so I'll be ready when it's my turn again.

"Mrs. Gibbs?" Ms. Leland asks, looking up from her orange copy of *Our Town*.

Mrs. Gibbs. That's me. I take a quick breath and start my line. The words drop out of my mouth, not singsongy like the boy's in front of me, his voice looping up and down. I grip the edges of the booklet, the sweat from my palms soaking into the thin cover. I try to hold the words down, but the letters skip and stutter.

Face? Fark? Farsee?

"Farce," Ms. Leland calls, and I repeat. Someone sighs. Ms. Leland reads the dark, wiggly lines telling the actors what to do. "She puts a plate before him."

Almost done. For this round.

"Here, I've made something for you," I read.

My head hurts. If I was home, I would take a scoop of yogurt from the fridge. Here, I'm afraid to move my hands and lose my page.

"This next line starts with a strange word," Ms. Leland says. "'T'aint.' That's just the playwright spelling out an accent. The words are really 'It ain't' or should be 'It isn't.' So, Lark, you'll start with 'T'aint.'"

I repeat, finishing the line and then scanning the page, seeing Mrs. Gibbs over and over again. *How long will I have to do this?* I never would have asked for a part. Would have just followed along. But we drew slips from a silk pouch. Now I'm Mrs. Gibbs, a woman in a play that doesn't seem to have a story. Dad says movies and plays are propaganda. This just seems like someone drove into town and wrote down anything someone said.

I struggle through the next few lines before Ms. Leland stops us.

"Let's mix up the reading roles," she says.

"Can I be Emily?" the girl named Jessica says, her hand arching above her head.

"Let me think."

Ms. Leland hands out the roles, mostly keeping everyone in their same ones. Jessica is Emily. Caycee is Mrs. Gibbs. I'm following along now. Ms. Leland looks over at me and smiles. I wonder if she knows I'm relieved.

Ms. Leland invites me back to her classroom for lunch. Alex says lunch is the best time for meeting people. Just join a table. Look for an empty seat. Start a conversation. But everyone's already asked me the same questions:

So, you were homeschooled? Yes.

Your whole life? Yes.

Was it lonely? I wouldn't know.

What made you want to come to Willow Creek? A shrug. An answer would mean more questions.

Are you saved? I didn't know the answer to that question, but realized soon the answer was yes. Another lie at school.

Alex says it's a small school, so it will be easy to make friends. Not many to choose from. But I haven't made any friends yet. When Ms. Leland asked me if I wanted to have lunch in her classroom, it was the easiest question yet.

She reminds me of Dad, the way she asks me a question, but then answers it herself. She tells me about the baby quilt she's making for her nephew. He's already a year old, but last year was her first year as a teacher, so she was too busy to finish it. She shows me a picture of the quilt on her phone. Then of the baby. He's the only baby I've ever seen that size. Our babies were always too small, some so tiny they didn't really exist.

Ms. Leland's lunch comes out of all these different-sized containers with bright-colored lids she sets in a row across her desk. Cucumbers, carrots, little brown twists, and chicken with rice. I've never had rice. I take a bite of bread, and Ms. Leland raises an eyebrow at my lunch but doesn't comment.

"So, do you have a favorite book, Lark?" Ms. Leland spears a cucumber with her fork, then salts it with a tiny shaker. "My favorite author is Francine Rivers, and out of all of hers, I'd probably pick *Redeeming Love*, but that's so typical. Everyone loves that book."

I've never heard of that book. I don't know if I'd love it.

"I don't really have a favorite."

I try to remember the name of a book, any book, but I

can only picture the covers and the ideas. Most I couldn't say I liked.

"Do you read a lot? Most homeschool kids I know read all the time."

"Not really that much."

"Does your family like to read, your mom or your dad?"

Ms. Leland smiles as she chews, but I feel sweat underneath my fleece jacket. Suddenly it feels like I have to answer these questions right, like Ms. Leland can tell something about me, about us, depending on how I answer these questions about books.

"My dad likes to read. A lot. But he can't read as much when he's on the road—"

"Your dad's a truck driver?"

I nod. "My mom reads the Bible."

She doesn't really, not like Dad, where the words jump from the page and into his brain. Mom uses the Bible like a map of a place she already knows. She has it just in case she loses her way.

"I love to read scripture, too. It's why I love working at a Christian school. It's part of the curriculum! What sort of books did you read as part of your homeschool curriculum?"

Again, the covers of a hundred books I've held in front of my nose flash in my brain: pioneers, horses, flags, bright red letters that pop off the cover. I remember the book Dad handed me before he left.

"The last book I read was *Undaunted Courage*." I never got past the first page.

"Wow! Really? That's a pretty advanced book for a

freshman. Benefits of homeschool, I guess." Ms. Leland reaches over and grabs her copy of *Our Town*. "Are you liking the play?"

"Yes."

"What do you like about it?"

"It doesn't make life seem that scary."

Ms. Leland laughs. "Even when Emily dies? I was horrified the first time I read it. My sister was pregnant with her first baby, and then I was all worried she was going to end up like Emily and die in childbirth! I had to pray about it because it got so under my skin."

I don't remember that in what we read. But it's not surprising, I guess—Emily dying while having a baby. Babies die, so the mothers can, too. Happens all the time at the farm.

And yes, I'm a little scared about Mom, too, each time she's pregnant.

She reaches across to grab my forearm. "Oh my gosh, Lark, I just spoiled it for you! Don't tell your classmates. I can't believe I ruined it."

"It's okay."

Ms. Leland flips through the script and then hands it to me with her thumb holding open a page. "Can you try reading this part again? It's from earlier, when you were Mrs. Gibbs."

I don't think I can say no.

I press a finger beneath the first word, "George," a name I remember because it's said a lot. One of the main characters. I start to read, and Ms. Leland holds the booklet for me. She reads the different parts as they come up, using different voices and making herself laugh.

"So how was that?" Ms. Leland stares at me with a smile

THE TRUTH ABOUT EVERYTHING

I don't quite trust because she knows how it was. Awful. She heard me.

"Fine."

"Correct me if I'm wrong, but it seems like maybe reading can be a bit hard for you at times."

All the time, really.

"You're not wrong."

The smile drops. Thankfully.

"I can tell you're bright, Lark. Your other teachers talked about how you pick up information quickly even though you've only been here a couple days. Ms. Bamford says you're doing fantastic in Spanish, and that got me thinking. Spanish is mostly learned by listening and speaking. Hola. Gato." She laughs. "That's the only Spanish I know."

I smile. I know more Spanish than that. Me gusta la escuela.

"Clearly your listening comprehension is really strong—your understanding of ideas—but the reading is difficult, and there's a lot of reasons that might be. I was thinking you might like to spend some extra time with me, working on reading. Maybe after school?"

"I can't stay."

"Okay, well, lunch then? A couple times a week?"

Lunch is the best time to make friends, Alex says. Guess I won't have any, but maybe, finally, the words will clear and I'll be able to really read.

CHAPTER 12

I rush through a list of chores I'll need to finish before sundown as I race to the Honda. Run water to the trees and the broccoli and cauliflower. Pick eggs and shut the chickens. Start dinner if Mom hasn't. She probably hasn't. She usually doesn't.

I hustle out the doors, adjusting my bag to the other shoulder. Across the parking lot, someone slams something metal so loud it makes me jump. I walk across the gravel, coming around one truck to see Jessica, the girl who walked me to class my first day, squatting low with her hands on the dusty tailgate of a gorgeous—expensive—black Ford F-250. She heaves and the metal clangs again before falling back down.

"Ugh, seriously!" She grabs the tailgate again, adjusting her feet to give her more strength.

"It's not going to latch that way," I say.

She lowers the tailgate. "It will if I give it enough push."

I shake my head. "You probably have something in the latch. You'll just damage it if you keep slamming it like that."

She runs a hand through her long blond hair. "I guess I can just leave this stuff here and come back and get it with the other truck."

She has two?

The bed holds a few black plastic containers—some with small holes in the front—and a thin metal pole. Toward the front is a cardboard box with a dented lid.

"We're having an open mic night at my youth group and the school said I could borrow their sound system. Are you in a youth group?"

"No." I don't know what that is: like a team? But she didn't say team. I'm not on any teams, anyway. Or groups. Just a family of eight.

"You can come to mine," Jessica says. "Only a couple kids from here go. Most go to public school in Wolf Point."

"My friend Alex goes there."

She smiles. "He should come, too!"

I've never heard Alex talk about a youth group. Thinking about hanging around other kids makes my stomach flip. But maybe in a good way, like driving the motorcycle on the small stretch of highway near the farm.

"Do you have a set of sockets?" I ask.

"Maybe. There's a toolbox in the back seat."

Jessica watches me as I dig through the disorganized tool-box; the socket set is missing a few pieces, but it looks like it has the right one. I hop on the truck bed, removing the bed liner and access panel, which is already loose. Immediately, clumps of dirt and small bits of gravel fall to the ground. I pull out some pieces of grass and straw and then blow into the space around the cam/lever area. Flecks fly in my eyes and I press them closed. *Stupid.*

"If you have an air compressor, you should blow this out when you get back and then apply some lithium grease," I say, blinking a few more times. "This'll get you home, but it's not a long-term fix."

Jessica nods, like what I'm saying is at least familiar. "I can have my dad check it out; I just need to get this stuff home."

I inspect both sides, brushing and blowing out whatever I can. A small rock falls out of the left panel, which might have been the problem. The tailgate closes on the second try.

"You're a good mechanic," Jessica says as I brush my hands off on my jeans. "My dad's always telling me I need to learn more about taking care of my truck, but I just don't care that much to learn more than changing the tire or the oil."

"It's not that hard."

"Probably not."

"I could show you. I taught my friend Alex last summer; he was restoring an old truck that was mostly junk, so with this"—I gesture to the practically new parts—"it shouldn't be tough."

"That's okay," Jessica says as she tugs on the tailgate, confirming it's locked. "If my dad won't do it, I'll just look it up. There's this girl I follow who might have a video; I used her oil-change video my first few times."

"On the internet?" I ask, and the look on Jessica's face makes me wish I had kept quiet.

"Yeah. YouTube."

I nod and look down at the ground, my cheeks hot. When I look up, Jessica is smiling.

"But you should come to youth group."

"Maybe."

Probably not. Just getting to school seems hard enough right now, but I smile as I turn, because maybe.

CHAPTER 13

I t's our first time studying together, and Alex sits beside me, his pencil tapping on his knee. Scratch, erase, blow off the pink bits, write again. Chemistry is kicking his ass, he says, and I'd never tell him, but it's nice to see him struggle. Makes me feel less stupid as I bumble through my assignments.

We chose the barn loft because of the breeze and the certainty that Mom will never climb the ladder to find out what we're up to. She didn't respond when I called into her room that I was leaving to hang out with Alex. Even if she decides to look for us, we could hide the books before she even stepped on the first rung.

It's dusty up here, the room filled with Uncle Charles's run-down equipment too small to move up to the junk hill: old buckets, a rusted-out stove, a leather saddle that could be nice with a bit of polish. I swept before Alex got here, sending dirt and straw down the wooden slats into the empty pens below.

"It's gonna get too dark to do this in a couple weeks," Alex says. "Sunset's already seven p.m. We'll have to find a new spot."

I wonder how he knows the exact time the sun sets. It gets darker earlier, yes, I know, but why? Something to ask at school later. If I can.

"Maybe." Who knows how long I'll be able to keep this up? Dad should be home in a couple weeks, and there's no way I can sneak out every day without him noticing. Will the school let me come back after being gone so long? I guess I'll find out.

Alex leans over to look at my paper. "Word problems. Those are the worst."

Problems with words. That's what I have. If it was just numbers, amounts or shapes I could spin around in my mind, it would be easy. I can do that. But here the words blur everything, the answers lost in the muck of sounds. Ms. Leland says I'll get better with practice. Hopefully we have enough time to prove her right.

"Want to do some together?" Alex asks. "I'm almost finished with this."

"I can do the math."

"Okay. Just offering."

"It's not the numbers."

Alex presses into me as he looks at the page of problems. "Do you want me to read it to you?"

No. I want to read it myself. But I also don't want to show up tomorrow with a blank page. And I can tell Alex wants to help. I nod.

"Okay. Which problem are you on?" he asks.

I point to number one.

"Jennifer bought five pints of frozen yogurt and a tray of jumbo shrimp from the Food Place for a total of $45—"

"What's jumbo shrimp?"

Alex smiles. "Really big shrimp . . . oh, you haven't had shrimp, have you?"

"I don't even know what it is."

"It's like a little pink . . . I don't know how to describe it. Here."

His phone. He types a few times—getting information, from the internet, like Jessica and her truck—and then sighs.

"Right. No internet." He puts his phone back in his pocket. "Shrimp are like . . . crayfish without claws."

Okay. I can picture that.

"Do you want me to keep going?"

I nod, pointing to $45 so I can follow along.

When Alex reads, it's for me. He stops to ask if I got it or if he should repeat. His eyes flick up from the page to see my face. His deep voice curls around the words, creating pictures in my mind. We're doing it together, even if I'm only listening.

When Dad reads, I could leave the room and he wouldn't notice. Doesn't really matter if I learn what he's saying as long as I nod along.

Isn't that great, Larkie? Mm-hmm.

What do you think about it? Crazy, right? A response before I have the chance.

I scratch through a mistake in my adding since my eraser was gone by problem three.

"You know you can use a calculator for those," Alex says. He gets his phone again, showing me a screen that looks like the blue calculator on my desk at school.

"This way's fine."

"But a calculator is lots faster." Alex holds the phone out to me. "You can use it. I don't get service out here, anyway."

I rip a page out of my notebook and set it on the dusty wood. I place the phone on the paper, not wanting to scratch it. Alex told me how much it cost. We work quietly beside each other, Alex's phone lighting up the space between us, until it gets too dark to see. Alex stuffs his books into his backpack but doesn't make a move to climb down.

"You finished your first week: what other typical school experiences have you had?"

"How would I know?"

"Good point. Well, did you eat cafeteria food?"

"Of course not."

"Right. Do you have a locker?"

"A what?"

"That answers that question." Alex blows at the dust on the railing in front of us. "Why don't you tell me? Anything weird? Not what you expected?"

It's all different than what I expected but nothing strange. It seems like exactly what people would be doing in a school. More computers, maybe. A bunch of time spent moving between classrooms. Lots of laughing. I guess I didn't expect that. Then I remember.

"The thing every morning where everyone stands and puts their hands on their hearts and says that speech," I tell him. "I don't like that."

"The Pledge of Allegiance?" Alex asks.

"I guess so. It seems like propaganda."

"It is," Alex laughs.

I tap the pencil on my paper. "I'm right? It's really propaganda?"

"Schools don't seem to think so," Alex says. "But why else would you make kids pledge allegiance to the flag every day?"

Dad was right about the government wanting to own me. Why else would I have to promise to . . . promise whatever it is they're asking of me? Loyalty? To say yes to any demands?

You're named after the Freemen, Lark, so you can be a free woman.

Free women wouldn't say the pledge.

The Freemen hung the flag upside down, Dad told me.

Would the Freemen even go to school? I don't want to know. Instead, I change the subject. "Someone invited me to youth group."

Alex smiles. "That's great! Are you going to go?"

I shrug. "Maybe. I don't know. I've got to get this sneaking out thing figured out first."

"You are doing a lot of that now. Your mom probably thinks we're making out up here."

"What?"

"Because she doesn't know about school."

"No, what's making out?"

"Oh." Alex turns, brushing a loose strand of hair behind his ear. "Never mind."

"Tell me."

"It was stupid. We better head down. It's getting dark."

In seconds, he's up, brushing the dust off his pants and tossing his backpack over his shoulder. He's embarrassed.

"You first," he says, and I grab the first rung, careful to miss the rusting nail. I don't know what "making out" is, but I'm guessing from Alex's reaction, I won't find out at school.

CHAPTER 14

L ark, you don't look so good."

Jessica waves her fingers in front of my eyes before pressing her warm palm against my head. How can she tell if I'm warm when her skin is already so hot?

"I'm fine," I say, even though it's getting even harder to swallow.

Jessica presses her palm to her head and then back to mine. "You're burning up."

I don't feel hot but the opposite. Ice cold, like the time I was breaking ice on the water trough with my boot and kicked all the way through into the freezing water. Now my entire body is under ice.

"Ms. Leland, Lark is sick," Jessica calls to where Ms. Leland is sitting at a round table in the front of the room with two boys. "Maybe you have the flu," she says to me. "It's going around."

I haven't felt this way before. My throat has hurt. I've had chills. Mom told me I've had a fever. But not like this, not all at once.

Dad told me this would happen. The school. It's a germ factory. My pure body wouldn't be able to handle the contamination—like the Indians and smallpox. Susceptible. I should have expected this.

I lay my cheek down against the desk, the cool both comforting and off-putting. A hand is on my shoulder.

"Not feeling too good, huh, Lark?" Ms. Leland asks, crouched down beside my desk.

"I'm fine. I'll be okay. Just tired."

She puts her hand against my forehead, more skin on my skin.

"She is hot," Ms. Leland says over my head. I close my eyes again. "Jessica, why don't you walk her down to the nurse?"

I lift up, pain slicing between my eyes. "No. I don't need the nurse."

"She needs to take your temperature because if you have a fever, you'll have to go home."

"I'll just go," I say as I stand up, looking around for my bag.

"Grab her stuff," Ms. Leland tells Jessica, and quickly my bag is strapped over her shoulder and her arm is looped in mine.

"I've got her," Jessica says, squeezing my arm a little tighter.

Jessica leads me down the hallway, talking the whole time about the one time at Christmas when everyone in her family got the stomach flu. Everyone except for a newborn baby and her Uncle John.

"Here, I'm going to say a little prayer for you," Jessica says as we walk, squeezing my hand tighter. I swallow, the pain stuck in my throat. "Dear Lord, you are our strength and all power belongs to you. I pray that you heal my friend, Lark, and return strength and wellness to her body. I thank you that as we trust in you, we find new strength and soar high like an eagle. Lark will run and not get weary. She will walk and not faint."

I might faint. Her words are soft, but I want her to stop, knowing Dad would laugh at her prayer, these magical spells he says can't cure shit.

"Here we are," she says, knocking twice on the nurse's door before turning the knob. "Ms. Fahlgren?" she calls into the small office.

"Hold on a minute!"

Jessica keeps our arms intertwined as we wait, her fingers drumming my palm. Finally, a woman in light blue matching top and bottoms comes into the room, drying her hands on a paper towel that she tosses into the trash.

"Well, hello there, Ms. Dennyson. Who's this?"

"Lark. She's new. And she's sick."

Ms. Fahlgren smiles, leaning down to look into my eyes.

"I'm fine. I'm just a little . . ." I swallow and grimace.

"Your throat hurt?" she asks. A third hand pressed to my forehead. "You're burning up. Let's check some things. Thanks, Jessica. You can head back to class. I appreciate you bringing her down."

"I can't stay here," I say, backing toward the door. My boot stumbles on Jessica's foot.

"Ouch!"

"I'm sorry," I say, and then repeat it to Ms. Fahlgren. "Thank you, but I'm just going to go home."

"Don't worry. We'll call your parents in a minute. Just let me do a quick exam while you're here. Save you a trip to the doctor."

No. Not the doctor. Being in here is bad enough with the bottles lined up against her shelf, the small drawers full of poison. I won't go to the doctor.

"No," I repeat.

Ms. Fahlgren looks at me, her brows furrowed. "Why don't you just lay down here a second then? Okay?"

Next to the wall is a bed of shiny green plastic. That can't be the medical establishment. It's just a bed. I lie down, curling my legs up tight to my chest.

"Here," Ms. Fahlgren says, sliding a pillow underneath my head. "Do you want a blanket?"

"No, thank you."

I let my eyes close, surprised how good it feels to be lying down. I hear the swish of Ms. Fahlgren's pants as she walks around the room. A cupboard opens and closes. Water glugs from a jug.

"So, how long have you been feeling this way?"

"A couple days."

"And did you take anything to help?"

See? Already she wants to pollute my body. "No."

"Nothing? No aspirin? No sore throat drops? It must really hurt."

"I gargled salt water."

A click of her pen. "Did it help?"

"Yes." Mom says it helps, even if I can't tell the difference.

There's a long pause, and then I sense Ms. Fahlgren standing beside me. I open my eyes to see her legs. I try to lift up on one arm.

"No, no, you can still lie down. Just put this under your tongue."

I clamp my lips together.

Her arm on my shoulder. "It's just to take your temperature."

Is it really? Mom's thermometer doesn't look like this. I can see the numbers on hers, the little line of liquid that squiggles up with the heat of my mouth.

"See," she says, moving the machine down toward my face to show me a small screen. "The numbers will show up here." She chuckles. "You haven't been to a doctor recently, have you?"

I shake my head. Never.

"Prayer can do a lot for the body, but sometimes you need an MD." A metal rod covered in plastic comes toward me. It's just a thermometer. I open my mouth. "Now close."

I wait. Nothing happens. She pulls the thermometer out of my mouth when it beeps. "101.8."

That's a fever. Anything over 98.6. I know that, without a prayer or an MD (whatever that is). I need to go home. I push myself to sitting, ignoring the chill that runs through my body. I want to lie down again, even on this cold plastic bed.

Ms. Fahlgren's hands are suddenly on my throat, pressing up and down the sides. Her fingertips are smooth, not calloused like mine. "Your lymph nodes are a bit swollen. Let me look in your mouth. I'm guessing it's strep. Open up."

She flashes a light in my mouth, her eyes flicking back and forth. "Hold on," she says before unwrapping a long cotton swab. My jaw begins to ache from holding it open. Quickly, she swipes the stick in the back of my throat, and I close my eyes to keep from gagging.

"I can't do the test here, but from the looks of it, this is definitely strep throat. You'll need to go home until you can take the antibiotics for at least twenty-four hours. It's very contagious."

She slips off her plastic gloves and throws them in the trash.

"You can lay back down while I call your parents to come get you."

"No." I try to stay calm. "Our phone line is down. I can make it home."

Ms. Fahlgren shakes her head. "You really shouldn't be driving when you feel like this."

I drop off the table. "It's not far. I'll be fine."

"Let me at least call you in an appointment with the clinic. The nurse practitioner goes to our church."

"I'll go. I'll do it," I say, knowing I won't. Would never.

I ignore the last things she says as I walk out the door. I hurry down the hallway, ignoring the pain in my throat, the throbbing in my head, only hoping I can make it past the office without anyone stopping me.

"Hey, Lark!" someone calls, but I keep my head down. Outside, the sun is so bright, and I close my eyes, squinting them only enough to make it to my motorcycle. I pull on my helmet and turn the key.

Slowly, I bump along the fields until I'm home, where Mom will be waiting with another glass of salt water.

At home, I lie under my quilt, wishing I had the energy to wash the sheets so I wouldn't have to lie here in dried sweat. My feet are wet in the cold socks I'm wearing beneath my wool slippers. For better circulation, Mom says, to draw the fever down. She's in the kitchen, making some elderberry tea. My mouth still tastes salty. *You'll feel better soon*, Mom said, though she doesn't know when. A few days. A week.

That's a lot of chores to miss.

Alex stopped by, she said, but no, he couldn't see me. No one can. I'm contagious. For a few days. A week.

That's a lot of school to miss.

And with Dad back in a couple of weeks, I'll be forced home again.

Will they let me come back?

For a moment, a small one, I consider those antibiotics.

# CHAPTER 15

The parking lot is still when I pull up to the school. I didn't want to be late, not again, but Mom wanted me to eat a full breakfast, make sure my energy was up. Then, she burned the eggs and had to remake them. Twice.

I stash my motorcycle by the pine tree and race toward the door, my legs still wobbly from four days in bed. I pause, resting my hands on my hips before heading inside, my boots clanging on the tile. It's almost the end of second period already. I could just hide out in the bathroom, wait for the bell, and slip into third period.

But I've already missed enough class.

I step gently as I pass the office, hoping no one notices me. I don't want any questions.

"Lark!"

I freeze. Turn.

Jessica pops her head out of the office. A momentary blossom of happiness. "You're back. Are you feeling better?"

I nod.

"We missed you."

I've never been away long enough to be the one missed. I wasn't sure they'd even notice.

"Wait, I'll walk you to class."

She's back at my side, her arm in mine. Alex would be proud.

I think I have a friend.

That afternoon, I weave through the school hallways, dodging classmates with nowhere to go, nothing to do. They punch shoulders, hold hands, stop and talk right when I'm ready to pass. They're in no rush to get home because this is what they have—school. But not me. It's only one part of my day. I still have a few more hours left of daylight and lots of work to make up after being sick. I brush past another shoulder, putting a hand up to keep someone else from stepping back into me. A few more feet, and I'll be outside in the crisping air, headed to the Honda and home.

Feed the . . .

Do the . . .

Wash the . . .

Smile for Mom. Kiss her cheek. Talk about a day that didn't exist. Someone calls my name. I turn.

"Glad to see you back, Lark," Ms. Schmidt, our counselor, says. "I'm headed your way as soon as I drop these off at the office."

A stack of paper in one hand. A coffee mug clutched in the other. A smile, a nod, more nodding. *What?*

"It will be so nice to meet your family! Normally, I talk to all family members before the school year even starts, but with yours . . ." Her shoulders up. A head tilt. A smaller smile. *Sympathy?*

"How . . . you talked to my parents?"

Not possible. Dad isn't home until next week.

Ms. Schmidt shakes her head. "No, not yet, which is why I'm going to do a little home visit today. I've tried calling, but it says the number is disconnected. And then you were absent for several days, which got us worried. It was really unusual for us to enroll a student without having met the parents, so Mr. Leibach asked me to stop by."

She steps forward. Reaches a hand toward me, sloshing her coffee up and over the rim. Brown spots dot the floor. "It's not like that! You're not in trouble. We just want to get to know them. Check in."

She won't bring anything but trouble.

Someone shouts across the hallway. I tug on my backpack strap.

"Today's not a good day. My mom's . . . she's feeling really bad, was bad when I left, and my dad's not home."

I suddenly realize today's my last day at school. I wish I would have planned for it. Asked to borrow some books. Maybe that small blue calculator from math. That bookmark with the names of scientists. I would have enjoyed today more, had I known it would be the last. I'll keep the school from visiting Mom, and then I'll be done. It will be over, but at least my parents won't know it ever happened.

Maybe after a while, it will be like it didn't.

The hallway is beginning to empty, fewer voices, some steps on the echoing floor. Ms. Schmidt is so close now, too close, her perfume stinging my eyes, catching in my nose.

"I won't stay long, but it's really important that I see your mom today." She leans. Whispers. "This visit is required."

"Okay, see you later." And then I'm out the door and running toward the bike, my bag of books slamming against my shoulders. No, *deltoids. Trapezius.* I know those now.

I've got to get home.

# CHAPTER 16

The yard is empty when I pull up. I loop around the house to make sure Mom's not in the garden or her flower beds. She's not. I leave the Honda next to the gas tank, tossing my book bag into the back of the old truck—I'll hide it inside later when this is all over—and race toward the house. On the stairs, I can hear music blaring.

She's up. Today of all days.

"Mom," I call as I open the screen door, leaving my boots on the mat. No answer, but from the familiar whir I know where she is. The kitchen. I come around the corner to see Mom swaying at the counter, her feet stepping together and apart as she swings her hips. The room is a disaster—apples, their peels and cores, are scattered around, some even on the floor. The apple peeler-corer-slicer is strapped crookedly to the counter. White trays from the dehydrator are on every surface. Even the floor. I pick up the two closest to me and move them to the table.

"Hey, Larkie," Mom calls over the music. She sings a line to me before shaking some cinnamon all over the apples in the tray in front of her. A plume of brown settles over the counter. "I was going to move those."

"It's fine." I reach over to click off the radio.

"Hey! I was listening to that."

"Can we just have quiet for a minute?"

Mom frowns. "Didn't you have quiet all day?"

What did I tell her I was doing today? Cleaning the water tanks? Bedding the garden? The coulee? Was it chopping wood today? It doesn't matter. I've got to get her out of the kitchen and preferably into her room.

"Are you almost done?" I ask, moving around her to swipe the apple scraps into the chicken bucket. She doesn't even have a complete set of dehydrated apples finished yet. I move a few more incomplete trays over to the table.

Mom laughs, gesturing to the pile of apples on the table. "No. Look at all this. And I still have three more buckets in the utility room. I thought you would be home earlier to help."

"Sorry. Took longer than I expected."

Mom raises an eyebrow. "Why?"

I really wish I remembered what I told her.

"Trouble with the saw again?" she asks.

Thank you. "Yeah, I need to resharpen the blade. Why don't you go to the living room for a little bit? I can finish this up. You did most of it by yourself, so I don't mind."

"No, I'm fine. I want to do it."

I glance out the picture window. No cars. I hurry to the living room, looking out the storm window for signs of a vehicle down our dirt road. Most of it is blocked by the shelterbelt. Back in the kitchen, Mom is turning the crank of the apple peeler, the whole machine bobbing since she fastened it wrong. I'll fix it later. When there's time.

I pull the curtains closed over the picture window. Then, the shorter one over the kitchen sink.

"What are you doing?" Mom asks. "Open those up."

"It's a little warm in here. I'm just cooling it off."

Mom brushes back a strand of hair. "It's fine. And I want

to see out. It's like a cave now." She pushes past me to yank open the kitchen window curtain.

And there it is. A blue SUV and Ms. Schmidt behind the wheel.

"Who's that?" Mom asks, leaning so close her nose touches the window.

"I don't know. I'll go talk to them. Probably just someone from the county."

"Why is someone from the county here?"

"I don't know. Maybe it's not. Maybe it's someone from Mike's church."

Mike's dropped off stuff from his church before: hand-me-down winter coats and boxes of dried goods. Tiny Bibles. Each year a few more tiny Bibles with different colored covers. Mom has a stack of them in her bedside drawer.

"Sure," Mom says, apparently accepting that answer, and I race to the door, closing it behind me. Ms. Schmidt stops at the bottom of the steps.

"Long time no see!" She laughs, shading her eyes from the sun. I don't move. "Nice house. You have a great garden."

I know what she wants, but I'm not going to let it happen that easily.

"I'm looking forward to meeting your parents—your mom, I mean. Your dad's out of town, right?"

I nod. That's what I said at school.

"He's a truck driver."

Another nod.

"So, can I come in?"

"I told you my mom isn't feeling well."

I flash a look over my shoulder, hoping Mom is back to

slicing apples and not peeking out the window. Ms. Schmidt steps one foot onto the stair and my stomach drops.

"I can be fast, but it's really important that I speak with her. Just for a minute."

"She can come to school later this week. When she's feeling better. Would that be fine?"

Another step and now one hand is on the rail.

"Lark, I'm starting to get worried—"

The door creaks, and I can smell cinnamon and apples behind me. Mom.

"What's going on, Lark?"

Ms. Schmidt is at the top of the stairs, reaching out her hand. Mom pulls back.

"Hi! Mrs. Herbst? I'm Ms. Schmidt, the counselor from Willow Creek Christian School. It's so nice to meet you. Sorry to hear you're not feeling well."

"Can I help you?" Mom asks, hidden behind the dusty glass of the screen door.

"I was just hoping we could talk for a few minutes about Lark's schooling: her attendance—"

"Lark doesn't go to school. She's homeschooled."

Ms. Schmidt's face falls, twists, a look of confusion. "Right, Lark *was* homeschooled, but she's been attending our school for the past couple weeks."

Now Mom's face freezes, a grimace, then a stiff smile. "Right, yes, your school. We decided she's not going there anymore. Thank you for stopping by."

Mom yanks my arm, pulling us both inside. She slams the inside door shut and turns the lock. We never lock that door. She drags me down the hallway, my feet puttering after her.

I didn't know she was this strong. She throws my door open, slamming it against the wall. "Stay here."

I sit on the edge of the bed, listening to her feet in the hallway and then the soft shuffle of the closing curtains. The click of her rifle. Knocks on the door. Again and again. Five minutes. Ten. Then, the creak of it opening. A conversation I don't hear. The door closing again. The locks. Then, Mom is back in my room, her face red as she stands over me with her hands on her hips.

"What the hell were you thinking?"

"I don't—"

"I said no. When you asked."

"I know."

"And you did it anyway." Mom rubs her eyes with the back of her hand, smearing cinnamon along her brow. "How did you pay for it?"

"They gave me a scholarship—"

She scoffs. "You? Why?"

"I . . . I don't know. Because I couldn't . . . we didn't have $5,000."

"And you gave them our information? Where we lived?"

I picture the birthday card from Grandma Betty. Our address on the front. The only mail I ever receive.

"Yes."

"They can find us now. Find you. They'll lie and say we're not taking care of you. They can take you away. Is that what you want?"

" . . . No."

Silence. Mom sighs, her body going limp. She'll be back in bed soon, sleeping it all away.

"Please don't tell him—"

"Don't you tell me what to do. I'm your mother."

"I'll stop. I won't go anymore. I promise."

"That's right you won't go!"

"He doesn't have to know."

"I'll decide that." Mom looks at me and sighs with disgust. "You can stay in your room."

She closes the door, and I brush my fingers along the red marks on my arm. It's not sore. Not yet. Suddenly, I hear her mutter, "My baby got a scholarship."

She sounds proud.

The next morning, Mom is leaning against the counter when I walk into the kitchen, a finger in her mouth as she tears the edge of her nail. She drops the piece to the floor. Beside her is a small yellow knapsack and a mason jar of tea, the bag still in it. I go to grab it and notice a stack of pictures—the top one a line of girls kicking their legs above their heads.

Mom leans over, points toward a girl in the middle. "That's me. Junior year."

I don't recognize the girl with the bright uniform and glossy hair. Her smile is too big. Mom grabs the stack.

"I got these out last night." She sighs at another picture. "I hated most of school, but I loved drill team. The girls. The bus rides. Even those awful early morning practices."

She hands me each photo as she finishes.

"This one's me and Kelsey after homecoming senior year."

Their faces are dark, huge orange flames behind them. Still, another smile. I didn't realize she could be this happy. At the last photo, Mom takes them back and pushes the knapsack down the counter toward me.

"You better hurry up. She said you can't be late again."

I pause. "What? Really?"

"You still have to get your chores done. And read whatever stuff Dad wants you to."

"I will. But . . . you're okay with me going to school?"

"I'm not happy about it, but . . ." She pushes back a curl, her lips in a firm line. "We gave up a lot to live out here, and I know you've had to go without. School's not just about grades. I mean, the only friend you have out here is Alex. I want . . . if you want to try school, then you should go."

She holds the tea out toward me. I grab it, certain school can't be this easy.

"What about Dad? Are you going to—?"

"Maybe. Not yet. Not today." She looks like she might cry. "You're a smart girl. Smarter than I was. Maybe you'll like it."

I cross over to her, pecking her on the cheek before she wraps her arms around my shoulders, pinning mine as she holds me. We rock side to side, her chin pressed to my head.

She pushes me back, a smile so big she's showing the chipped tooth she normally hides. "Do they have a dance team at your school?"

She's too happy for me to tell her no. I kiss her one more time and head out the door, on my way—on time—to school.

It won't last. Not forever. Probably not even past the week until Dad returns. Because she says yes, for now, but she's a petunia to Dad's frost. She'll hold up for a while, but he'll get to her and she'll turn—drooping, limp, the truth seeping out of her withered veins.

But for now, she said yes, and this secret is wrapped up with the host in my hand on Sundays and the pork roast we eat for dinner at Grandma Betty's. My secret is strengthened by those, hidden in the bundle, protected from the wind.

It might not last much longer, but still, it's happening. I'm in school.

CHAPTER 17

A re you going to sign up?"

Jessica looks at the flyer in my hand. Driver's Ed. Information session tomorrow after school. Classes starting next week.

"I know how to drive."

But I might still want to learn. Dad will be home, so I'll have to miss the beginning. If I come back to school, maybe they'll let me start late.

Jessica pours some red sauce on her hamburger—ketchup. "You have your license already?"

Right. I forgot you needed one. Dad had to renew his CDL to start driving truck even though he hates that he can be tracked again, identified. But there's no other choice.

Maybe I can skip that part. Take the class, learn whatever it is I'm surely missing about cars, and then be done.

"I got mine last summer," Jessica says. "I almost failed my test because I couldn't get close enough to the curb when I had to parallel park. But when would I actually do that? I just drive around now 'til I find a better spot."

"Does it cost money?"

"The license or the class?"

"Both."

"Not a lot. Classes here are part of the school, so it's not much. And the license itself is like $75 or something."

Not much? That's gallons of propane, a tank of gas. Good

thing the class is less. We have the bug out money in the cellar, but I wonder how much more I can take—how much I'll need to take—before Dad notices.

"Do you want my fries?" Jessica scoots her plate toward me. She doesn't look funny at my lunch anymore. She's stopped asking, "Is that all you're going to eat?" The vegetable soup in my thermos is still warm, but yes, I do want her fries.

I take one, its end limp between my fingers. Jessica squeezes more ketchup onto an empty spot on her plate.

"We should go to the A&W. Their chili cheese fries are amazing."

She dips her fry and I do, too.

A mix of salty and sweet. Too sweet, but I kind of like it. School food feels normal now. Harmless. Ketchup isn't as dangerous as everything else at Willow Creek.

Our hands bump when we both reach. She laughs.

Grandma and Mom wouldn't notice if I left for a while after Saturday dinner; they'll both be asleep on the couch, the TV too loud in the background. If I bring Mom back a pop, she might not even mind. "Maybe. Sometime."

Not this weekend. I have to finish all the chores I neglected before Dad gets back. But soon.

Jessica smiles. "You just let me know. I'm always ready for fries."

A group of us stand around the only car in a parking lot full of trucks. Inside, we got all of the basics for the driver's ed course: the textbook, a calendar marking when we'll take classes and when we can go for the test, a permission slip I'll have to get

Mom to sign. Now Mr. Schmidt, our math teacher turned driver's ed instructor, is giving us a "hands-on lesson." Mr. Schmidt pops the hood of the school's driver's ed car, a gray Cutlass Ciera, and slips the metal pin in the hood to hold it up.

"Before you can drive a car, you need to know how it works. Today, we're going to talk through the basic skills you will be able to do by yourself by the end of the course."

The group moves closer to peer under the hood of this unremarkable car. They seem more focused here than they ever are in class. For once, I'm not nervous, not flooded with the knowing that I don't know. I get cars. I understand engines. I have answers to most questions waiting under that hood.

"First, can anyone identify this?"

Radiator. A boy beside me gets it.

"And this?"

The battery. Same boy answers.

Mr. Schmidt points and names the engine, the battery, tells us where we will refill the windshield washer fluid, antifreeze for the radiator.

"This will be another assignment," Mr. Schmidt says as he pulls a dipstick. "Can anyone tell me what this is used to measure?"

I decide to raise my hand. "Transmission fluid levels."

He shakes his head. "No, this is the oil dipstick."

I lean forward. No, it's not. Mr. Schmidt keeps going, talking about oil changes while holding the transmission dipstick.

He's wrong.

Is it a mistake? He just said the wrong thing? Or does he not know?

It's strange to not be the only one who's wrong.

When I pull up to Mike's, Alex is playing basketball with a girl in glasses.

I thought he'd be alone.

His arms stretch out in defense as she pushes him back toward the barn door. Her short dark hair swings as she moves across the dirt, placing the ball perfectly to miss the many ruts. Alex swipes, reaching for the ball, and she calls a foul, taking two quick steps before releasing the ball in a jump shot that sails through the rim.

She's really good.

Alex hasn't seen me yet, and I don't want him to now. He looks happy. I'm interrupting. I would just go back home, but I need the free gas, and there's no way I can fill these two canisters without them noticing.

"Lark!"

Ready or not. Alex waves me toward him, the ball on his hip. He's breathing hard, his chest heaving as he calls my name again. The girl turns, watches me.

Alex crosses the dirt to me. "What are you doing here?"

"Mike said I could fill a couple of gas cans."

Alex pushes back a loose strand of his hair. My body buzzes with him so close.

"This is my cousin, Kyla. You've met before, maybe, long time ago."

I glance at her face, trying to place her in my memory. I haven't met many people, so it shouldn't be that hard to remember.

"We went swimming in the stock tank?" I say finally, a memory of a little girl in a pink bathing suit and me in a long T-shirt. Alex jumping from the fence into the murky water, splashing us both. I don't know how old we were. Young, since Alex was still living with Mike then.

"Do you want to play?" Kyla blows on her glasses before putting them back on.

"I'm not good."

Alex laughs. "You can be on Kyla's team. Two against one."

"She should be on yours. You need the help," Kyla argues.

"We'll see about that," Alex says, tossing the ball at Kyla's chest. "Your ball."

She dribbles toward the basket with Alex racing at her side, leaving me standing at the top of their dirt court. Kyla shoots and Alex blocks it, grabbing the ball and dribbling in an arc toward me.

"You're on, Lark," he says, dribbling close to me, his smile growing as he nears. I put my arms out the way I've seen him doing, bending so I can move with him. He fakes a left and dribbles past me where Kyla is waiting. I watch the two of them battle back and forth before she steals the ball and passes it to me.

"Take the shot!"

I'm too far. I won't make it. Suddenly Alex is on me, his body so close I can smell him. His hands brush my arms, my hips, as I hold the ball, deciding where to go.

"Get off her!" Kyla shouts, running toward me with her arms above her head. "Pass it!" I toss it to her, wanting the ball out of my hands, and Alex grabs it before it leaves my fingers.

"Thanks," he says, before heading toward the basket. The

ball sails through the hoop and off the barn door, sending red chips of old paint down to our feet.

Pink and blue clouds streak the sky as the sun disappears behind the barn. Kyla and Alex sit on the top of the gas tank drinking Mountain Dew while I fill up the gas cans. Mike lets me fill up whenever—he says Dad is good for it, or will be at the end of the run when he gets paid, but we both know that isn't always true—and I wish I could have filled up without anyone watching Mike's act of charity. As the gas pumps, Alex and Kyla talk about the upcoming basketball season, which teams lost seniors and who should be captain. They argue so much it would seem like they hate each other, but then they're laughing, smiling and hitting each other.

I have cousins, but we're not like this. I haven't seen them in years, not since they stopped coming to the farm. I don't know why. Dad always complains about his brother the know-it-all, so maybe he told him to stay away. I stopped asking about them, wanting to see them. Like with school, once Dad made a decision he was done. No use trying to change his mind.

It would be nice to have cousins around since I don't have siblings. Live ones, that is. Ones I could play basketball with. Or drink Mountain Dew.

"You still homeschooled?" Kyla asks, and I shake my head.

"Lark goes to Willow Creek," Alex says.

"The Christian school?"

"Yeah." I tap the nozzle on the rim of the gas can, catching the last drops. "Only for a couple of weeks."

Alex jumps down and grabs the first can, heaving it back into the truck. "But she's already learned Spanish!"

"I have to take French," Kyla says. "I can't say anything yet except 'bonjour.'"

Me gusta la escuela. Me llamo Lark. Está … estoy feliz. Estoy mal. Estoy … cansada? No, estoy canstada.

I crank the handle, letting the gas flow into the second can. I'll only fill it partway. Just enough gas to get me to school and top off the generator.

"I'm going to take driver's ed." If I can get back to school after Dad's return.

Alex frowns. "You're going to get your license? I didn't think your dad would be cool with that."

I shrug. "I might not take the test."

"It's not that hard," Kyla says. "Just pay attention to the road conditions. And use your blinkers."

"The teacher didn't know the transmission from the oil dipstick," I say, capping the last gas can.

Alex laughs. "Not everybody knows engines as well as you."

"But shouldn't he know that? He's a teacher."

"Teachers don't know everything," Kyla says. "Some of them know nothing."

That can't be right. Everyone makes mistakes, but they're teachers. They went to school. To college. They have to know.

Alex swings the second gas can over the side of the truck and leans against it, his arms crossed over his chest. "You can't be surprised. You're going to a Christian school and you're not really a Christian. Aren't they saying stuff all the time that you don't believe? Like creationism or … I don't know … anything in the Bible they take literally."

I don't know what he means by literally, but no, school hasn't felt that way. There are prayers and talk of Jesus and god, but that doesn't feel different than Mom and her Catholic Sundays or Dad and his rants about the damage done by religion. It's words. It can't be seen. It's not the same as being wrong about the transmission dipstick, something that is so obviously true.

Kyla hops down from the gas tank. "Our school is trying to include more real history, but it took until I moved here to learn anything about Indians that didn't have to do with the damn Pilgrims."

Alex nods in agreement. My chest is tight, a surging fear I can't quite explain. I thought teachers would know. School would have the truth. And maybe they do.

Probably.

But if they don't? How will I know?

Times the Government Came for the Patriots

Ruby Ridge

Waco

Montana Freemen (Justus Township)

Bundy versus the BLM

The draft

Chem trails

FEMA concentration camps

Gun confiscation (not yet, but happened in Australia)

High-frequency Active Auroral Research Program: surveillance, directed-energy weapons, mind-control

CHAPTER 18

Dad says I'm a fast learner. He taught me to drive truck when I was nine, and the only reason I couldn't handle a manual transmission then was because my legs couldn't reach the clutch and the gas pedal at the same time. I got it by the time I was ten.

Mike says I'm good with my hands. He showed me how to rewire the fuse on his old tractor, and then I figured out how to do it on the motorcycle myself. Show me once, and I can do it again. I'm the same with directions. I can picture the path to the field Mike's describing, even as he stops and starts and forgets and changes. And once I've driven there myself, I'll never get lost.

On the farm, once you learn something, your part never changes. The tractor might be different, but the start is the same: left foot on the clutch, right foot on the brake, transmission in neutral. Each field brings different ruts, new paths, and a bunch of pheasants flying up to shake you out of your daze. But you don't change. You know what you know, and you do it again and again.

School's not like that. At school, the information varies—the books, the videos, the handouts, the places you go on the computer—but you have to change, too. Sometimes I turn numbers into new ones, and other times I guess how much vitamin C is left in an orange after it's picked. Not guess. *Predict*. *Hypothesize*. Sometimes I'm writing about my life, my ideas, and other times I'm just trying to guess what words the teacher wants to read. So much reading, always reading, and coming up with the questions. At home, Dad always asked the questions. And answered them. All I had to do was listen.

At school, I'm not a fast learner. I'm not a quick reader or an efficient writer and most of the time, I don't even know what the teacher is talking about. *¿Me gusta la escuela?* Maybe. Most days.

The boy in front of me, Mark, turns in his desk to pass me a blank white note card.

"I want you to list everything you know about September Eleventh," Mr. Havens, our history teacher, says. "You'll have two minutes to write down as much as you can and at least one question." He flips over a timer and white sand falls to the bottom. "You may start now."

Around me, pencils move. Not mine. Today is September 11. They said it during announcements. We said a prayer this morning the same way we always do, but today we prayed for the victims. For their families. People died today, but I don't know why. I look down at my card.

Victims, I write. Lots? I don't know. More than one, because they said *victims* with an "S."

Mourning families. I know that word from Mom. From us. We've been a mourning family.

I search the room for a clue. A poster of the presidents. Lots of words in red, white, and blue. Buildings that are important enough to have their picture taken. I should recognize them but don't. Nothing says September. Not that I can tell.

"You have one minute left," Mr. Havens says, "and then I'm going to collect your cards."

I can feel my heart pounding in my chest.

"Okay, time's up. Go ahead and pass them forward."

A hand taps my shoulder, and I reach behind me to get the card from Jessica. I pass her card forward, sliding mine under my leg. The stack of cards makes it to Mr. Havens's hand without mine.

Mr. Havens turns off the classroom lights and starts the projector. We wait while he clicks on his computer until the screen is filled with old newspapers. Then the title "9/11 Attacks."

9/11. I know that! My heart skips, but this time, the good kind, like when I'm a few turns of the screwdriver away from a fix. 9/11. September is the ninth month. Today is the eleventh day. How did I never realize? I grab my card and start to write.

9/11 was an inside job.

Detonators set inside the towers and a fighter jet targets the Pentagon.

Rogue planes flown by government military.

Secret landing base.

Real Flight… What was the number? Ninety-something… ninety-three? *. . . shot down, eliminating all witnesses.*

The video stops, and my heart is still racing because I know this. I could raise my hand. I add *massive conspiracy* and *coordinated within the government* to my card before tapping Mark's shoulder. He turns.

"Pass this up."

He frowns but grabs the card. It travels over shoulders until Mr. Havens has it in his hand. He sets it at the bottom of the stack.

"Okay, let's share some of these," Mr. Havens says as he

sits on the edge of his desk, one ankle crossed over the other. His tie is red, white, and blue like most of the room.

"Andrew writes, 'When planes crashed into the World Trade Center—"

World Trade Center?

"—and into the Pentagon. Thousands of Americans died.'"

"May they rest with Jesus," Jessica whispers behind me.

Mr. Havens flips another card. "Jacob writes, 'A terrorist attack by al-Qaeda.'"

He would think that. He barely does better in school than me even though he's gone here his whole life. Of course he wouldn't know the truth.

"Same, same," Mr. Havens says, then stops on one card. "'It changed airport security.'"

Jessica raises her hand but doesn't wait to talk. "My uncle's a pilot, and he remembers that day and how everyone was freaking out because they had to ground all the planes in like twenty minutes. He said he's never seen anything like it in his entire life."

Mr. Havens nods, rubbing a hand on his beard.

"And now we have all these security measures, even at tiny airports like Glasgow. Before, you just showed your ticket and got on the plane, and now, well, everybody knows."

I don't know. I've never been on a plane. Mom and Dad flew on a plane once to go on their honeymoon to Las Vegas. But that was long before I was born.

"This one's from Lark," Mr. Havens says, looking surprised. I've never said anything in his class before. Until today. "She writes, '9/11 was an inside job.'"

Someone laughs. Maybe a cough.

He reads the rest of the card without saying anything out loud.

I talk without raising my hand, needing to explain myself, because his face says he hasn't put the pieces together like Dad and me have. "There wasn't enough jet fuel to weaken the steel. The buildings wouldn't have collapsed completely or that fast if it wasn't a controlled demolition."

Everyone is looking at me, listening to me. I keep going.

"And think about Tower Seven? It wasn't hit with a plane and it didn't collapse until hours later and the government left it out of the first report. And all these government people used that building, like the CIA and the FBI, and it even got reported to have been destroyed before it really was. Steel doesn't collapse. Fire doesn't burn that hot."

Mark looks over his shoulder, his lip curled above his teeth. "Is this a joke?"

"No."

"So, what, you seriously think 9/11 was some government conspiracy?"

I look to Mr. Havens, who is still staring at my card. "It was."

People start saying things all at the same time so that I can't catch them. *Awful. Nut job. How could she say that?*

"Enough," Mr. Havens says, setting my card down on the desk. "We appreciate differing opinions in this class—"

"But that's not an opinion, that's bogus—"

"I said enough."

Mr. Havens looks at me, and I don't want him to say it. Not out loud. Not in front of everyone. *I take it back. You don't have to tell me. I know now.*

"Lark, while there are some people who have questions

about the events of September Eleventh, these events occurred. Members of the al-Qaeda terrorist organization developed a plan to train as pilots and to crash highjacked planes into important American targets, resulting in the catastrophic loss of human life and the disruption of the entire American society. It was not a conspiracy. Or a hoax."

The room is quiet as he grabs a stack of papers off his desk and hands them to someone to pass out. "We'll get started with the timeline of events. Seems like we all have something we can learn today."

A hand on my shoulder. I turn to see Jessica looking at me gently.

"Don't be embarrassed."

I nod, turn away, not sure how I can be anything but ashamed. I may be a fast learner at home, but here I don't know what I'm supposed to learn. Finding truth is like predicting the rain. Nothing I can hold on to. Nothing to be sure about.

Dad is not sure about some things and one hundred percent sure about everything else. He was 100 percent sure about what happened on September 11.

Maybe he was wrong.

"You're getting it, Lark! That's three in a row." Alex high-fives me, his fingers then curling around mine until our palms press together, our fingers overlapped. We hold them together in the dark of the barn, his phone lighting up the science book on my lap.

"You've gotten so much better and it's only been a couple weeks."

Genius. Brilliant. Mom and Dad say that when they don't actually know if I've gotten the question right. It's hope, not truth. But I can tell Alex means it when he says I'm improving.

I want to ask Alex about what happened in class—9/11 and the other events on the timeline of history that might only exist in my head. Ruby Ridge. Jade Helm. But I don't want him to stop looking at me like he is now—like I'm smart, like I'm normal. Someone who isn't only good at fixing trucks. I don't want to be "Home School" again.

Just Lark. And Alex. Two people—friends—that aren't that different.

For tonight, I let that be true.

Dad's not coming home for another two weeks, and even though Mom is crying like she'll never see him again, I can't stop smiling. Problems with his rig again. Radiator. Maybe fuel pump line. He's already lost days making repairs. Doesn't want to lose more time driving home just to get back on the road a few days later.

Fourteen days total. Ten more days of school. Hours of opportunity to search for answers to the questions I'm still too afraid to ask.

I'll take what I can get.

CHAPTER 19

'm not allowed to touch Dad's computer. It's almost hidden in the bedroom, pushed in the corner on an old sewing machine table, the parts buried under piles of clothes and newspapers and the packets of seeds we were going to plant last fall in a windowsill garden. I never touch Dad's computer. Not even when I clean their bedroom. I just skip over it. Dust has collected between the keys and even a few dead flies, but I don't remove them because the computer is not for me.

I'm not allowed to get on the internet. I used to listen to the sound from outside the closed bedroom door—sometimes voices, other times music, mostly clicking—wondering what was happening, how those sounds turned into Dad's ideas. I still wonder, but not as much, because the results are the same. A couple years ago, Dad got the good internet. Not having a TV meant we had the extra money. The internet puts us on the grid, but Dad said we needed it to stay ahead of the government plans, to keep one step ahead, not let them pull the wool over our eyes.

Mom uses the computer, too, but what she sees, what she does—that stays behind her closed door. When Dad is on the internet, his brain fills up like a grain bin, packed so tight with words that for a while nothing can escape. It might be a couple hours. Once, it was a couple of days. Then, something jostles the words—the bin door thrown open—and they begin pouring out, the words rushing so fast Mom and I have to jump back so we don't get buried. The weight of the grain can suffocate you in seconds. Dad's words are the same.

At first it was fun, listening to him share the ideas he'd learned about how to make the farm better. He'd stay up all night reading about composting or solar panels or echinacea and then the next day, we'd hop in the truck and park in a field and start digging up the plants by the root. Mom was supposed to make tea out of them. Or a compress. We ended up just washing them and chewing the roots.

Sometimes, the things Dad learned on the internet helped, like how gnats hate vanilla. Now when they're bad down at the dam, we hang a few air fresheners to the back of our caps. That was from the internet.

But other times he wakes me up, tells me to ignore whatever book he gave me the week before and sit and listen. For hours, I'm trapped across the table from him as he paces and yells, the words he learned, the stories he's read—*Can you believe it, Lark?*—and I do because I have to. I didn't read it. Dad says the elites are always working to centralize their power and their money by poisoning our bodies and our brains. *Did you know, Lark?* I didn't. I guess I do now?

The truth is on the internet, Dad says, but also lies. And creeps who will post pictures of nasty things. But I think the real reason I can't use the computer is because of the fantasies the government will tell. *It'll sound so good, you'll want to believe it, Lark.*

Maybe I would.

I've never had to tell the difference between truth and lies for myself. Maybe I wouldn't know. Maybe I would be fooled.

Alex uses the internet, but he doesn't believe all the

government lies. He can't have: he's too healthy, too normal, still seems in control. But where did he learn: school or the internet? Or maybe school means they can fill his brain, but not suffocate him. He can shake the truth from the chaff. Alex is allowed to use the computer, and he's turned out just fine.

And today, at school, it's my turn.

Mr. Havens said we're supposed to research the Declaration of Independence. Listen to people read it out loud. With the internet.

I shift in my chair, feeling the wetness of my hands on the keys. I'm allowed to use the computer here. Mr. Havens told me to. Still, my stomach churns as I follow the steps Alex used when he filled out my application. I click the eye-like circle—yellow, red, and green surrounding a blue dot. Around the room, people are clicking and searching just like Alex. They know where to go, what to do, clicking on lines and dots like code to a language I never learned. But I know about Google, now. Alex says it's the basics.

I type the first word, "Declaration," then stop. Delete it.

Look it up. That's what Jessica said. She found what she needed on the internet.

Maybe I can, too.

Mr. Havens is across the room, curved over the screen of another student, his finger pressed to the glass. I'll come back to the Declaration of Independence. In a minute. Instead, I type, "Was 9/11 real."

Enter, and the page floods: *The people who think 9/11 may have been an inside job. 9/11 conspiracy theories. Was the US government behind 9/11?* I delete the words, letter by letter. It's too much. I can't tell what's real and what's not.

A new question. The word Mom taught me in the bathroom. "Period."

I click the first link and scan the words until I come across a picture. Two red arms attached to a purple something. A picture where this thing—uterus—is inside my body. I go back to the search, write "inside my body," and hundreds of pictures pull up. Familiar outlines I've seen in the mirror, but then pictures of parts I didn't know existed. Blue *veins* and red *arteries*. Bones that curve and others made up of more parts than I ever imagined. Curls and coils—*intestine, colon*—jammed inside a space I would have thought too small. And names for all of the muscles that stretch across the bones, overlapped like woven yarn. *Gluteus maximus. Palmaris longus.* Words I can see but am afraid to say.

I click again, a picture with the word "microscope." Bright colors and unrecognizable shapes. Bright red dust clutching a green strand—*blood clot.* A strand of hair ridged like waves on a lake. The red sea between blue cliffs, like Moses passed through—*nerve dentin.* I click and click, finding picture after picture.

My throat tightens and I wipe a tear from my cheek.

It's beautiful. Overwhelming. I thought I knew how much I was missing, but I would have never guessed all this.

Even if I never get to learn it all, at least I know it exists.

"Everything okay?" Mr. Havens says from across my computer screen. He's looked at me with familiar sympathy ever since the 9/11 lesson. I click the "X" like Alex taught me, disappearing the images on my screen.

"Yes, everything is fine."

List of Things to Look Up on the Internet

9/11 attacks

Conspiracy theories

How to make money

Most productive vegetables to grow

How are human babies made?

Why do they die?

Directions to the A&W

What are chili cheese fries?

CHAPTER 20

A breeze catches my ears, and I pull my cap down farther as I scrape underneath Grandma's lawnmower. Dried grass and mud are caked on the underside from the last time I mowed a few weeks ago. I don't mind mowing. It's better than sitting inside while Mom and Grandma argue over the right way to do anything.

I reach my hand into the blades, plucking out clumps and tossing them onto the sidewalk so it doesn't get clogged again. The blades need to be sharpened, but I doubt Grandma has the tools for that. A beetle crawls beneath my knee, and I toss it on the sidewalk before flipping the mower over. I pull back to the start of this run and yank on the cord until it putters into action. Rabbit, not turtle, on the throttle and we're off.

Mom waves out the window, and I keep pushing. Then she knocks. I wave. She knocks again, points. *What?*

I stop the mower—I'll never get this done, and I still have a few assignments to finish when we get home—and throw my hands up at Mom.

"What?"

She points again toward the driveway. I turn.

Alex. Smiling. A zip-up hoodie over shorts and a tank top.

"Why are you just standing there?"

He lifts a hand in greeting to Mom, who's waving both hands at him from the window. She mouths something I can't understand. "I called your name," he says.

"How'd you know I was here?"

"I drove past. You're standing outside. Wasn't a mystery. Whose house is this?"

"My grandma's."

"I didn't know you saw yours." Alex stretches his arms across his chest, then swings them back and forth a few times. "You never talk about her. Is she like forbidden for being . . . I don't know . . . normal?"

She is actually, but he doesn't need to know that.

But he could.

He knows my other secret, about school. "We only come here when my dad's gone."

"He's gonna have a pretty big shock when he comes home one day and realizes that while he's gone his daughter is at school and his wife is . . . "

"Eating pork roast and watching TV."

He laughs. "Living the big life."

He sits down at the edge of the grass.

"You want to come inside? I can finish this later."

"No, I need to shower still. This is fine."

"You're just going to sit there and watch me mow the lawn?"

"It's a good view." A grin. A flush to my cheeks. Maybe he'll think it's the cold.

"I was thinking we could meet up at the Quonset now that it's getting dark," he says, twisting a blade of grass between his fingers.

"My mom knows."

"Seriously?" Alex sits up. "How did you not tell me this before? And she's fine with it?" I shrug. "I guess you are already sneaking out to your grandma's house, so what big a difference does school make?"

More than he knows. More than I expected. I thought school would just feel like more. More work. More time. Like the packets but with extra pages. A layering of information on top of the little stack I already had.

But it's everything. It's lined my insides. I see things now, and I know. Words, numbers, clouds moving, and we're connected. They're a part of me. Not a pile outside, a collection waiting for dust. School is the difference between the Lark I was and the me I am now.

I leave the mower, walking closer to where Alex is sprawled out on the sidewalk. I sit beside him, our knees touching. Almost.

"I'm going to a restaurant to see a friend after this."

"Really?" Alex high-fives me. "That's awesome! From school?"

I nod.

"That's really cool. I guess school is changing you quite a bit."

It is. In a lot of ways. I have a friend. Use the internet. Can read better. But I can't be that different yet when there's still so much I don't know.

"Do you know about 9/11? September Eleventh?"

Alex raises his eyebrows. "Uh. Yeah."

"What do you think about it?"

" . . . That it was awful and changed America in a lot of ways. And it led to some terrible country music songs that they still play at football games."

Heat climbs up my chest. "But, okay, I know you probably don't think this, but can you just answer a question?"

He leans closer. "Yeah."

"It wasn't a hoax, was it? Like, it happened to real people?"

He doesn't smile. Doesn't laugh. Just looks at me.

"No, it wasn't. It was real."

"Okay."

"But why are you asking?"

A rush of shame fills my stomach. "We talked about it at school, and it's just . . . not what I thought. Not what my dad told me. I've been trying to research it, but I can't tell the difference in what the internet pulls up, and now I wonder all the time, like about FEMA camps or the United Nations—but I can't ask my dad."

"Why not?" he asks.

"Because . . . I just . . . I thought a lot of things were one way, but now . . . they aren't."

"Well, yeah, because sorry, Lark, but you believe some pretty out-there stuff. Your dad tells Mike his conspiracy theories any chance he gets. Government takeovers. Chem trails. He even tried to convince Mike to trade in all his savings for gold."

I don't know whether our beliefs are unreasonable—conspiracy theories—but some of them might be wrong. I know that now.

"Some of the things my dad told me—like September Eleventh—I just believed him."

"Of course you did," Alex says. "Kids believe their parents all the time. And parents lie. Some parents tell nice lies like Santa Claus and others say everything's fine when they're getting a divorce and your parents tell you that the government puts fluoride in the water to numb the masses."

"They didn't say that."

"Well, maybe not that, but something like it."

"It lowers kids' IQ."

Alex laughs. "Point made."

He leans toward me, his bare knees pressing against mine. "Your parents are going to lie to you. Again and again. When do you stop believing them?"

I don't know.

Maybe today.

The afternoon light on the A&W windows makes it impossible to see inside. Where I should be. But I can't go in. Not just yet.

I've never been to a restaurant before, but I'm not afraid of the food. Chemical toxins from the plastic, white sugar and iodized salt, food that fills but doesn't satisfy. I don't care. It can't be that different than the meals I've had at Grandma's or the leftovers I've taken off Jessica's plate at school. I'm not here for the food, anyway.

I wonder if Jessica is sitting at a table, waving at me through the glass. Maybe she can't come, and I'm standing out here alone for no reason. She wouldn't have a way to tell me if it happened.

The wind whips my hair across my face, flutters the flags across the street. American. Montanan. A blue one for the Fort Peck tribes. Another I don't recognize. A couple passes by me, and the door rings, a small bell attached to the top of the frame. Jessica expects us to be regular friends. Friends who sit and talk about . . . things I should know to talk about, and neither of us worrying about paying with cash so we can stay anonymous. Yes, Jessica knows about homeschool and me not going to the doctor, but she still thinks I can be a normal friend.

I'm not sure I can be.

With Alex, it's different. He knew me before I knew things. The Lark that goes to school and eats fries with ketchup is part of the person without a birth certificate. They're not separate, not yet. Probably will never be. I can still see who I was—who I still am—when I'm with him. But with Jessica, I'm someone new. Someone with homework. Someday maybe a license. A person who might get a high school diploma. I'm louder with Jessica, too. I talk more. Laugh at jokes I don't always understand. And I don't know if I can be that Lark for an entire conversation when there aren't teachers or assignments to fill up the space.

The door swings open, ringing the bell again.

"Are you coming in?" Jessica smiles, pops the end of a fry in her mouth. "I ordered a couple things already because I was too hungry to wait."

She leans into the door, swinging it farther open.

Yes, I'm going in. Ready or not.

Jessica sits across the table, her dusty boots propped up on the bench beside me. Between us are trays of half-eaten fried foods—onion rings, two kinds of cheese curds, and chili cheese fries. They're cold now, less crisp, and even though I'm not hungry anymore I keep eating. Because they're here. And it keeps me from having to say much, though Jessica doesn't give me much space. She tells me about school, her family, asking me questions but not lingering when I don't have much to answer.

Where did your name come from? *The state bird and anti-government patriots.* I just tell her about the bird.

What do your parents do? *Evade the government.* No. Not that. A truck driver. A mom.

What type of music do you like? I should know this. It's so simple. Not a hard question. But I can't name a song *I* like, that isn't just a favorite of my parents.

My answers aren't lies but incomplete truths. I don't tell her everything. Still, Jessica doesn't push. Doesn't look at me like I'm one of the crazies Grandma Betty describes.

It's easier than I expected, having a friend.

Jessica fiddles with her gold cross necklace. "I did what you said with my tailgate, but it might not even matter. Dad told me he'd take my truck if I didn't get at least a C in all my classes."

I wonder what her dad is like. If he's anything like mine. Sounds like maybe. Her dad went to law school before he decided to come back to the farm, she said. My dad escaped to the farm, but now he's left again.

"By the grace of god, I'll pass all my finals and I can stop stressing," she says. The cross twists in her fingers. She sees my doubt. "He arranges all things in my life."

"But how do you know?" I don't want to hurt her feelings, crush her with reason the way I know Dad would try. "Because you don't have . . . proof."

Jessica smiles. "I don't need proof. I have faith."

Mom says that, too, about faith, but really it doesn't look

that different from hope. No matter how much faith Mom had that the babies would be okay, it didn't make a difference.

"People believe in things they can't see all the time," Jessica continues, dropping her feet so she can lean on the table. "You believe in gravity but you can't see it."

Gravity. I try to remember. A push or a pull? Falling?

"Radio waves. Wi-Fi. The air." She breathes out into her hand. "You can't see it, but you can feel it. You know it's there. Or what about emotions? Love. You wouldn't say those things aren't real."

No. She's right. I never saw the Twin Towers fall, but I believed it was by government design. I've worried about antibiotics even though I've never felt their effects. So far everything I know has come from two places: my parents and the farm.

If I stop believing them, then I'll only have what I can see. But there's more than that to know. Things I'll never feel but are still true.

"Believing without seeing," Jessica says, dropping her rumpled napkin onto her empty plate. "That's faith."

It's not enough for me. I might not see gravity, but I want to know how it works. Radio waves make sense when I hold the deconstructed parts in my hands.

I can't just believe anymore. I need to be certain I'll know the truth when I hear it.

Things Jessica Says I Absolutely Have to Try

Leggings

Prayer

Spinning snow cookies in her truck (once I have a license)

Charcoal face masks

Ramen noodles

Gum

Listening to music

CHAPTER 21

Two days later, Mom is on one of her evening walks with Gizmo, the kind that bridges the days she spends in bed with those she whirls around the house, and I use the time to study. Back before Willow Creek, the evenings stretched on even before winter when the dark came early. Dad read. Mom puttered in the kitchen. I waited for the next day, sometimes playing with Gizmo, other times darning socks. Nothing to break the routine.

Now there's never enough time. I can barely finish my chores before I have to ride over to school. When I get home, I battle the sunset to do everything before it gets dark. It's impossible to get it all done.

I pull my large government book out of my bag and toss it on the bed. I flip to today's chapter, knowing I'll have to read it again: three times, maybe four.

The Constitution. Federalists. Anti-federalists. Centralized government. States' rights. Dad's used some of these words, talked about our Founding Fathers and the Constitution, but he never told me this. That they didn't agree. That those men had different ideas for how the country should be. To Dad, the original Constitution was perfect. But even the men who wrote it worried things could go wrong, that their big plan could be ruined.

According to Dad, it was. Government today is corrupt, yeast that won't rise.

I wonder if the Founders would agree. If I do.

I reach over to take a sip of the Coke sitting on my nightstand. Alex gave me a six-pack after I told him I kept falling asleep as I tried to finish my homework. He said the caffeine would help, but exhaustion still tugs at my eyelids. I take another sip. I still don't really like the flavor, but hopefully in a few minutes I'll be more alert as I track my finger along the page. Most of the words are lost to me, so I look at the pictures—men with pointy noses and ruffled white shirts. A map of revolutions. A drawing of nine statues—the states—and one falling over. Or being put back together. *United we stand. Divided we fall.* Dad would agree with that.

The screen door opens. She's back already?

"Mom?"

The door screeches shut. Thuds on the steps. I poke my head out the bedroom door.

"Mom?"

No answer. I take a few steps down the hall, peering around the corner and out the picture window.

Dad's truck.

I run back to my room, grabbing the book and tucking it underneath my covers, scattering the pillows around to cover the bump. I toss my bag underneath the bed and grab the can of Coke. Poison. At my door, I listen over the pressure of my heart in my ears. I let out a soft breath, trying to slow it all down. He doesn't know yet. The front door opens, and then a thud. His bag. Then he's back down the front steps. He's only got his coffee mug and his spit cup left to grab before he's inside for good.

Four days. He shouldn't be back yet.

I race down the hall to the bathroom, pulling the door shut and wishing it locked. I pour the Coke down the sink, the brown liquid swirling against the white. I hope it doesn't stain even though Dad says it's corrosive, like battery acid. I rinse the traces down the drain. Where to hide this can? I don't have time to run it to the barn, where I've shoved the rest underneath a bed of hay in an unused trough.

"Lark! Come help me with this!"

My heart jumps. "One sec!"

I look around the bathroom, opening the closet door and grabbing a towel. I wrap it around the can, trying to make it as flat as possible, and then move it to the bottom of the stack. I move some cloths to the front. I'll have to come get it before Dad takes his shower.

"Lark, now!"

One last check of my room for any signs of school, and then I'm in the pantry, where Dad stands at the sink, a cardboard box at his feet.

"Take this," he says, holding a dented can out to me. "One of these is leaking and it's all over the place." *Green Beans*, says the damp label, the paper torn at the edges. Must be from the food pantry in Billings. "Start wiping them off as I hand them to you."

I grab a cloth off the shelf and reach past him to wet it. One by one Dad hands me the cans and I wipe them down, stacking them on the shelf behind me. All beans. I was hoping for corn. Or beets.

"I didn't think you were back 'til the end of the week."

Dad frowns. "That piece of shit truck. I told Mike that part he gave me was crap, but he swore up and down it was still good. I started smoking again ten miles out of Pocatello. Barely made it back."

"How long you back for?"

"However long it takes me to fix that damn truck."

"I can help."

Dad smiles. "I'm sure you will, Larkie. It'll be nice to have a few extra days home. Just me and my girls."

I smile, hoping he doesn't see the guilt in my eyes. I used to love having him home a few extra days. Couldn't wait to spend the time fishing or hunting, my chores faster and more fun with company. Now I can only think of what I'll be missing. No way I can sneak off to school with him here.

"We can go pheasant hunting tomorrow if you want."

I want to debate about federalism. Or at least listen to others. I want Jessica to show me the videos of transmission repairs she promised.

"Or we can go down to the dam and fish a bit."

I want to take my math test. I want the Spanish word "familia" to roll around my mouth and off my tongue. Padre. Madre. Abuela.

Hermana.

Hermano.

"You don't seem too excited." Dad turns, looking at me with thinned eyes. "You got other plans?"

He laughs, wrapping an arm around my shoulder, because he doesn't know that I do.

A flicker in my bedroom window. Three bursts of light. Black.

Then three more. Up from the hill, the light flashes again, but it's too dark to see exactly who it is.

But I know.

I pull a jacket over my nightdress and tiptoe through the hallway. Their bedroom door is closed, the muffled sound of an internet video escaping beneath the doorframe. I grab a flashlight from the shelf by the door before pulling on my boots. The screen door creaks—why didn't I spray it with WD-40 like I meant to?—and I pause, waiting to hear their door open, his feet following me.

Nothing.

I stumble through the shelterbelt, the flashlight barely broad enough to create a clear path. By the Quonset, Alex sits on the four-wheeler, the light of his phone brightening the curve of his nose, adding a shimmer to his eyes. The flashlight on his phone keeps pulsing as I sprint up the last part of the hill, making my lungs burn.

"You can stop that now," I say. "I'm here."

Alex flicks off the flashlight and stuffs the phone into his pocket. "You were in bed already? It's like eight p.m."

"I wasn't asleep."

"But you're in your pajamas," he says, gesturing to my nightgown. "Your grandma pajamas."

His laughs fills the dark.

"What?"

"You're like *Little House on the*—yeah, makes sense." Alex sighs, resting his hands on the handlebars. I pull my jacket tighter against the breeze.

"Well, I knew we couldn't meet with my dad home."

"How long is he here for?" Alex asks.

I shrug. "However long it takes him to fix the truck."

"With your help it shouldn't be long. A couple of days?"

Another shrug. I never know with Dad. He often has a plan in his head that I don't find out about until it's already in action.

"So, your mom hasn't told him?"

"Not yet."

"I guess no study sessions, then? 'Til he's back on the road."

I nod.

"Well, hopefully it's not too long, then."

Alex's frown makes my guts smile. I'll miss him, too.

CHAPTER 22

A hand rocks my shoulder, its fingertips cool against my skin. The room is black, and it takes a few seconds before my eyes catch the outlines of Dad's face.

"It's time," he whispers, his teeth glinting in the dim morning light.

"Today?"

"Yes. Now."

"For real? Or—"

"Treat every time like it's the one."

I swallow a sigh. "What about Saturday?"

"No. Now. They aren't going to let us pick the day."

I ignore the fact that he did. He picked the day. The day of the math test. The debate in government. Now this. He can't fix the truck if we're bugging out. Another day lost, maybe two if he wants to stay out there.

Dad presses his watch, the screen lighting up green. "Let's go. You know we only got four minutes and we're already down eighteen seconds."

I flap back my quilt and Dad pats my knee. "You know what to do."

He's right. I do.

The next steps are familiar, and I count the seconds as I move, the way Dad taught me. Eight seconds to pull on my jeans and a sweater. Two seconds to grab the prepared bag from my closet.

I peek around the corner of Mom and Dad's room to see Mom hidden under the blankets, a mound in the darkness. Dad brushes past me in the hallway.

"Why isn't she up?"

Dad reaches into the closet to pull down our handguns. He shoves his in a holster and hands mine to me.

"Aren't you going to wake her up?"

Dad shakes his head. "Not today."

"Why not? We always go together."

After Mom lost Avery, Dad didn't have her help set up the cabin, but she always does the drills. Leave no man behind. Or mom.

"She's just not today." He drops his eyes. "She said no."

I wish I could say no. Dad's watch flashes green again. "No time to talk. I'll grab the safe and meet you outside."

No. He can't go down there. "I'll get it. I moved it when I took some new cans down. You get the bikes."

Dad frowns. We don't change the routine. I run down the stairs before he can say anything else. The safe is where it always is, beneath the bench where we'll sit and wait out the nuclear winter. I grab the key off the hook and grab out the envelope of cash.

It's only a drill. He won't look inside. He won't count it and see the missing $250.

I shove the envelope in my backpack and race back up the stairs.

Twenty-eight seconds.

In the shop, Dad rolls out the Honda before getting his old dirt bike. The front axle's wonky, so it's not great for every day, but bug outs only happen once in a lifetime. We hope. Gizmo races between the two of us, sensing our flight. I hop on the Honda, feeling the lightness without Mom clinging to me. *Travel fast. Travel light*, Dad always says. No Mom means we can probably do both. Dad revs his engine, hollering into the wind.

"Gizmo! Larkie! Let's go!"

He takes off so fast his wheels skid in the dust, but he rights himself before diving down into the ditch and heading up the north hill. The Honda bumps along the grass-worn path, and my bag jostles on my back. I should have tightened the straps. Gizmo huffs behind me, his big paws kicking up dirt as he races to keep up. I follow Dad's red taillight, the cold air catching in my throat when I try to yawn. I'm awake now.

When it's real—if it's real—I'll need to be ready from the beginning.

I wonder when they'll notice I'm not at school. Will Jessica think I'm sick again? Maybe she'll still save me a seat at lunch, thinking I'm just late like usual. I might have passed my math test. I finally know how to do math with letters: equations. Variables. Words I have now.

I would have passed it this time.

At the top of the hill, Dad pulls up next to the watering tank. A couple of Mike's cows hover nearby, their heads hung low as they yank mouthfuls of grass. Gizmo stands between our bikes, ready to run again as soon as the engines start. The kickstand is jammed on the dirt bike, so Dad rests it against a fence pole before hopping up onto the edge of the water tank.

"Wooo-ee!" he shouts, his boot splashing in the water,

and the cows scatter. He balances himself against a fence post. "Hand me the binoculars."

I shove the Honda kickstand into a clod of grass and walk to Dad's bike. The binoculars are in the second front pocket. I dig them out, a few batteries falling to the ground.

"You can get those in a minute. Get me the binocs."

I leave the batteries and hold the binoculars up to him. He teeters as he leans, but soon he's standing tall again, the binoculars pressed to his eyes.

"Road clear."

Of course it is. He scans to the left.

"House is clear."

Of course it is.

"Ah, look, there's Jefferson. Good for nothing donkey. Wish we could bring you, buddy."

Dad tosses the binoculars at me and I barely catch them by the strap. He jumps down, his smile even wider. "Let's give those government goons a run for their money."

He grabs the binoculars from my hand and I scramble to pick up the batteries and shove them in his pack. "I got it," he says, swatting my hand. "Go load up."

I run back to the Honda and hop on, Gizmo at my feet. I pat his head, trying to avoid the slobber dangling from his lips. It's a long ride ahead, but he never seems to mind. Maybe he's made for wandering.

I'm not.

After forty-five minutes of zigzagging and circling back across empty fields, we make it to the tiny cabin Uncle Charles made to store his fishing supplies, but which now must protect us from the post-collapse of society. I wonder if the cabin knows so much rests on its tilted frame.

Dad's out collecting wood from the pile we stacked last spring. The cold slips through the cracks in the logs to sting my cheeks as I sit surrounded by plastic containers I pulled out from under the floorboards. Inventory. Knives. Fuel. Batteries. Cooking utensils. Puzzle. That's what I'm supposed to be doing. Counting the lifelines in each box, sweeping out any spiders, checking for signs of mice or bugs in the rations. Simple math. The most basic when I could be doing algebra. I yank a coat out of one of the containers and lay it on my lap to warm my legs.

Gizmo bursts past Dad as he opens the door, running to slap his tongue all over my face.

"Go, you goon," I say, pushing him with my hand, but he only turns to stare at Dad, his tail whopping me in the face.

"How's the count?" Dad asks as he begins to build the fire in the black wood stove.

"Same as it always is."

He turns from where he's crouched by the open stove door.

"But you inventoried, right? That's step two upon arrival to the bug out."

"What does it look like I'm doing?"

"Honestly? Sitting on your ass."

I stand up, bumping into Gizmo. "You can count it yourself, then."

Dad drops his log, brushing his gloves on his canvas pants. "I don't appreciate that tone."

"I don't appreciate being drug out here for no reason. It's not even a real drill. We didn't bring Mom."

"It's still a real drill."

"So, we're gonna bug out without Mom?"

Dad huffs. "No, course not."

"Then it isn't a real drill."

"Why don't you take Gizmo and go find some kindling so I can get this fire started? Take your pissy attitude out for a walk."

"Fine," I say, kicking a container as I make my way to the door. Outside, Gizmo races along the edges of the pond, kicking up birds and sending the cattails bobbing. I gather a handful of dried grass and leaves for the kindling and shove them in my pocket before stopping to sit on the dock. Gizmo splashes in the edges of the water. I hope he doesn't get too close. I don't want to get sprayed, not when it's this cold.

I used to like bug outs. Liked the break from the routine. The adventure. The rush in my veins as we raced away from the enemy. I didn't mind setting up camp, checking the inventory, and building the fire. I liked choosing my MRE—my favorite is beef ravioli. Seems fancy, like you'd get at a restaurant in town. I'd beat them both at Gin Rummy, and sometimes Dad would play the harmonica. It was a nice way to wait away the post-collapse, even if it was just practice.

But now it feels different.

Alex said when he was a kid, his cousins told him that the bogeyman lived under his bed, and if any part of his body slipped over the edge of the bed at night, it would yank him down into the depths of hell. So, for an entire summer, Alex slept wrapped up so tight in his blankets he could barely breathe, let alone move his arms. One night, he heard scratching underneath his bed and then saw a hand reaching up toward him. He screamed, rolled off the edge, and smacked his face on the ground so hard his nose gushed blood all over the carpet. His aunt came in when she heard the screams, and once the lights were on, the bogeyman was revealed to be his cousins. He never slept rolled up tight like that again. He knew the bogeyman wasn't real anymore. He learned. He grew up.

But here we are, Dad and I and Gizmo, miles away from anyone, hiding out from our danger. It used to be real. I could smell the smoke of fires scorching the cities, hear the gunshots as people fought over the last stores of food. I'd never seen a government agent before, but I could imagine their tight fingers on my arm as they dragged me away to a life of confinement. I felt safe here, miles away from a home that was hundreds of miles away from the cities of corruption.

Now I wonder if maybe when the lights get turned on, there won't be anything to see but the two of us and Gizmo in a rickety cabin next to a pond no one knows exists.

It's not like I can ask Dad if it's all real—elite control, 9/11, impending martial law. How would I explain knowing something he didn't tell me? And wouldn't his answer be the same? Bugging out is his answer. The prepped materials are his answer.

Our life, this life, is the answer.

"Lark! You got that kindling?"

"Let's go, Gizmo," I call, and he follows me up out of the pond, shaking droplets onto my legs. I walk back toward the cabin, deciding to look for the cards, because even if it isn't real, and the government will never come, and the sky will never darken in a nuclear night, I still have nowhere else to go.

CHAPTER 23

I t's my first day back, and I'll be late to school again. I was going to get up an hour early. Finish chores even if it meant the chickens would stay roosting in the coop because of the dark. Make it to school before 8:00 a.m. so I could ask Jessica to catch me up on the missing assignments. Copy her notes. Slip back into life as a normal student.

That was before Dad decided to stay one more night. Now I'm waiting for him to pack the truck, kiss the top of my head, yell goodbye to Gizmo, and pull the rig out of our driveway and down the dirt road on his way back to Pasco.

He's still drinking his coffee. Second cup.

It's 7:45 a.m. I should have left fifteen minutes ago.

My books are ready in a bag underneath my bed, pushed behind some old boots that don't fit and my tackle box. I can't pack my lunch while Dad's here, watching me from the table while he pretends to read. Instead, I hover around the kitchen, rearranging jars of dried herbs and straightening the dish towels.

"Got ants in your pants?" Dad asks, setting his book down on the table and creasing the corner with his stained thumb.

"Yeah." It's better to tell as much truth as I can when the rest is a lie.

He smirks. "Thought so. You've been bouncing around the kitchen like a chicken with your head cut off. What's the deal?"

"I don't know."

"If you want something to do, you could head down to the far end of the garden and start putting it down for the winter. I can bring you the rototiller before I head out."

I don't want to start down at the garden. "Do you have a new book for me to read?" Distract him.

Dad tilts his head and smiles. "Why, Larkie, yes I do."

He reaches into the backpack at his feet, loosening the strings at the top and then digging his massive hand inside. He pulls out a stack of books and rests them on the table. He slides a red book covered in blue eyeballs across the table to me.

"Here. Try that one." I sit down in a chair across from him, holding the book in my hands. *The Trial*. It's not too thick. I flick the pages with my thumb. "Didn't expect you to want to read."

At first, asking for a book was just a way to kill time without having to start a major chore I wouldn't be able to get out of, but now I realize—I might be able to read this. I skip through pages that don't look like the actual story until I come to the first page. *Arrest*. I read the first three sentences, pausing on a name I don't recognize, but moving forward like Ms. Leland taught me.

"What?" Dad asks.

"What?"

"You're smiling."

"Oh." I didn't realize that.

"It's not a funny book."

I set it down, holding my place with my thumb. I should be more careful. Not show the learning on my face. "It's not that. It's just . . . I can read this book."

Dad frowns. "Of course you can. You read all the time, way harder books than that."

But I'm really reading this time. Or at least trying to. I'm not just looking at the words and waiting for Dad to fill in the answers.

"Right. Reading this book just feels easy today."

Dad smiles, stretching his arms up and over his head. "That's because you're a genius, Larkie."

I know he believes that. I'm not a genius, but I am reading. 8:03 a.m. I'm also late.

I pick up the book and finish a few pages, knowing I'll have to come back and read them again, not because I can't understand the words but because my brain's too focused on Dad. Mom rustles in the bedroom, but I hope she stays asleep long enough for us both to leave. Dad and I watch each other over the tops of our books, quick glances in a game of chicken. Dad slugs back the last of his coffee.

"Okay. It's time. Gotta hit the road."

I keep my eyes on the page as Dad walks back to his bedroom. A whispered conversation with Mom, and then he's back with his bag. He pauses to kiss my forehead.

"Take care of your mom. See you in a few weeks."

"How many exactly?"

Dad rests a hand on the back of my chair. "You want your dad back already? Wishing we were still splitting the chores?"

I nod as if that's why I want to know. As if I'm wondering when I can go fishing again, when someone else can feed the cows.

"Short trip this time. Just to make up for those lost days. Ten to Pasco. Three down to Willamette. Four days over to Cheyenne if the weather's good, and then home. You do the math."

Ten plus three plus four plus a handful. Three weeks?
Maybe more. I wave to Dad before he heads down the stairs,
yells goodbye to Gizmo, and pulls the rig out of the driveway.
In minutes, I'm gone, too.

CHAPTER 24

What are you working on tonight?" Mom asks, bouncing on the edge of my bed when she sits. She's more interested in my lessons now than she ever was in the years she was homeschooling me and actually in charge of what I learned. She never even asked where I was going on the nights I studied with Alex. But now that I do my homework in the house, she comes in multiple times a night, sometimes to drop off a snack, other times to give me a break I didn't ask for. I think she's bored. Or lonely.

"Is it science?" She sticks out her tongue. "I hate science."

"It's not science."

"Good." She flops behind me, shoving the pillow under her head. She leans on her side, one arm wrapped around my waist. "Can you read me something?"

She also does this, asks me to read out loud, but she's usually asleep within minutes. Sometimes snoring. Always drooling. I don't mind the warmth of her beside me, as long as she's quiet. She did stay up when I read the poems from Ms. Leland's class. Emily Dickinson. She liked the one about hope like a bird. Said it reminded her of the babies.

"Please? Just for a few minutes," Mom begs.

I look down at the workbook in my hands. "It's not really that kind of book."

"I don't care. I just like listening to you."

I'm still grateful she didn't tell Dad when he was home, so

this is an easy thing to give her. I flip the spiral cover, glancing over my shoulder to see her eyes already closed, her arms crossed over her chest. Her nails look better. She must not be chewing them.

"'Blind spot. The area in the rear passenger side of the vehicle that is difficult for the driver to see when looking over their right shoulder. Modern vehicle . . . design . . . intended to limit—'"

Mom props herself up on her arm. "What class is this?"

"Driver's ed."

She frowns. "I didn't sign you up for driver's ed."

"It started a couple weeks ago. I have the papers in my backpack for you to sign."

Mom pushes up higher now, her back flat against the headboard, her arms crossed.

"You don't need driver's ed. You already know how to drive."

I place a scrap of notebook paper in the workbook to mark my place.

"I know, but I actually don't know a lot of this. Like a blind spot? I didn't know about that."

"Your dad taught you about blind spots!"

"No, he didn't."

"Of course he did. That's basic. You just don't remember."

Her throat is flushing red. She tugs at one of her fingernails.

"Okay, maybe I knew about blind spots, but there's lots of other things in here: tips for maintaining the engine and driving on ice. Also, I don't have a license and you're supposed to have one if you're going to drive. Like to town or something.

It's a crime if you don't. I could get pulled over by the police. Then what?"

Mom starts mumbling, her eyes telling more of a story than her mouth.

"What?" Nothing. "Mom?"

"No."

Suddenly, she is up and marching out of my room. I leave my books and follow her to the kitchen, where she starts yanking pots out of the cabinet.

"No what? Mom? No what?"

She slams a pot down on the stove. "No license. No driver's ed. No."

"What, why? I can get the money. Mike said he'd pay me to repair a few things."

She rolls her eyes before attempting to open a jar of stewed beef and tomatoes. Her fingers go white as she tries to remove the lid.

We already ate dinner. This doesn't make sense.

"You said it yourself, Lark. You already know how to drive. So why would you need a license? Why would anyone? You don't get a license when you learn other basic things. You don't get a walking license. Or a school license. There's only one reason you would need a little plastic card with your picture on it." I reach for the jar, and she yanks it back. "Because the government wants to track you!"

I move out of her way as she pushes toward the sink, running cool water over the lid.

"It's like we taught you nothing. You've been at this school, what? A couple months? And suddenly you want a license and . . . and . . . and to . . . there's a reason you don't have a birth certificate, Lark! You belong to me and to your dad and to the land. And to god. Not to the government. You give them your name and address and then it's over. You're in their system forever. You're theirs."

I reach for the jar again, and this time she hands it to me. I twist twice and it releases, sourness biting the air. Rancid? Botulism?

"I loosened it," Mom says, snatching the jar from my hands and dumping it into the pot from so high the droplets splatter the stove and counter. "Maybe your dad was right about school. I let you talk me into it—"

"No. I won't do driver's ed. I don't need a license. It's okay, Mom—"

Maybe I can at least keep the book, the chance to know about insurance and warranties, even if I'll never need them. As long as I can stay in school.

Mom sighs as she stirs. "Homeschool was fine. You learned, right?"

"No, I didn't. Not really."

"How can you say that? After all your dad has done for you—"

"Dad hasn't done real lessons for years."

Mom scoffs. "You're in high school now at some fancy private school, so you must have learned something!"

She can't actually believe that. She has to know my home-school hasn't been anything real. No science. Simple math. Only books I can't read.

"I'd think you'd be more grateful for all we've given you, all we gave up for you," Mom says. "Your dad was right. Government school only corrupts young minds."

I reach for her. "It's not like that. I am grateful. I'll tell them I'm not going to take the class. It's not required. I don't want to, anyway." I run a hand down her arm. The lies and my touch soothe her. "Mom?"

She swirls a spoon in the stew, the gas flames flickering blue beneath it. Low. I might need to check the gas line. We'll need more heat if there's bacteria.

The room is quiet. We're together in the kitchen.

Like it used to be.

Maybe the way she wants it.

"Why are you looking at me like that? It's true!"

Alex smiles from his spot leaned back against the barn walls. The wind finds us through the cracks in the beams, and he pulls the collar of his jacket up higher. It's getting too cold to keep studying in the loft and too dark, but even though Mom knows about school, we'd rather be up here. Alone.

"Some are going for $100,000. $500,000," I say. "I don't have all the tools for some of those big repairs, but the videos show you the whole thing, start to finish. If I could fix up one of those cars Mike has in the south barn, it's . . ."

More money than I can imagine. I could buy a lot with that much cash. Gas. Food. A new jacket and work pants. Maybe even my own truck.

"If anyone can do it, you can."

I tuck my fingers under my legs to warm them. "I can't stop watching the videos anytime we're in the computer lab. It's amazing! If I had this back when I was working on your repair, I would have been done way sooner. Have you watched YouTube?"

Alex laughs. "Yes, Lark, I know about YouTube."

"Right." My cheeks flush. I bite my chapped lips. Shiver.

"You're cold. We should go inside."

I shake my head. "I'm fine." Gizmo barks at the sound of a truck driving past. The chickens cluck below us. "Why are you looking at me like that again?"

Alex pats the dusty barn floor beside him. "It's fun to watch you like this. You've always been kind of shy, uncertain about yourself, and it's like this person was always waiting to come out, but you couldn't because of your parents and everything, but now you're getting to experience all the great things in life—chocolate, YouTube. Nothing's too cool for you. It's all new and amazing. You remind me how lucky we are."

I scoot over to him, and he wraps an arm over my shoulder.

Lucky, yes.

For now.

CHAPTER 25

ootsteps in the hallway, and no one turns as the door opens. The room is dark except for the small rectangle on the screen, a video explaining photosynthesis, the reason plants need the sun. I track the tiny balls of light, watching them move from the sky to green and purple compartments within a plant, still amazed at how small the world is. The room is dark, yet I recognize those boots and dusty jeans.

I would throw up if my stomach wasn't empty.

"Excuse me, sir, can I help you?" Ms. Mullins says, standing up behind the desk where she's been grading our most recent quiz. I might have gotten some right this time. Letters pop up on the screen, E and ATP and so many tiny balls moving and humming and becoming food for the plants. I thought they ate water.

"Let's go."

"Please, Daddy," I whisper as his fingers wrap around my forearm. I didn't get a chance to write the last word.

"Now, Lark."

I trip on my bag as I stand, grasping the desk beside me. "I'm sorry," I whisper as my hand clasps Andrew, the boy who sits beside me.

Jessica's mouth opens, her eyes hidden in the dark. Goodbye.

"Sir!" Ms. Mullins says, but Dad doesn't pause.

"I already checked her out at the office. She's not going to school here anymore."

His fingers are warm, the heat pulsing through his palms. Has he absorbed the colors of the sun? Are those rays heating up his skin? I didn't know the sun does more than burn.

"I'll walk. I'll come with you," I whisper as Dad pulls me through the hallways. I don't hear any feet on the tiles behind us. We're a few steps from the front office window, and I breathe out. They might stop us. Ms. Frandsen will turn, her lips forming an "oh" of surprise, and she'll call for Mr. Leibach.

No. They don't stop us. Do they even try?

"I'm sorry, Daddy," I cry as he slams against the front door of the school, his hip pushing the bar and letting us out into the crisp air. I look back for someone, anyone, but he shoves my shoulder and I trip down the front steps.

"Get in the truck."

Dad's red semitruck is parked across the gravel parking lot, blocking cars on both sides. He opens the passenger door, pushing me up faster than I can climb, and I bang my shin against the metal doorframe. My hands scramble for the back of the seat so I can hoist myself up before he slams the door shut. Once closed, I squeeze near the door, out of his reach.

Heat builds behind my eyes, but I won't cry.

Dad jumps in the other side, slamming the door and turning the engine. He reaches across to lock my door, as if I would jump out.

As if I had anywhere to run.

The truck hums down the highway until we reach our driveway. Can he hear my heart? Dad doesn't park the truck like normal. He leaves it across the circle drive, the wheels smashing the stems of the flowers I planted this summer.

Will they do photosynthesis anymore? Did he break the delicate light-changing rooms inside?

Mom stands on the wooden steps, a hand pressed over her eyes to block the sun. Does she know it's not just yellow, not just white? It's full of colors, all the colors, we just can't see them. They're hidden like the tiny balls of energy inside the plants. I scramble out of my seat, not wanting Dad to yank me down again.

"Do not move!" Dad yells as he marches over to the garage. He comes back with his shotgun. And mine.

Mom calls to him, "Brett, come inside. Bring her inside. She's home now."

Why isn't he yelling at her, too? She let me go. It was my choice but she said yes.

Dad shoves the shotgun in my hands. "Walk."

I stumble behind him as he trudges past the barn, his feet on the worn, familiar path. We walk for fifteen minutes until we're up on the ridge behind the house. The grasses scratch against my legs as I follow steps behind, the air dry as it begins to cool. My feet search for space between the clumps of wild grasses as we zigzag back and forth, making sure the pheasants don't circle behind and into safety. I need to retie my boots.

I walk and wait, and then a rush of movement and flight. Two pheasants soar into the horizon, their bright red breasts the perfect target against the gray sky.

One, two. They fall, their outstretched wings collapsing against their sides.

"Will the government teach you that in their schools?" Dad shouts even though I'm only steps behind him.

"They aren't the government."

We look for the spots where the birds fell, but the grass absorbs them, the wind swaying the blades across the entire hill.

"Do you think your Jesus Freaks would teach you this?" Dad shouts again. "To be self-sufficient? To know the land? No. They only care about hooie-wooie magic and judgment. But I judge them."

He turns. He judges me.

Dad reaches down, pressing aside a tall piece of brush, and grabs the first pheasant by its legs. It flops, its wings pattering until he picks it up. Its wings lift again, ready to soar, and then he shakes. Once. Twice. And hands it to me. We find the other a few paces away. It doesn't flop, doesn't soar. He drops it in my hands.

We're silent as we walk back to the house, the birds swinging at my side.

At home, Dad prepares one pheasant at the counter, his hunting knife moving quickly around bones and through ligaments. He palms the gizzard, holding it toward me.

"Here, your own science experiment."

His knife slices through the white layer, the deep purple muscle. He pulls it open, revealing the green grit inside.

"And what's this? It's what the pheasant ate."

I know. I've seen it before.

I know about pheasants. Where to find them, how they

move. Their breasts, their legs, their gizzards, which Mom will never eat.

I know about pheasants, but I don't know about photosynthesis.

And now, I never will.

Things Jessica Says I Absolutely Have to Try

~~Leggings~~

~~Prayer~~

~~Spinning snow cookies in her truck (once I have a license)~~

~~Charcoal face masks~~

~~Ramen noodles~~

~~Gum~~

~~Listening to music~~

In the quiet dark, Mom sneaks into my room. She exhales as she sits on the bed beside me. I close my eyes and pretend to sleep.

"I didn't tell him, Larkie," she whispers, reaching up to touch my cheek. I pull the sheet up higher. "I swear."

Dad's footsteps in the hallway and she pauses, her hand resting on my hair. Inhale, exhale, a sniffle, then a whisper.

"Please don't be mad. I don't know how he found out."

I roll over, away from her and the lie. Of course she told him. There isn't a world in which she doesn't. It's how the machine works, the spark plug, the on-switch. I started up school, but she was always ready to turn it off.

All he probably did was ask, *Where's Lark?*

"Larkie?" I hold still. "I know you're not asleep."

There isn't anything for me to say. I knew she'd tell. She did. It's over. She brushes back the hair on my forehead, and I pull from her grasp. "Stop."

"Maybe it's a good thing. That school . . . it wasn't right. It's better this way. Like before."

Three flashes in the window from Alex's flashlight, but I pull the curtain closed. I can't risk sneaking out. Not tonight. No matter how much I want to hear his voice.

It'll be okay, Lark. We'll figure it out.

I want to hear it even though I know it's not true.

I close my eyes, knowing tomorrow I'll wake up one day closer to forgetting.

It works when we lose the babies.

The Montana Freemen

Patriots

Held off the FBI for 81 days

Protected their land: Justus Township (my namesake)

Fought for freedom

Defied tyranny

Knew the laws better than those damn lawyers and
government hacks

Sovereign individuals

Died in prison

CHAPTER 26

Mom's head rests on my shoulder, her curls tickling my neck, my arms, her breath warm on my skin. I tried to tilt her toward the window twenty miles ago when she first fell asleep, but she tucked her arm around mine, holding me like her pillow. Dad hasn't spoken since he woke me up this morning. One of his arms rests on the windowsill and the other on the stick shift. My legs are tucked over by Mom so he has room to shift gears. I wish I could be farther away this morning. Dust blows in through the air vents, and I sneeze, the only sound for the past two hours.

I don't know where we're going, or when we'll get there.

Not enough supplies packed to be camping. Wrong road for the bug out.

Two hours puts us just outside Havre, where we've gone to get seed. Nothing to plant this time of year, anyway.

We're halfway to Great Falls. Mom had a family reunion there once. We didn't go.

I picture the map on our wall, trying to measure out the distance from our home in two hours' worth of thumbs.

This morning before it was light, Dad shook me awake, barking at me to get dressed. Hurry up. He'd be waiting in the truck. No hint of the excitement that comes from a bug out or an early morning hunt. Mom was in the cab when I got there, her eyes closed, her mouth tilted open as she slept against the head rest.

Now we're driving on Highway 200, the fields of brown, cut wheat passing by the windows. Dad isn't listening to the radio like normal. We aren't sharing a bag of sunflower seeds like usual. I keep my eyes on the road and wait for something familiar.

Finally, as the light peeks over the rusty hills, Dad pulls onto a dirt road. No sign. No particular mile marker, but he seems to know where he's going. The truck bumps along the gravel ridges, waking Mom up. She yawns, rubs her eyes, and then leans her head against my shoulder.

"Almost there?" Mom asks, interlacing our fingers. She glances at Dad, hopes for him to respond. When he doesn't, she pretends like she never asked. "We shoulda packed breakfast. I'm hungry."

"Check the bag on the floorboard," Dad says without looking at her.

Mom pulls a plastic bag onto her lap, digging around to find a bottle of water, several pieces of jerky wrapped in a cloth napkin, and a mason jar of nuts. She unscrews the lid, shaking some straight into her mouth.

"You want some, Larkie?" She holds out the jar, and I shake my head. The gravel road and the unknown are making me carsick.

In the distance, a shelterbelt of pine trees looms in front of a tall, rocky hill that could almost be a mountain if it wasn't alone. The road curves and then I see it: a small white farmhouse surrounded by run-down corrals, a tilted barn, everything weathered gray. A paint-chipped gas tank next to a rotting wood box. A smaller shelterbelt of bushes with few leaves surrounds the house, the branches not protecting

THE TRUTH ABOUT EVERYTHING

anything from the wind. Dad pulls the truck into the driveway and parks.

No cars. No other trucks.

"You know this place, Lark?" Dad asks.

"No."

"You sure? You should."

"No."

"The spirit of this place, it's in your bones. It's in your name."

Oh. In all the stories, I never pictured it like this, a run-down farmhouse in the middle of fields just like ours. "It's Justus Township."

"I gotta get out," Mom says. "Stretch my legs."

The open doors send a rush of cool air into the truck. Mom hops down, slamming the door behind her. Through the rear-view mirror, I see her walk down the road behind the truck, her arms swinging in circles.

She's left me alone with him. On purpose? Maybe.

"Your name was supposed to be Adeline," Dad says, his eyes staring at—what? The old house? The barren trees? "Your name was Adeline until the moment I held you at the picture window and looked out on the hills, the big open sky. I wanted you to soar, Lark, not be trapped in the ground. You couldn't fly if you were Adeline."

Adeline. I feel this new-old me inside my mouth. Adeline.

"So, we called you Lark, after the meadowlark. Montana's state bird."

That I know.

"You didn't have a middle name until the day you were born, either. The babies, they didn't need middle names, but you, I wanted you to be free. To live without chains, without lies, without anyone holding you back: not your body and not your mind."

Dad turns. Looks at me.

"See, when I was a kid, I didn't know better. I went where they said and did what they wanted, and it felt wrong. The wrong crawled under my skin, but I just kept doing it. I never questioned. I sang the hymns and sat in the classes. But why, Lark? Did it teach me to be a better man?"

Together we shake our heads.

"Did it teach me to see clearly? See for myself?"

Again, no.

"All the truth, the truth I'm trying to teach you, Lark, I had to find on my own. I was trapped for my whole life, but not you. You're free! You've been free from the day you were born! Lark Justus. You don't belong to the state or to the government. You belong only to yourself."

In this story of him I've heard a thousand times, he's never talked about me. Not like this.

His eyes wrinkle, his throat catches. "So why?" Not here, in the truck, with me there to see it. He only ever cries alone. "Why would you want to give it all up?"

I didn't think about it like that. Not giving something up, but gaining something.

Out the window, Mom is swaying side to side, her sweater hanging off her shoulders as she stretches her arms, the wind blowing them like a weathervane.

"If there's something you want to learn, I can teach you. If there's something you want to know, we'll find out."

Dad grabs my hands, his calluses scratching against mine.

Underneath his fingernails, a thin line of black. His thumb-nail is still split from where it got slammed in the hood last summer.

"Anything," Dad says, squeezing my hands. "Just name it."

I think of the books at school, the shelves and shelves, more books than I've ever seen and all the colors of paper and the microscope in Ms. Mullins's room and the copies of *Our Town* and the entire roomful of computers. A computer lab. *Me gusta la escuela.*

"Do you know about photosynthesis?"

Dad frowns. "Isn't that how plants get food?"

I nod. "Yeah, from the sun."

"That's what you wanted to go to school for? Photosynthesis?"

"Not just that."

"Write it down, then. Make me a list of all the things you want to learn. And we'll do it."

"Really? Every day?"

"Yes!"

"What about my chores?"

"We'll figure it out. I promise. If you wanna learn, Lark, you'll learn."

At home. I'll be homeschooled again. Or maybe for the first time really since before was home without school. But can it even be different if he's still the one teaching me?

"And you'll have to tell me the truth."

"What's that supposed to mean?"

"When you tell me things, you have to tell me what really happened. They talked about 9/11 at school. They said—"

Dad shakes his head. "See! You're already buying into their lies."

"But how would I know differently! You haven't given me any proof."

His head drops. "You're right. That's my fault. I wanted to shield you from it, keep the ugliness away from you, but I was wrong. There's proof, Lark. I just haven't shown it to you, and they never will because they don't want you to see it. They don't want you to know."

Dad lets go of my hands. "Don't put yourself in a cage, Lark, not when you're already free." He turns and pops open the door. "And now I gotta go find a place to pee."

For the next few hours, we peer into darkened windows, trying to glimpse the life behind the dusty blinds. Gold hidden from the government, the New Federal Reserve, a courthouse siege in Garfield County. The same stories Dad's told a hundred times but this time, in the real place, they seem more ordinary and, surprisingly, more real. Not simply heroes, but farmers with a fence that needs mending and a shelterbelt that won't stop the wind. Proof I can see, touch with my chilled fingertips. Being in this place moves them from Dad's mind to Justus Township.

Maybe makes them a bit more a part of me.

CHAPTER 27

I'm shutting the chickens," I yell as soon as I see Alex's head-lights out the picture window. He can't come here. Not yet. I'm not sure what Dad would do if he knew Alex was part of it—school, sneaking out, studying. When no one responds, I grab the bucket off the hook and head out and around the house.

Gizmo bounds alongside me as we race through the ditch. "Go home!" I tell him, but he sticks to my side.

A deer in the dark, his loud barks—that's all it will take—and they'll wonder why he's on the hill and not with me check-ing the chickens. I can't sneak with him loping beside me. "Here, fetch!"

I toss a thin stick into the air, but it doesn't have enough weight to fly farther than a few feet. Gizmo nuzzles the grass but moves on when he realizes it's just a twig.

"Stop following me!" I plead even though I know it won't make a difference. "I'll be back!"

Up the hill, parked behind the Quonset, is Mike's nice truck. The navy-blue Chevy he only drives to church or wed-dings and vacuums after each ride with the Shop-Vac. Alex jumps out and runs toward me. He's wearing a T-shirt and gym shorts, the neck of his shirt still ringed with sweat just like the edges of his hair. He's not supposed to be here—it's a practice night—but I'm so relieved to see him.

Two more steps and his arms are wrapped around me.

The empty egg bucket falls to my feet. My cold cheeks warm against his chest, my head rising with each of his breaths. His heart beats, slowing mine.

"Oh my god, Lark, I was so worried when you didn't come out last night." He holds me back, peering into my face. "Mike said he'd never seen your Dad so pissed. Are you okay?"

Mike? But Mom? She didn't . . . she was telling the truth?

"Mike told him?" I ask. "How'd he know?"

"Church," Alex says. "Apparently someone at the school was talking about this homeschooled girl who started there and Mike asked questions and figured it out. He told your dad when he came over to bitch about some part."

I never even considered Mike. After all the planning, fearing the ways Dad might find out, picturing Mom whispering in his ear. A broken part and Mike's big mouth.

Doesn't matter now.

Alex slides his hands up my arm. His fingers are cold. "Are you okay? How mad was he?"

I shake my wrist even though it's not sore anymore.

"I'm fine."

Alex's fingers find their way back down to my wrists and I grab his hands, holding him close for a few more minutes. The yard light fills up a bigger circle as the hills darken around the house. Gizmo disappears into the dark. I want to stay here with him smiling at me, but I can't be that Lark, the one he believes in, the one he's proud of. Not anymore. "I have to get back."

"I'll walk you down."

I shake my head. "You don't need to do that."

"Then I can come later this week," Alex says. "We can keep

working together—keep you in shape. You have the books still, right?"

I nod. For now. They'll be gone by morning.

"We can plan for what's next. Are you thinking Wolf Point? I can talk to the counselor and see what you need for registration. I mean it's far, but—"

I pull my hands back. Step away. Grab the bucket off the ground. An ache tears through me, knowing what I have to tell him. He won't want to hear it. I'm not certain I want to say it.

"I have to go. We'll talk later. Gizmo!" I look past Alex, searching for movement. I can't look at him. "Gizmo, let's go!"

Alex reaches for me. "Lark? What's going on?"

"I have to check the chickens," I say, heading back down the hill, ignoring the tightness in my throat, the sting in my eyes.

Alex follows. "Okay, but why are you running from me?"

"I'm not running. Gizmo!"

I can't yell any louder.

"Lark, stop!" Alex says, his cold fingers grazing mine.

He won't understand. He can't. Alex has always been different. He knows me, but he doesn't know this—the stories and beliefs that I can't separate from, even if I tried.

"I'm not going to Wolf Point. Or any school." Quick. Sharp. Tell him. "I'm going back to homeschool."

Alex stops. "Seriously? Why?"

"It's going to be different. Dad said he will buy me real textbooks and I'll have time now, it won't be just chores. He says I can learn whatever I want; I can use the internet." Maybe. I don't know if that's what he meant about proof, but I hope so. "It will be real school."

Gizmo catches us, tagging Alex's legs before returning to mine.

"After fifteen years of nothing, why would you believe that?"

"It's not nothing."

Alex crosses his arms, the wind catching the ends of his hair. "Okay. Can you do long division?"

"Maybe."

"How can you 'maybe' do long division?"

I press Gizmo away with my palm again his wet nose. "I might know how to do it but just call it something else."

"Fine," Alex says. "I'll give you that. Long division is when you divide with the little box. One number, the divisor or the dividend, I don't remember, goes inside the box. And then you divide it and bring the numbers down. You might have a remainder."

I stare at the dirt, trying to picture the numbers and lines he's describing with words I remember seeing in the math book Dad bought me years ago. It doesn't match up with the math we were doing at Willow Creek, either. That was algebra.

"I don't know how to do that."

"Who was the first president of the United States?"

"George Washington."

"Bravo!" Alex says as he claps for me, the sound sharp in the quiet night. "Do you know any other presidents?"

"Yes," I say, finally grateful for all of Dad's history lectures about our Founding Fathers. "Thomas Jefferson. Paul Revere. Abraham Lincoln. George Bush. Benjamin Templeton?"

"Who?" Alex says. "You mean Benjamin Franklin?"

I blush. "Yeah. I just forgot."

"He wasn't a president. Neither was Paul Revere. What was the Civil War about?"

I search my mind, but it's as messy as Mike's shop, random names and broken facts scattered too far from each other for me to put them back together.

"States' rights."

"Uh, no. Slavery. What are the continents?" His words are fast, cold.

"Can we stop now?"

"Just one. Name one continent."

" . . . France."

Alex takes a long breath. "France is not a continent. It's a country. Europe is the continent and it's full of countries. Germany. Spain. Italy. The Netherlands—"

"Okay."

"Doesn't it bother you, Lark?" he asks, his eyes hidden, the moonlight outlining his body.

Does he think I don't know? That I didn't feel shame every day at Willow Creek when every lesson, each book contained something I had never heard of? The second-guessing I do about the smallest parts of my life—can I eat this? Will this hurt me?

I knew, and I made a change.

"It's going to be different this time," I say. And it could be because I'm different. I won't just believe Dad without question. School will be something we figure out together. "We talked about it. I can still learn things. I just can't go to Willow Creek or any government school. It's the only way I can be free."

"I don't even know what that means."

I step toward him, wanting him to understand this the way

he gets poetry or basketball. "It's like my name, Lark Justus. I'm named after the Justus Township and the Montana Freemen and they fought the government for their freedom—"

"Hold on. Who?"

"The Freemen. Patriots. They created the world they wanted, their own area free from tyranny."

"I've heard of them, but I don't think . . ." Alex grabs his cell phone out of his pocket. He taps on the screen and holds it up. "Not enough service here. Come on."

"I'm not finished," I say.

"I can get a couple bars on the top of the hill. It'll take two seconds."

He turns and jogs back up the hill. Gizmo darts beside him and I follow behind. Our breath is heavy, weighted with the cold. At the top of the hill, Alex stops and taps on his phone. In the blue light, his eyes zip over the words.

What does it say? My stomach sinks. I don't want to be wrong again.

"An armed antigovernment militia . . . " *Yes.*

"Lark, they led a standoff against the FBI and got charged with fraud." *Necessary actions. False charges.* "They tried to kill a judge!" *What? I don't remember that . . .*

He reads again, recoiling. "Whoa, these guys are super racist."

Racist? I shake my head. "No. They're not." Dad never said that. Antigovernment. That's all.

"Yeah, like not even hiding it. They don't believe any of the amendments to the Constitution are legitimate. That means they don't support ending slavery or women's suffrage."

Women's suffering? Why would they—

"God, Lark, there's a Confederate flag and a noose on the wall!" I don't know exactly what that means, but Alex looks at me like I'm them. "These guys are your role models?"

"No . . . it's just . . . my name, but that can't be right. They're sovereigns, like Dad, but not racist. And they didn't kill anybody. Are you sure that's actually them?"

Alex turns the phone and there it is. The white farmhouse. The barren trees. The bluff behind them.

Should have known. But could Dad still be right? I'm believing the lies the government wants me to see. Is Alex the one who doesn't know the truth?

"These guys are the reason you're not going to school?" Alex asks. "I mean, I'm happy to help you with your geometry and answer your questions about current events because I know you've had shit for an education, but I'm not going to teach you about racism. I get asked to do that enough at school."

A sigh, the cloud of his breath swirling around his face.

"Is this what you want for your life? To live on some tiny farm with a bunch of white supremacists, hoarding rifles and canned food in your cellar, waiting for the government takeover?"

"No. Not that."

"But you just said—"

"I don't know!"

My voice booms across the empty pasture. Alex stills.

"My dad isn't going to let me go to school," I whisper.

Alex closes the space between us. "Are you afraid of him?"

No. Not in the way he thinks. I'm not scared of the pitch of his voice or his fingers around my wrist. He won't hurt me. I know that.

I'm afraid he's right. About everything—the county, government schools, the pork chops I've been eating at Grandma Betty's.

My parents gave me a chance to be different, separate from the binds of the Feds and the poisons of processed food. The government overreach didn't extend to me. Their greed didn't slip through my blood. I was prepared—to flee, to fight, to survive in a world where those dependent on the government wouldn't.

And I gave it up. Tried to.

Now Dad's offering me a chance for both—to learn and to be free. I'm afraid to give up that chance.

Alex taps my palm with his fingertips. "You can't give up. Not after all the progress you made. I'll help you. We could talk to my old caseworker, Ms. Bearcub. Or a lawyer."

I pull back. "No."

Alex frowns. "What your parents are doing isn't right, Lark. They're good to you, but they're not teaching you what you need to know. That's child abuse."

His words burn, a searing red pain across my mind.

"No. They don't do that."

"It's not hitting you or screaming at you—"

"They don't do that. They don't hurt me."

Alex stares at me, a look of pity in his dark brown eyes. "You're fifteen years old and you can't name a continent, Lark. Hurt you? They already did."

It's the right choice.

Homeschool is freedom. Useful. Practical. My mind is my own.

Alex says Dad is wrong. The Freemen are criminals, racists. Sugar won't kill me. He's sure of this in the way Dad is certain about everything else. But he's young, barely two years older than me.

If Alex is right, I'm a foolhardy patriot hiding from imaginary dangers.

If Dad is, I'm dead.

CHAPTER 28

The days slip back into the routine of before as softly as winter approaches with decreasing light. The same chores await me, along with the projects—mended fences, repaired water lines—I only finished in the stories I told Mom when I got back from Willow Creek. They'll be done quick now that there's no homework and no Alex. And Dad's here to help, too. I'm not sure when he'll be back on the road, though we can't afford for him to stay. He must think he can't afford to leave.

I'm not bored—there's too much to do for that. I just wonder what I thought about before, during all the hours and days I had working alone. Now I have bits of books we read in class or images of internal organs to tumble around in my head while I sit on the tractor. I wonder what Jessica is talking about at her youth group. Would I have liked leggings? Or gum? What did I think about back then? Maybe my head was empty? Maybe I was.

There's no proof now that I ever went to school. Dad inspected my room—under the bed, in my sock drawer—and had me hand over any books or journals. They weren't much use anyway—pages of unfinished learning—but I liked knowing I could go back to them someday. More is coming, he said, to replace them. The right books. Just what I need. Homeschool for real. Trust him, he said.

I really want to.

I'm the only one who still feels it, though, like school was the thick coat I grew for winter and haven't been able to shed even though I was thrust back into summer. It's too much weight for me now, but I can't let it go.

I learned things. They're mine, at least until I forget. Like the babies, just because we can't see them doesn't mean they don't exist.

For the past two weeks, Dad and I have gotten up before light to scout out whitetail deer. We've already shot a doe and a tiny buck, but Dad's eager for the big one Mike told him about, a 10-pointer spotted just north of the farm. Enough meat to last us through the winter and into next spring. Although we've done this same thing every day, this morning feels different, the cold below thirty degrees, the wind chill dropping it even more. The heat in the truck sputters, so I wrap my hands tighter around my thermos of hot tea.

This morning Dad chose talk over music, so I can't just lay my head back on the rest and sleep a few extra minutes. I have to listen. Say, "Mmhmm" and "Yes," an active participant in Dad's lecture. Today, it's the Second Amendment. Not the first time I've heard this speech. Not the last.

"It's right there in the words—*'shall not be infringed.'* People try to argue, but they knew what they were writing. Now all these guys are saying they support the Second Amendment, but they're still pussying around the government: *'Okay, sir, I'll buy this baby nine millimeter. I'm sure it will keep me safe when martial law begins and you're knocking down my door.'*" He slaps his palm on the steering wheel. "Gun control is people control!"

On the rack behind us are our two rifles, his 270 Winchester that used to be Uncle Charles's and the 30-30 Remington Dad got me from some guy at an Idaho truck stop. No licenses. No permits. Maybe Dad's right about this, about the guns: I don't see why we'd need a license for guns we shoot on our land. But maybe there's something I'm missing. Another blind spot.

Dad sips his coffee. "It's the most important amendment, why?"

He turns to me. I flicker open my eyes.

"Because it's the one that protects our freedom."

"That's right, Larkie! If we can't defend ourselves from tyranny, then nothing else matters. It's what protects our life, liberty, and pursuit of happiness, just like the Constitution promised."

"That's in the Declaration of Independence, not the Constitution." I bite back a smile. As much as he hated the idea of Willow Creek, looks like it did teach me something.

Another glance. Another sip. The truck hits a rut, and we swing to the side. I clutch the armrest while we bounce along. Dad finally finds a smooth patch along the path's edge.

"I've been reading up on these militias that are forming all around the country, and it's like people are finally getting it," Dad says. "Hell, the Montana Freemen knew what needed to happen decades ago!"

Even though Dad's already revved up, this is my chance to ask about what Alex found. To see how his beliefs compare: if he'll be willing to tell me the truth this time, not leave anything out. Dad's still going on about the militias and waste-of-time politics. I feel my stomach rising into the back of my throat.

"About the Freemen, did you tell me everything?"

Dad frowns. "What do you mean by that?"

"I'm just wondering." I twist the thermos in my hands.

"Are there parts about them—bad things—that you didn't tell me because—"

"What do you mean 'bad things'? Those men were patriots."

"I know, but Alex says—"

"What does Alex know about it?"

Another rut jostles me toward the door. I grasp my thermos to keep the tea from splashing out.

"After we went to the township, I was telling Alex about them, and he pulled up this article—"

"You can't believe everything you read on the internet."

"Stop interrupting me!"

The truck is quiet. I stare out the frost-edged window toward the icy ground. I've never done that. Yelled at him. A sense of fingers tightens around my chest. I keep an eye on his hands.

"Go on."

I turn and Dad looks at me, his eyes soft. His fingers aren't clenched on the wheel.

"Did they try to kill a judge?"

He taps his thumb along the wheel. "That writ of execution was just a threat."

"Okay . . . were they racist against Black people and Indians?"

Dad rolls his eyes. "People always want to make everything about race now, but it was a different time back then."

"So, yes?"

"It's complicated. Did they say some racist shit? Sure. And I've had to wrestle with that, but it doesn't change that they fought for justice. For freedom. They didn't bow down to tyrannical government."

"Alex said there was a noose."

"They didn't use it," Dad sighs.

"But why didn't you tell me? You said that guy Sam was an idiot for the things he said about Indians and you've always said that all men are created equal—"

"And women," Dad says with a smile. I won't give him one.

"After all the stories you told me about the Freemen and my name, how could you leave that out?"

"I told you. It was a different time. Lots of people believed—"

"You should have told me!"

"I didn't tell you because it didn't matter!"

"But I get to decide that! You have to tell me everything, and then I'll figure out what I believe. It can't just be you telling me what to think anymore."

Because it does matter. You can't be a patriot and a racist. A darkness twists through the golden legend of the Freemen heroes, my namesakes. It's stretched from their farmhouse to my veins, carried by Dad's repetition and pride. Their memory, their tainted ideas, are part of me now. Their story is my present.

Dad's jaw clenches as he shifts his hands on the steering wheel. "I always wanted you to think for yourself. Have a mind of your own."

Maybe. We'll see if he still believes that once I start using it.

The Montana Freemen

~~Patriots~~ *Racists*

Held off the FBI for 81 days

~~Protected their land:~~ Justus Township (my namesake)

Fought for ~~freedom~~ what exactly?

Defied tyranny *Maybe*

Hung a noose on the wall. And a Confederate flag

Knew the laws better than those damn lawyers and
government hacks

Wrote a writ of execution—to kill—a judge

Sovereign individuals . . . *or fools*

Died in prison *Where they should be*

CHAPTER 29

A few nights later, Dad has Mom blindfold me in the kitchen with a dish towel. "Close your eyes. Close 'em," she says, giggling as she tries to secure it. It's musty—dirty sink water, no proper rinse—and damp, cool against my skin. The towel droops down my nose, my eyelashes peeking over the edge.

"Whoops," Mom says, reaching around to lift it up. She pulls the towel ends, catching some of my hair. "Is that too tight?"

"No. It's fine."

"Come on, Larkie," Mom says, laughing, her smooth hands in mine. "Follow the sound of my voice."

Together we shuffle into the living room, my foot catching on the lip between the linoleum and the carpet edge. I've been meaning to replace the metal strip that came loose months ago. Mom only laughs more, her excitement pulsing into my hands. She pulls me forward until my toes bump into something else.

"Okay, let her go," Dad says, his voice high, too. They're excited. Thrilled. Their energy takes the edge off not being able to see. Last time they did this, Gizmo was waiting to be dropped into my arms. I love him, but I really hope they didn't get me another dog to take care of. Mom reaches behind me, loosening the knot, and the towel drops to my feet to reveal a large cardboard box in the center of the living room. A couple corners are dented, a slash of black something along the side. Dad's already hacking at the tape with a knife.

"Wait," he says, sitting up on his knees. "You do the honors."

He sets the knife in my open palm, and his excitement begins to bubble within me. I've gotten presents before. Mostly things from home—a collection of agates, a jar of my favorite jam (sometimes that I've made myself), a pillowcase embroidered with my name. My shotgun would have been a present, but my birthday had passed and Dad didn't want to wait until Christmas. None of my gifts have ever come in the mail, our house a stop the mailman never makes. I try to quiet them, but the ideas race in my mind—a computer for just me? A phone like Alex's? No, too expensive. Too big a box. I push back my hope so I'll be ready to smile at whatever I see.

I slide the knife through a white sticker with Mike's name and information. I pull out some brown paper and there they are.

Books. Textbooks. For *real* homeschool.

Mom is beaming from the couch, and before I can move, Dad is kneeling beside me, yanking out books and talking about them faster than I can follow. He drops two blue-and-white books in my lap.

Adventures in Reading. Someone has scribbled out something on the cover in blue pen, but the owner's name is still in the corner: John Safanto. The books smell like dust. I flip them over. Harcourt, Brace & World. 1963.

"I got a great deal on those, $1.99 for the two. These textbooks are a rip-off. No wonder so much of our taxes go to public schools. The books cost more than my truck!" Dad hands me a heavy blue book with a wheel on the cover. *Conceptual*

Physics: Teacher's Edition. "That one I did pay a lot for—$22.99 plus shipping—but I figured the teacher's edition would be best for physics since it's so advanced. It should have tips and stuff for us to use to figure it all out."

I flip to the table of contents: *Newton's First Law of Motion* and a word I don't know. In-er-tia. I picture a poster in Ms. Mullins's classroom, a man with flowing hair kicking an apple. *Linear Motion. Speed. Velocity. Free Fall.*

I've never taken physics.

He didn't even ask.

"And this I got," Dad says, handing me a white box of AP United States History flash cards, "because, honest, the more I looked at history and government books, the more I remembered they're such crap. Total propaganda bullshit. We can do these cards together, and I can make corrections. But at least they've got the dates."

"Isn't it going to be great, Lark!" Mom says from her spot sprawled out on the couch. She tugs the afghan tighter around her shoulders, leaning forward to grab one of the notebooks off the ground. She twirls it by the metal spiral.

"Your dad got you a bunch of notebooks and journals for all your notes and essays. It's going to be like real school, but better!"

I can tell she means it, believes it, the same way she swears yogurt cures my stomach pains though it never really does. Mom tosses the notebook back toward the box. It hits the side and slides to the floor.

"We'll make a schedule with time for chores and lunch and I can even ring a bell or something to mark the change in periods," Mom says. "I think I have a bell in my bedside drawer. Maybe a whistle. Did you borrow it, Brett? Brett?"

"No, I don't have your whistle."

"Well, if I can't find it, I'll think of something. Maybe even a spoon on a glass like a celebration!"

Dad hands me a stack of small books with a penguin at the top of each one. The pages feel fragile, some of them curled at the tips, small snags ripped out. *The* something *Diamonds. Oliver Twist. The Moon Stone. The Woman in White.* I don't recognize any from the Willow Creek library, but I honestly didn't spend that much time in there.

"Those are supposed to be the classics," Dad says, adding *The Mystery of Edwin Drood* to the pile. "Hopefully classic doesn't mean boring."

He digs around in the box before pulling out a small square envelope with a circular see-through window. "This, you'll actually have to use the computer for, so it will be part of your lessons when I'm home." He hands the envelope to me. A woman with brown skin and black hair pulled into a bun smiles off into the distance. *Mavis Beacon Teaches Typing.* Six million sold. Better typing guaranteed.

"I could type ninety words a minute," Mom says from the couch. "Almost fastest in the class, but Lisa D. could do like one twenty or something ridiculous. But she never had a boyfriend."

"I'll have to figure out how to load it onto the computer," Dad says, taking the envelope so he can inspect the back. "But then you can learn to type. I got this cursive workbook so you can learn that, too, cause despite what people think, not everything is online."

"I can use the computer now?"

Dad frowns. "No, not just yet. I got to set up some parental controls and stuff first, but maybe, yeah, eventually."

He pauses to survey his bounty, then me.

"So, what do you think?"

I don't know what to say. This is what I said I wanted: actual school with real textbooks and time in the day meant just for this. And these are official textbooks—older than the ones at Willow Creek, but ones students use in regular schools. They seem to mean it—Mom and Dad—school will be a priority now, but I don't yet believe it won't be chipped away at by chores or Dad's speeches or Mom's too-tired days.

And even if it becomes a priority, it doesn't feel like enough.

Before we went to Grandma Betty's, I didn't think about myself as hungry. We had food, almost every day. The pangs in my stomach weren't any different than the ache of a sunburn in July or the sting of horseflies on my ankles. Some days we had more and others less. Then, I ate dinner at Grandma Betty's: mashed potatoes and gravy, Shake 'N Bake pork chops—not one but two. Three, even, some days. Green beans, dinner rolls with margarine, a bowl of lettuce salad with flecks of tomato and cucumber. And then dessert—white Texas sheet cake, raspberry oat bars, cinnamon-swirl coffee cake. It wasn't until dinner at Grandma Betty's that I knew I was starving.

This box of old books would have filled me up six months ago.

Now I only see what's missing: a microscope, a calculator, the internet anytime I need it. And teachers. Yes, I'm finally getting better at reading thanks to Ms. Leland's help, but—physics! That's for seniors and I'm just a freshman—by age not ability—and I don't think I can teach this to myself.

I don't think I want to.

And school wasn't just books and teachers. With Jessica, I was starting to have friends. At least one. Going back to home-school is a return to being alone.

"Oh, and one more thing." Dad grabs a yellow envelope from the floor behind him and rips open the top with his pocketknife. "You said you wanted to stop listening to your old man's stories and read the truth for yourself."

He holds the book out toward me.

The farmhouse with the bare shelterbelt. Pine trees, the bluff blurred behind it. I recognize this place now. Justus Township.

The Untold Story of Government Suppression and the News Media Cover-up.

Untold, yes, but which parts? *Confederate. Noose. Racist.* Or will they leave those out? Worse, will they be there on the page, but I won't be able to see them, not able to tell the truth from facts? Their untold story will be the only one I know.

"It's what you wanted," Dad says, his lips pulling his smile together, smaller, and I'm not ready to see it go.

"Yes, thank you," I say, clutching the cursive handwriting booklet to my chest. "It's perfect."

And now who isn't telling the truth.

CHAPTER 30

The red tips of my fingers peek through the holes in these hand-me-down gloves. I tuck them under my arms, lift them to my lips, and breathe out warm air. A momentary cloud forms: I wonder why. The question disappears like my breath.

"Why don't you go inside and warm up a minute," Mike says from the other side of the garage. "You've been out here for hours. I'm just going to wrap this up, and then I'll come make us some coffee. Right, no coffee for you. I might have some decaf or I can make you tea."

"Are you sure?"

Mike nods, and I set my tools down in the box at my feet. Outside, the wind bites my cheeks, and I race toward the house, wishing I could feel my toes. At least at Mike's, I'll be able to warm up; he always has heat. I stomp the dirt off my boots on the cardboard at the base of Mike's stairs before slipping them off. The cold wood finds the holes in my socks, but in seconds I'm inside.

In the dining room, a newspaper sits beside a plate with crumbs and a coffee cup a quarter full. Drawings of animals are everywhere. Smiling cows on the dish towels. Leaping sheep on the platter above the bar. Multicolored roosters on the place mat. I sit at the end of the table, rubbing my toes together to gain some feeling. Across from me, a yellow phone hangs on the wall, a whiteboard next to it with names and numbers.

Alex. His name and number, there on the board.

I haven't seen him in a few weeks. He's never here when I am, and, of course, he hasn't stopped by the house. I've been alone so much of my life, but now I actually feel lonely without Alex, without Jessica.

I've never called anyone before. Dad takes his cell phone when he's gone, and we don't have a landline anymore since the only person who ever called was Mike. Grandma Betty has a phone I can use, but even though Jessica gave me her number I never called. I didn't have Alex's until right now.

I can't see Mike from the window. He wouldn't care if I called, I don't think. But does it cost money? For each phone call?

I just want to say . . . I'm sorry. Maybe not that. But it would be short.

I grab the phone. A buzz. I punch in the numbers.

It rings, my chest vibrating with each round. A click.

Hey, this is Alex. Leave a message, though I gotta be honest—I probably won't listen to it.

I set the phone on the hook and sit back down. A glance out the window. Still no Mike. A stuffed sheep with a black face looks down at me from the top of the cabinet. At least my fingers are warming up. I tuck them under my thighs, realizing how much I do want coffee if it does the same as the pop Alex snuck me. I miss the caffeine, the jolt of energy that I don't get from Mom's homemade mint tea.

The phone rings. Do I answer it? It could be Alex. It might not be, and then what do I do. My feet bounce on the floor. The ringing stops. Exhale.

It rings again.

Before the second ring, I answer.

"Hello?"

"Hello? Who is this?" Alex's voice sounds almost the same as when he's with me, his voice through the phone a near perfect mismatch. "Lark?"

"Yeah, it's me."

"Is something wrong? Is Mike okay?"

"Yeah, everything's fine. He's fine." The looped cord curls around my hand.

"Okay . . . so why did he call me?"

"I called . . . I just wanted to talk to you."

"Oh." A slight buzz at the end of the line, like the electricity humming through a hot wire. "What did you want to say?"

The door opens, a brush of cold air filling the room.

"Hoo-wee it's cold. I'll get that coffee started—" Mike freezes in the arched entry. He mouths, "Who is it?" his face scrunched up in confusion.

"It's Alex," I say, holding the phone out to him. "He just called."

Mike shakes his head, crossing the room to grab the phone. I take a seat back in my chair.

"Hay-lo," Mike says, his hand stuffed in his pocket. "Yep, just gonna make me and Lark some coffee to warm us up a bit. I know. I think I still got some decaf Aunt Janette brought last Christmas."

Alex says something I can't hear. They make plans for the weekend.

"He wants to talk to you again?" Mike says, a smile on his face as he hands me the phone. My cheeks warm, faster than the rest of me. I press the receiver to my ear.

"Hello?"

"So, what did you want to talk to me about?"

"I forgot."

"Lark."

"I think you were right," I whisper, looking over my shoulder to see Mike scooping coffee grounds out of a small green container.

"I'm right about a lot of things." Alex's laughter melts the last frozen bits. "But seriously, you mean about school? About your parents?"

"Both."

"You're ready to do something?"

"Maybe. Yes."

A loud buzzer behind Alex's voice. "I gotta go now, Lark. That's the tardy bell for eighth period."

Right. He's still at school, his day split into even segments, marked by a bell and not the sun.

"I'll come by tonight. Meet me on the hill at eight." A moment of just our breaths, behind it, the sound of closing lockers and shouted greetings. "I missed you, Lark."

The heat in my cheeks slips down my spine. "I missed you, too."

I hang up the phone, cradling it gently in the metal hook, before sitting down again at the table. Mike sits a cup of steaming coffee in front of me. For now, I don't need its warmth.

It was easier than I thought, closing the gap between the two of us.

"Mike? Can I use your phone?"

He looks up from the kitchen sink. "Sure. Take your time. I'll meet you in the shed when you're finished."

I pick up the phone, pressing the numbers I have memorized after they spent days on my wrist written in thin blue ink.

"Hello?"

I wasn't sure she'd answer. She has school, too.

"Hi, Jessica. It's Lark."

A gasp. "Oh my gosh, Lark, what happened to you?"

Too much.

"Are you okay?" Jessica asks, her voice as gentle as I remember. "They said you went back to homeschool, but I didn't think you wanted that."

I don't. "I'm not coming back to Willow Creek, but I might be in town some more—I don't know when exactly—but I thought maybe we could get together again?"

"Yeah, sure, of course, but are you sure you're okay?"

I think I will be, even though it's probably going to get worse before it gets better.

"I'll be fine. Just have to figure out some things with my parents."

"I understand." And I believe she does, even though she doesn't know everything. Jessica never needed all the details to trust me. "I'm not supposed to be on the phone right now, but just call me when you know, okay? We still need to introduce you to ramen."

I smile. That's right. We do.

Hopefully, someday soon.

It's already dark when the headlights flash. I slide the steel Quonset door closed before racing over to Alex's truck, Gizmo jumping in circles at my feet. Alex leans across the seat to open the door. For a moment, we sit with the sound of the heater.

"Your parents didn't notice?"

"I told them I'm walking Gizmo." Dad's been watching me more carefully, so it was better to only half lie. Outside, Gizmo races up the hill barking at something in the moonlight. Alex smiles at him. At me.

"I was pretty surprised you called."

I turn toward the window, pressing a finger on the foggy glass. "I never called anyone before."

"Well, that makes me lucky number one." He reaches across the truck to tap my hand. "Lark. Did you mean it? You want to do this?"

It's not about wanting anymore. It's about needing. I can't go back to a life of chores and lectures about martial law. I don't want to live with questions and no way to find the answers. Even though Dad says it will be different, that he can do better, those new-old books are proof that he can't. Not fully. I can't picture a life outside this farm just yet, but I want options when the time comes. "Where do I start?"

"I've been thinking about it," Alex says, taking off his stocking cap. "It's possible you could emancipate."

"What's that?"

"It's like getting freedom from your parents. You're in charge of yourself and can make your own decisions, like being able to go to school. But I'm pretty sure you have to be able to support yourself, and you don't have a job or any savings, I'm guessing."

I shake my head.

"The easiest first step would be to talk to my old caseworker,

Ms. Bearcub, and see what she thinks. There's got to be a law about teaching your kids something."

"When would we go?"

"When's the next time your dad leaves town?"

I shrug. He hasn't talked about leaving yet, but we both know about our dwindling reserves of canned food. The low propane tanks. We need the money, so he'll have to leave. Eventually.

"I'm proud of you, Lark," Alex says, his brown eyes glowing in the dashboard lights. I want to move toward him, to get back to the place where we sat in the barn with his arm over my shoulders. But he might not want that anymore. He might be only here to help.

Better than nothing.

"I have to get back."

I hop out of the truck, the cold racing up my body. I call for Gizmo and head down the hill toward home, grateful for Alex's lights behind me, revealing the path.

CHAPTER 31

The next week, Dad makes a short run to Boise and the next day Alex pulls up to a brick building just off Main Street. *Montana* is written in huge letters on the door glass. Below it: *Roosevelt County Child and Family Services Division.* My stomach churns, burns, maybe from the non-decaf coffee I drank on the way here. Or the government trap I'm about to walk into. Not that Alex would knowingly lead me into one.

"What is this place, exactly?"

Alex turns off the truck.

"CPS office. It's where Ms. Bearcub works."

"It's a whole government building that . . ." *Tracks children and families? Counts them? Monitors them?* All our fears of the government are beginning to pulse within me. This is what Dad's been talking about. An entire building dedicated to—

"What do they do?"

"A bunch of different things. Mostly respond to reports of child abuse. Or if families can't take care of their kids, they step in with foster care." Alex drums his fingers on the steering wheel, squints a smile.

"But is that the government's problem? Isn't that a family thing?"

Alex pauses. "I guess maybe, but if the problem is in the family, it doesn't really make sense for them to try and solve it themselves. And I'm guessing a lot of families do. This is for the ones that can't."

A man in a brown jacket walks past the door behind the glass. The rest of the windows are too high to see inside. Only brick walls. What don't they want us to see? It's getting harder to breathe beneath my wool coat.

"And what is she going to ask me, again?"

Alex scoots closer. "I don't know exactly, but she'll probably want you to describe what homeschool has been like, how things are with your family. Nothing big is going to happen today. We're just here to talk."

"What about tomorrow? Could we come then? I can tell Mom I'm working at Mike's again. She won't check."

"I can't do tomorrow, but if you want, we can come back another day. Whenever you're ready." He reaches across the seat to grab my hand. His fingers are cool as they link with mine. My breathing slows a little. If we weren't sitting outside a government office, I would be able to just enjoy Alex beside me, our hands intertwined.

But I can't. Not yet. I don't know what I'm actually scared of. I just know I should be.

"What are you worried about? They won't tell your parents you're here."

I'm not worried about them right now.

"Can they keep me here?"

"No."

"Or take me to some holding pen for kids?"

"Well, if we were at the border—"

"What?!"

He grabs my arms. "Sorry. Wrong moment for that. I promise nothing bad will happen to you if we go inside. You just decide if you're ready."

We sit together in the truck. No one comes in or out the door. Are they watching us? Waiting for us to come inside? Right now, Dad says I'm invisible to the government, but once I tell them my name, maybe they'll have me. I try to think about what Alex said—it's just a conversation, a chance to get more information, see what my options are—but it's not quite loud enough to drown out fifteen years of fear and preparation against the people sitting inside, the organization they represent. I want to believe Alex.

But I don't.

Not all the way.

I don't trust anyone fully, not anymore.

Alex squeezes my hand, rubs his thumb across my veins. "Obviously I don't share your dad's views about a lot of things, but I get why you're scared. Do you know all the shitty, brutal things the US government has done to Indians? That they still do? And even a place like this—supposedly protecting children and families—they had to pass a freakin' law to keep the government from stealing our babies and giving them to white families."

"But," he continues, his eyes on my gaping mouth, "sixteen years ago, Ms. Bearcub showed up at a trailer across town when neighbors reported a baby screaming for hours. My dad was passed out in the living room, and my mom was unconscious from where he'd shoved her against the wall. Ms. Bearcub got me to Mike and then helped my mom get the support she needed."

I suddenly imagine Alex as a baby, crying out into a frosty night. I want to hold him closer.

"The thing with you, Lark, is that everything is black or

white. Good or evil. Poison or food. But life's not like that."
He squeezes my hand one more time before letting go. "If you
want to go home, we'll go home. If you want to go in, we'll go
in. It's up to you."

He turns away, giving me space to decide. He flickers with
the radio, catching the scores of last night's divisional football
scores. He swears. His team must have lost. He blows on his
fingers before tucking them under his legs.

It's just a conversation. A start. No different than showing
up at the private school. "Okay. Let's go."

Alex beams, hopping out of the truck. He meets me at
the glass door.

"Do you want me to go first?"

I shake my head, ignoring the surge in my body telling
me to flee. Alex follows me inside.

"Alex Marshall, look at you." A Native American woman with
gray-streaked black hair and a thin smile reaches out to grab
Alex's shoulders. Her wrinkled fingers squeeze tight, and he
pulls her into a hug.

"Hi, Ms. Bearcub. Long time, no see."

"Aren't you supposed to be in school?"

He shakes his head. "Exam day. I'm off for the afternoon."

"You're a junior now? I saw your picture in the paper this
fall from that game against Dodson." Suddenly she notices me.
"Who's your friend?"

"This is Lark Herbst. She's hoping to talk to you."

Ms. Bearcub's eyes crinkle as she scans me. "Come inside."

Alex looks to me for direction.

"You can wait here," I say.

He nods, moves toward the gray chairs along the wall. "I'll be right here."

I follow Ms. Bearcub into a small white office, the only furniture a wooden desk and three chairs, one across from the desk and two pushed against the wall. Ms. Bearcub gestures for me to take the seat in front of her desk.

"Tell me what's going on," Ms. Bearcub says, a yellow notepad and pen ready.

"I . . . Alex told me . . . I want . . ." The words catch in my throat like they don't want to be here, either, betraying me. And Dad.

"I used to be homeschooled—still am sort of—and I . . . don't want to be."

"Okay. Tell me about that."

Suddenly, I realize there isn't much to tell. In minutes—seconds maybe—I've told her all about the past promises of school and it never happening. The books I can't really read and the weeks at Willow Creek. I mention that box of new-old books.

But not Dad's ideas. Conspiracies.

"How old are you?" Ms. Bearcub asks, her pen still gliding on the page.

"Fifteen."

"From what you've told me, I'm guessing you don't have a birth certificate, then? Or a social security card?"

I shake my head. Ms. Bearcub pauses, her pen hovering over her yellow notepad. Behind her is a whiteboard written on in different colored markers. A few pictures of kids are clipped to the side. In the one photo she's in, her smile fills up her face.

She doesn't smile that much here. I appreciate that.

Ms. Bearcub bites on her lower lip, her dark eyebrows arching as she thinks. "Are you a member of any tribe? Maybe a tribal membership card?"

No. According to Dad, we're original American, true patriots.

"My name's in our Bible. Does that count?"

She nods. "It does." She writes for a few more minutes, flipping back and forth in her notes while I wait. Did I say the right thing? Was there something important I left out? What does she need for proof that my life should be different?

"It's your parents' legal right to homeschool you, but there are registration and attendance requirements, as well as minimum hours of instruction and mandatory course subjects. Unfortunately, the laws aren't strong and you have to have someone to enforce them." Ms. Bearcub gestures around the empty office. "All cases go through our centralized intake to get screened for a response, but based on this information alone—you said you're not in any immediate danger?" I shake my head. "Your education at home seems insufficient, but I still have some questions, if that's okay with you, Lark."

Her eyes are gentle. I nod.

"Why did you parents decide to homeschool you?"

They had big dreams: a farm overflowing with homegrown food. A space free from surveillance. An education that would open my mind. Lots of babies.

It would have been nice.

"They don't believe in public school."

"Don't believe in it?"

"Well, because of the government."

A tilt of Ms. Bearcub's head. She scribbles something. "Like sovereign citizens?"

Yes! I'm surprised by the comfort I feel in her knowing who I am. "You know about that?"

"I've had a few clients who shared those beliefs. It's more common than people think. And growing." She glances over her notes, then back to me. "I'm going to assume that your dad isn't working somewhere that would require him to pay taxes. Does he farm?"

"Not really anymore. He drives truck."

"Okay. And your mom? Does she work?"

"She can't. She's sick."

"Sorry to hear that. What's her illness?"

"I don't really know."

"Can you describe it? Does she cough? Is it her stomach?"

"No. It's not really her body. Some days she's normal, and some days she can't get up."

"So more mental health issues?"

"Maybe."

I wait while she writes.

"These might seem personal, but I'd like to know a bit more about your home. Do you have electricity? Running water? It's pretty cold already. What about heat? What food is in your house right now?"

I tell her about the generator that mostly works. The lanterns. Yes, to the water, except that one time the well pump was on the fritz. A wood stove that warms the kitchen pretty well as long as I have enough firewood. Food? Jars of canned vegetables. Venison when we hunt. Eggs from the chickens. Just enough. Most times.

"And what would happen if you got sick? Would your parents take you to a doctor?"

"No. Never."

"Do you have any illnesses now, like asthma or diabetes?"

I don't know what those are, but . . . "No?"

"Have you ever gotten hurt really bad before? Or gotten really sick?"

A broken toe from when I dropped a metal chute. Sore throat Mom said was strep, this year and years past.

"No."

"Say you got hurt on the farm—broke your leg? What then?"

"I don't know. My mom has some books. Maybe my dad could—" *Look it up on the internet*? I don't finish the thought, hearing how ridiculous it sounds. "Are we almost done?"

Ms. Bearcub sets down her pen and waits for me.

"Alex says that you helped him when his mom couldn't take care of him and he had to go live with his grandpa. This isn't like that. My parents take care of me. I have food. I have clothes. My dad bought me these new packets and books to study, but some of it's still wrong, and I can read, even though it's hard, but it's . . ." I could learn something, scrape some ideas from those dry bones. But no. "It's not what I want."

"Okay, Lark, thank you for sharing." Ms. Bearcub glances down at her version of my life, looks right at me. "I'm glad you came in today because otherwise, we would never have known you needed some help. According to the State of Montana, you don't exist."

Alex takes us to the McDonald's drive-thru after the meeting. A double Quarter Pounder. No cheese. And a medium fry. Large, if I want to share. I don't.

"You sure you don't want something?" Alex asks as the truck rolls forward toward a board covered in pictures of food. "They used to have salads and a yogurt parfait, but the healthiest thing they have now is a smoothie."

He leans out the window to better read the sign. "Strawberry banana or pineapple mango."

I've never had pineapple, rarely strawberries. I've never heard of mango.

"I'm fine."

"You sure? I'm paying."

My stomach rumbles, a familiar motion, but I can't eat this fast food. Ammonium hydroxide, preservatives, artificial colors, pink slime. Maybe it's all wrong, more lies about truth, but I just spent the past several hours stretching into a new world. I leapt out of my skin today. Maybe too far this time.

A voice crackles through the window. "Welcome to McDonald's. May I take your order?"

Alex leans, one arm on the window. He repeats the order he described to me on the way over. He turns. "Last chance."

I shake my head. Still, no.

"Add a strawberry-banana smoothie. And then that's it." He looks over at me. "You don't have to have it. I'm curious to try one, but it's yours. If you want it."

Once Alex has his order, he sets the fries on the paper bag and nestles it on the armrest between us. He sets my—his— strawberry-banana smoothie in the drink holder, a napkin around it. Inside the cup is something like pink snowdrifts, speckled with dark red.

"Just in case you change your mind."

He smiles, laying out the burger wrapper on his lap like a napkin. He takes a bite before pulling forward, a bit of ketchup on the corner of his lip.

Water droplets form on the smoothie cup as we drive, soaking the napkin. Something's happening between the heat in the truck and the melting, pink ice. It probably has a name I don't know. Alex turns down the radio.

"How are you doing?"

"I'm fine."

"It's okay if you're not. That was a big step."

The paper crinkles as Alex folds it into a square, shoving it back into the paper bag.

"How do you think it will go with your dad if she does a home visit?"

Worse than before, with Ms. Schmidt and Mom. That's the only possible way. Ms. Bearcub is the government at our home-without-an-address to check up on his daughter, who doesn't exist to the State of Montana. Slammed doors. Loaded guns. A bug out. His fingers tight around my arm, maybe even across my cheek for the first time.

"He might not be home."

"I wish I could be there. Maybe I'll give Ms. Bearcub a call and figure out when she's planning to go out and then I'll come over, too."

"No." That would be worse. More people. More outsiders. "I'll be fine."

"You don't have to do this alone," Alex says, a sheen of grease on his lips.

I smile because he wants it, close my eyes and rest my head against the cooling glass. Alex is here, with me, but he's wrong. This, whatever it turns out to be, is something I have to do alone.

Flurries have started to fall when we pull into Mike's driveway. Alex leaves the truck running while we sit in the quiet. He unwraps the wet napkins from around the smoothie.

"Sure you're not going to drink it?"

I shake my head. No. Too many leaps today. Too many decisions with potentially hazardous outcomes. I don't want to waste any decisions on a fast-food smoothie. Alex takes off the lid to swallow down the pink ice. He sets it down, smiles, his face so close and exactly what I need and before I can think anymore, I lean over the console and kiss his cold lips.

"That was unexpected," Alex says as I rush back to my side, my cheeks flaming. What was I thinking? I hope I did it right. Did he even want it? Want me?

"Lark, look at me."

His eyes are soft, the way they always have been. He reaches out a hand, tugs me gently toward him. "Can we try that again? Now that I'm ready for it?"

My heart races, the way it has all day, but this leap has deep waters underneath, a floor of hay to soften the fall.

Our lips together again, his parting so mine do, too. His hand behind my neck, the smell of him so familiar and still new. Everything slows, the blood in my veins, the thoughts in my mind.

Alex I've always known to be good, to be true.

Alex's mouth is sweet like summer.

Alex is the easiest decision I've ever made.

CHAPTER 32

A couple days later, I get back from fixing the battery on Mike's truck to find Mom and Dad huddled at the dining room table, Dad's rifle propped beside him, his handgun inches from his tapping fingertips. The room is dark, the curtains closed, the lights off.

"Mom—"

Dad shushes me with his hand. I move closer to the table, trying to keep my footsteps light.

"What's going—"

Mom shakes her head, then leans past Dad's shoulder to peek out the closed curtain. A triangle of afternoon light hits the table, revealing a smear of jam from this morning's breakfast.

"Coulda been Mike," Dad huffs, his voice just above a whisper.

"I don't think so. I told you, probably the school."

"But she hasn't been there in weeks. Why send someone now?"

"I don't know. Maybe her attendance or something."

"I told them she wasn't going there anymore."

They both look at me.

"What's going on?"

Then, I see it. The white rectangular card clutched in Dad's hand. I recognize the round seal with mountains and rivers from the stack on Ms. Bearcub's desk.

She came.

The guns are out.

"What happened?"

This time Mom looks at me, her palm to her cheek.

"Someone showed up at the house. From"—she whispers the rest—"Child Protective Services."

"And she was kind enough to leave us her card," Dad says with a sneer.

I sit down at the table. "What did you do?"

"Nothing this time," Dad says, his eyes on the Ruger. "She's just lucky I wasn't home."

"Your dad was down at the south side checking the water tanks. Her lucky day." Mom pats Dad's knee, and he smiles at her. Just for a minute.

"Will she come back?" I ask, careful to keep my voice neutral so they don't guess my connection to her visit.

"Not if she knows what's good for her." Dad lets out a long, heavy exhale. "But probably. Yeah. Those government types are always getting in somebody's business. Just wish I knew who talked to her so I could shut them up."

Since you're the reporter, your name will be kept confidential, Ms. Bearcub said. *I'll have to tell your parents about the accusations, but that's it.*

I watch them, waiting to see if their glances change, if they start looking at me as an outsider.

My right leg bounces beneath the table. I tighten the muscles, hoping to hold them still. "But if she does come back, then what? You wouldn't actually shoot her."

"I'll do whatever I need to, to protect my family."

"But if you—if she died, wouldn't that be worse? The police?"

Mom scoffs. "Your dad's not going to kill anyone."

"You don't know *what* I would do," Dad snaps.

"It would be his right," Mom says, correcting herself. "A man's got the Constitutional right to protect his home and his family."

I wonder if I can tell Ms. Bearcub to forget it. I was stupid to think they'd allow her in the door, let alone listen to her. Maybe I can get Alex to call her, tell her to back off.

"I don't even get what they're looking into us for?" Mom says as she twists the end of a split curl. "What they got to investigate? You've got food, a roof over your head. We don't even use the belt like my dad did. You're our baby." Her throat catches. "Why would they want to take you away from us?"

"No one's going to take me away," I say.

"Damn right, they're not," Dad says, standing up and grabbing the guns. "Next time we'll be ready."

Mom follows him down the hallway, and I pull back the curtains. The sun is starting to set behind the trees, sending a shimmer of pink across the skiff of snow. I grab Ms. Bearcub's card off the table and tuck it into my pocket.

Just in case I need it.

A knock at the door and no one moves. It's rare for us all to be inside at this time of day, not out in the fields or on the road. But here we all are, where we've been for the past three days, sitting around the dining room table without plates. A knock again, a little louder this time, as if the reason we haven't answered is because we didn't hear.

We did.

Dad decided to let her in—we got nothing to hide—to show her enough to shut her up and check us off her list. He made us scrub down the house earlier this week, dusting the shelves and sweeping the floors. He had Mom tidy up their bedroom, or at least throw all the clothes and blankets into the closet. Dad even put some of Mom's dried flowers in a mason jar on the table. He said it needed to look perfect.

Another knock.

"Answer it," Dad says from his end of the table, his eyes peeping over the thick book in his hands. Mom's eyes don't leave the hands twisting in her lap.

"Maybe you should go, Brett," Mom whispers.

"No," Dad says, a flicker of fear across his face. "I need a minute. Go. Now."

I stand and push in my chair, crossing toward the door. Out the picture window, I see a blue pickup truck, but not a farm one. This one is mostly clean except for a skiff of frost and dirt on the wheel wells and some streaks on the windshield. Something dangles from the rearview mirror.

When I open the door, Ms. Bearcub's fist is up, ready to knock again.

"Hello. I wasn't sure anyone was home. But I saw the vehicles in the yard, so I kept knocking. Your parents are here?"

"Yes, they're waiting for you." I step back into the house. Her face doesn't give off any acknowledgment of me and the conversation we had at her office. "You can come in."

THE TRUTH ABOUT EVERYTHING

"Thank you," she says, stopping to stomp her shoes on the mat.

"You can leave your shoes on."

She won't bring in dirt. The black leather on her shoes is unscuffed, the soles clean. She nods, sliding her shoes back and forth on the rug a couple more times, and then follows me inside.

Mom is sitting upright now as if pressed up against a pole. Her hands still flutter, occasionally up to her face to push back a wayward curl. Dad's holding the book up by his nose, but he's not reading. His glasses are lying on the table beside his coffee cup. Ms. Bearcub stops at the end of the table.

"Mr. and Mrs. Herbst? Hello. I'm—"

"We know who you are," Dad says. "We got your card."

"Hello," Mom says, suddenly getting to her feet, as if she just remembered hospitality. "Would you like some coffee? Lark, get—I didn't get your name—"

"Loretta Bearcub."

"Get Ms. Bearcub some coffee."

Mom pulls out the chair at the head of the table, and Ms. Bearcub takes a seat across from Dad, setting her small black briefcase on the floor beside her. Dad puts down his book.

"You came to check on Lark?"

"Yes, and to get to know your family a bit better overall. I know these visits can be stressful, especially for a family like yours that doesn't normally engage with the county." Dad snorts. "However, someone did make an allegation to our office, outlining two primary concerns—"

"Who was it?" Dad demands.

"I can't tell you that. All reporters are kept confidential."

"So, they can just lie about us and save face?"

"I understand how this is frustrating, but we take all reports seriously, regardless of the veracity, which is why I'm here today."

Dad sets the book down on the table, his hands now free to grab the rifle beside him. Ms. Bearcub glances at the gun. Mom nibbles on her nail. "We don't hit our kid."

"As of now, I don't have any concerns of physical abuse." Ms. Bearcub takes the coffee from me. "Thank you, Lark. The report expressed concerns about a lack of regular schooling for your daughter, Lark, as well as some possible issues with access to adequate food and heat."

"Told you it had to be Mike," Dad whispers to Mom. "We never should have let him give us that meat. Charity."

Mom pats his hand, her eyes locked on Ms. Bearcub, her smile too still to be natural.

"There's no judgment if your family has needed support in the past or if you do now. That's part of why I'm here. To see if there are any services we can offer to help your family." Ms. Bearcub waits, maybe for Dad to jump in, and then continues. "Lark is your only child, correct?"

Mom shakes her head. "She's the only one still with us, but we have six children."

"Oh. I wasn't aware. And where do these other children live?"

"They're dead," Dad says, his words crumpling Mom, who droops in her chair. "Why don't you tell us what you need to know about Lark?"

Ms. Bearcub takes a slow breath. "Homeschooling is the

right of parents under Montana state law, but it is also a big responsibility. We want to check in—"

"Who's we?" Dad asks.

"Well, the Child and Family Services Department. The superintendent of schools also has an interest in the education of students in this county."

The government. That's who wants to know.

Dad leans back in the chair, his hands behind his neck. "Well, what do you need to know?" Before Ms. Bearcub can answer, he leans forward. "What is the supreme law of the land?"

"Excuse me?"

"The Constitution!" Dad slaps his hand on the table. "What are the rights of every American citizen?" He turns. "Tell her, Lark."

All eyes are on me. "The right to bear arms. The right to freedom of speech . . ."

"Freedom of assembly." Dad jumps in. "Freedom of religion—or no religion if you're not a brain-dead idiot." Mom drops her eyes as Dad keeps going. "Freedom of expression. Freedom to petition the government despite how useless that exercise would be."

"Mr. Herbst—"

"See, I've taught my daughter what she needs to know about our country and the way it should be run. She can read. Here—" Dad slides his book down the table and it crashes into my tea mug, tipping it onto its side. The remnants of brown liquid drip onto the table and soak into the pages. I swipe the book off the table and wipe it on my pants.

"Open it to page one twenty-seven—never mind, you tell her, Ms. Bearcub. You pick a page, any page, and she'll read it."

I flip the worn pages with my thumb, my eyes scanning the words, desperately seeking familiar shapes.

"This really isn't necessary," Ms. Bearcub says. "I'm sure Lark can read. What would be helpful is to see the curriculum you're using to instruct her. Maybe you can walk me through a typical day. The law requires that families notify the county superintendent of schools—"

"Where does it say that?" Dad leans toward her, daring her to answer.

"Section twenty of the Montana—"

"Come look at it, if you don't believe me." Dad hops up from the table, splashing Mom's coffee. Startled, Mom stands, too. "See what she's been learning. I guarantee you it's better than anything she could learn in those government schools."

"That would be great," Ms. Bearcub says, pausing to blow on her coffee before taking one last sip.

"You can follow me." I lead her down the dark hallway to my parents' bedroom. Dad charges past me, kneeling down on the carpet as he pulls books and cardboard boxes off the shelf by his desk. He slides one across the floor toward us.

"Here. This is the old packets she's done: math, reading, science. All of it."

He turns back to the shelf, and Ms. Bearcub crouches down beside the box. She pulls out loose leaf notebook paper with my handwriting, assignments I don't remember. She flips through a social studies workbook, the one with the Chinese emperor who put all the statues of men and horses into his grave. She

THE TRUTH ABOUT EVERYTHING

lifts out a math workbook, scanning the pages before setting it in the pile on her floor.

"Here's all the new materials I got her, now that she's in high school," Dad says. Ms. Bearcub reviews the physics book, the reading manuals, even Mavis Beacon's smiling face. Dad brings over a stack of books and begins handing them to Ms. Bearcub. "*The Papers of Thomas Jefferson. The Wealth of Nations. Cujo.*"

Ms. Bearcub raises an eyebrow. "The Stephen King novel?"

I never read that book. Half read the others.

"It's literary. She can't read all nonfiction."

Ms. Bearcub sets most of the books down beside the pile before skimming the pages of *The Case Against the Fed*. I recognize the cover, but don't remember what the problem with the Feds was: banking, maybe, or the electrical grid?

"The reading level on these novels is very high for a student Lark's age."

Dad shrugs. "Lark's really smart. Way smarter than other kids. If she was in public school, they would have held her back. Kept her going as slow as the dumbest kid in class. But not here. Here she could move as fast as she wanted. She can read anything. Right?"

He looks at Mom, who is leaning against the doorjamb, her cheeks pale as she rests her head against the door. She pulls her sweater tighter around her, tries to smile. "My baby is brilliant."

"That's right," Dad says, grabbing a book from the stack. "Here. Larkie. Read this."

He hands a thick book to me. I stare down at the cover, the strange horses leaping across letters I can barely read. Dad grabs it out of my hands, flipping a few pages before handing it back to me. Some of the lines are already underlined in blue pen, Dad's tiny handwriting filling the sides of the page.

"Start at the star," he says, and I find a tiny blue star marking a paragraph in the middle of the page. The words jump, startled like a deer in headlights, and I try to pin them down with my gaze. My breath flutters in my chest. I hold it, needing everything to remain still.

"You got this, Larkie," Dad says. "You've read this hundreds of times."

I haven't read it even once. Not really.

"Now I love my dad. He is my friend," I read, squinting my eyes. "He is an . . . in . . . indi . . ."

"Independent," Dad corrects.

"Independent, gre . . ." I run through guesses in my head. *Great*? Too short. *Gorgeous*. Wrong for a dad. I force my eyes back to the page. "Gree—gray—gair—"

"Gregarious."

I nod at Dad. "Gregarious. Feasty."

"Feisty."

"We don't need to keep going," Ms. Bearcub interrupts as she stands. "You did a really nice job, Lark. Thank you."

"She's not done!"

The room goes quiet. The words get longer, more tangled, and Dad's anger builds as I stumble down the page.

"I don't know why she's reading like that," he says to Ms. Bearcub. "Come on, Lark, read it right."

"She doesn't need to keep going. I can see how—"

"No. She's not—this is not how I taught you!"

The veins in Dad's neck swell, his face darkening in the

shadowed room. I keep trying, willing the sounds to slide out of my mouth. Finally, sentences from the bottom of the page, Ms. Bearcub reaches out her hand, taking the book from me. I move closer to Mom, and she reaches out, tucking an arm around my waist.

Dad stands, too, running a hand along his chin. "That was sort of a hard one, and she's stressed out about all this. You being here and all."

"It's no problem. It is hard to read on the spot." Ms. Bearcub turns over the booklet in her hands. "I noticed, Mr. Herbst, that while the books you have Lark reading are high school level, this reading packet is from sixth grade, but the physics is traditionally for seniors. The older workbooks you had are around grade three. Can you tell me more about Lark's academic level?"

"Why would we bother with grade levels? No need to stick her into some arbitrary group that defines what she should and should not know."

"Understood." She turns to me. "Can you tell me how many hours you spend a week on schoolwork, Lark? I understand you have a lot of chores here at the farm as well."

"Um, well, it depends. It's harder during busy times like harvest—"

"She spends several hours a day reading and doing lessons, but her learning isn't confined to this house, to these papers. The whole world is her classroom," Dad says, draping an arm around my shoulder, his fingers tucking into my bones.

"And Lark has really great penmanship," Mom says, gesturing toward the box. She reaches over and plucks a notebook out and hands it to Ms. Bearcub. "See. Everything is so even.

Not like my chicken scratch." Mom laughs, her voice high like it is when she's trying to get another invite from Grandma Betty.

Ms. Bearcub smiles as she looks at my perfect penmanship, the comforting curves of letters I could copy, shapes I didn't have to yank out of my brain like weeds in dry dirt. She turns, taking in the shelves, the books, us.

"This is it?" she asks, the booklet still in her hand. "This is everything Lark's been learning since she started school?"

It's such a small pile. One box. A shelf of books.

"Are we done here?" Dad says, walking to the door. "That's all you need to see."

Ms. Bearcub sets down the workbook. "Yes, thank you. I was hoping we could take just a few minutes for you to show me your pantry."

A storm sweeps across Dad's face. "You want to see our food stores?"

"That would be great."

"And the fresh water we have saved up?"

"Yes, thank you."

"What about our medical supplies? Lanterns? Fire-starters? Our generators?"

"I'm mostly concerned with the food items, but it sounds like you have quite the reserve."

Dad starts to slowly applaud. "Thank you! Finally! For saying the real reason you're here."

"Excuse me?"

"You don't give a shit about Lark's education. You saw— she can read. She has books. She learned way more than I ever did in that bullshit high school in town. You and your government cronies don't care about what she learns. That's just a cover for what you're really after—our stockpile."

Ms. Bearcub shakes her head, her clipboard at her side. "No, Mr. Herbst, I'm not—"

"We all know what's going to happen post-collapse: electricity cut, those little green bills you let run your life won't be good for anything but wiping my ass. And when it gets bad, when the people are starving and there's blood in the streets, where will you go? Here. To people like us who have been preparing for that day for years."

Dad leans in toward Ms. Bearcub, stepping closer with each word, while Mom and I press tight to the wall.

"You think you can just come into my house and tell me I'm a shit parent and embarrass my daughter and then count all of my stockpiles so you can report it back to your government cronies? You don't want to do the work, but you want the fruits of my harvest. Well, I have two words to say about that: Hell. No."

"I hear your concerns, Mr. Herbst," Ms. Bearcub says, retreating out of Dad's range. "But I'm really only concerned about Lark's well-being and finding ways that I can support your family."

"Lies!"

Ms. Bearcub rubs the back of her neck, then smooths her palms on her pants. "If today isn't a good time for me to finish the visit, I can come back at a later date."

"No. You want to see it? Let's go."

Dad storms out the door, pushing Mom and me out of the way. We stand frozen for a few seconds as the kitchen cupboards slam open. I hope he doesn't break anything. Finally, we lead Ms. Bearcub back to the kitchen.

"Here it is!" Dad shouts, opening the refrigerator door. "Do you want to count each jar?"

Ms. Bearcub only nods from the edge of the kitchen, leaning slightly so she can see inside the open doors. Maybe she really is counting. With a smack, Dad closes each cupboard.

"And there's more!"

We follow him down the stairs into the cellar. The familiar musty scent mingles with Ms. Bearcub's soap. Dad tugs on the lightbulb string. The faint outline of our breath is visible now in the cold. He spreads his arm wide, his fingertips inches from the cement walls.

"All my progress, everything needed for my family to survive, is here in this room. Look. Look for yourself."

Ms. Bearcub scans the room, her eyes dashing from jar to lantern to rifle. Behind her Mom folds a misplaced towel before adding it to the stack. Dad yanks the metal money box from beneath the seat. Suddenly, I remember the $250 for my application. The $50 for driver's ed. I hope he doesn't count it.

"In here, $3,000—some cash, but mostly gold and some antique jewelry. More than you have saved up at your bank, probably. It's not your money now, anyway, it's the bank's." Dad's voice is measured as he nears Ms. Bearcub, his chest lifted like a buck ready to clash. "You think you're better than us, coming here and telling me how to raise my daughter. And that's okay." His smile is dangerous. It makes my stomach clench. "Because some day, it will happen. And you'll remember me, Brett Herbst, and the things you saw here at this house.

And you'll wish you were prepared. Mostly likely you'll already be dead."

Ms. Bearcub waits, not needing to respond. She closes her notebook, placing the pen in her back pocket. "Thank you for your cooperation today. I think I have all I need."

Dad scoffs before turning out the light.

CHAPTER 33

We wait at the door until we can longer hear her tires on the gravel. Mom pulls at the edges of the curtain, trying to block out the light, as if Ms. Bearcub hasn't already seen inside. Dad's breathing is heavy, but no one moves. Not yet.

Gizmo barks. At a bird? Or Ms. Bearcub returning?

A hiss from the heater.

Dad turns from the door. "It's time."

"What?" I ask, following him into the kitchen.

"We're bugging out."

"Now?"

Dad looks at his watch, the seconds already ticking down. "You know what to do."

Mom clings to the hallway corner, her eyes wide. She shakes her head, but I don't know what she means. No, she isn't going? No, this isn't happening?

"Lark! Go! Get your stuff."

"Are you sure? Won't it look suspicious if we go now?"

"Who cares?" he says. "We're not sticking around here. We'll leave, hide out at the cabin for a few weeks, maybe a couple months, long enough for them to forget we were even here. By the time we come back, they'll have moved on to sticking their noses in somebody else's business."

A few weeks? Will Ms. Bearcub show up again with her clipboard and a plan, only to find an empty house? Lark Herbst just a name she'll scratch off her list? Dad charges down the hall to their bedroom, and I plead with Mom, who still hasn't moved. "I don't think we should go."

"Your dad says it's time."

"But we've never actually stayed at the cabin for longer than a week. Will the supplies actually last a couple of months? It's almost winter."

Jars of canned veggies, canisters of gas, piles of wood, yes, but enough? I can't do the math based on a recollection. All we have is a half-assed inventory from last time when I was pissed to be there. Now we might actually need those numbers.

"We'll be fine. It's all right," Mom says. "It will be sort of fun."

"It's not fun!" I take a few steps closer, dropping my voice. "What about Grandma Betty? Won't she worry if she doesn't see us for a few months?"

"She knows we come and go."

"No, she doesn't. Since we started going last year, we go every—"

"Enough chitchat!" Dad shouts as he comes back into the hallway, his body weighed down with gear. "I said we're going. You have thirty seconds to grab your shit and meet me outside."

"Please, Mom—"

"We're going," she snaps, pulling her hand from mine. She pushes past me on the way to their bedroom, and I rush into mine. Two seconds to grab my bag out of the closet. Another second to grab a pair of wool socks to replace the worn ones I'm wearing. A few seconds to tear a sheet out of one of Dad's new notebooks. Four seconds to dig in my dresser for a pen that takes several swirls and my spit to write.

Bugging out. I'm okay. Gone for a few weeks. Maybe a couple months.

For Alex. For Grandma. Or Ms. Bearcub. Even Jessica, if she ever found her way to the farm. For anyone who comes and wonders where I am.

I toss my duffel over my shoulder and sprint down the hallway. Outside, Dad is rolling the bikes out of the shed, Gizmo pacing beside him.

The front door creaks. Mom's outside. He'll be ready for me soon.

I race downstairs to the cellar and throw open the lid of the tool kit, digging around the pliers and wrenches, sifting through nails and snips of wire. No tape. I scan the room. We should have rolls of it—duct tape, electrical tape, surgical tape. I dig in the first aid kit, finding a small roll and yanking off a jagged piece.

"Lark, let's go!"

"One second!"

My throat burns as I try to swallow down the fear.

"Lark, now!"

My heart races and I feel wild as I push the kit back on the shelf, holding the tape on my thumb. Where will I put the note? Someplace they'll see but Dad won't? The door? The mailbox?

"Lark!"

His feet on the stairs, and he can't find me down here with empty hands. I grab a handful of batteries from the box on the shelf and shove them in my pockets. I wipe my eyes, catching the sob in my throat. Should I have written the location of the cabin? No, not enough time to describe a place without a specified location.

I crumple the note and shove it in my pocket. Press the tape against my jeans.

They couldn't find us, even if they tried.

We'll be back. Eventually.

Bug outs aren't meant to last forever.

The cabin looks smaller than I remember, the gray afternoon light peeking through the gaps in sealant I didn't repair this summer. Winter will blow through those spaces, too, sharp cold to pinch our cheeks. I hope it doesn't snow. Up ahead, Dad drives his motorcycle over the south hill to scan for invisible followers. Mom and I park near the cabin while Gizmo races around the edge of the dam, already splashing and barking and flicking up mud. No use trying to hide with him around.

After a few circles around the perimeter, Dad buzzes down to the cabin, parking so close to us Mom has to jump back.

"What are you standing around for? You know what to do."

"I just did inventory a month ago," I say.

"Well, it isn't a month ago, so count it again."

"I'll make dinner!" Mom says, stepping between us.

"Why? It's the middle of the goddamn afternoon," Dad says.

Mom flinches before reaching for his hands. "It's always nice to have a snack. Some soup?"

"We don't have a fire made yet. How are you going to make soup?"

"Some sandwiches?"

"We'll get started inside," I say, grabbing Mom's arm and pulling her up the cabin steps. She pauses at the door, her hair blowing in the wind. Her eyes dance along the stove, the bed (her first quilt), the shelves of jars we canned together.

"I love it here," she says, her palms pressed on the cold stove. "We used to spend every summer out here. Did you know that? It wasn't nice then. Not like this. Just the cabin your dad had finished that fall and some blankets. But he did fill it up with jars of wildflowers."

How she can be here, now, and be thinking about wildflowers?

Mom sees what she wants, hears what she wants, tells herself the lullaby to put herself to sleep.

"Will you count the supplies in this one?" I push one of the containers toward her. "On the top is the list. You just have to check that the numbers are the same. It should all be there since I just did it, but we need to count it again."

This time we can't be careless with the inventory. We're seventeen miles from the house and our major first aid supplies. All we've got now is the travel kit.

Mom sits on the edge of the bed, the tub on the floor between her feet. One by one, she pulls out the items, holding them for a moment in her hand before setting them around her, a bed of bandages. While she works, I crank the radio, testing for the AM station that we can access on dry days. The propane tank for the lantern is empty, so I replace it with one of the last three. I prop a few candles in mason jars, filling them with sand so they stand upright in case we need them. When the propane runs out. Three tanks. Seven to nine hours. Multiply. Twenty-one. A few short evenings of manufactured light.

Gizmo races back inside, torn between us and Dad outside chopping firewood.

Mom yawns. "I wish we could stay out here forever."

No. She doesn't. Not really.

"It's nice, just the three of us. Oh, and you, too, Gizmo. Wouldn't forget about you." She squeezes his face, his tongue heavy against her palm. "If only we could bring the babies. Then our whole family would be here."

Augustine. Ashton. Aspen. Avery. Ave.

I might have learned from them. Together we might have been more.

"This will be fine," Mom repeats. "Everything's going to be okay. We've got a fire. Our family. Some fresh food. See, Lark? We've got all we need here. Anything we could ever want."

Mom smiles at a tube of capsaicin cream. I don't tell her she's wrong.

I think she already knows.

CHAPTER 34

*P*hotosynthesis *making that easier?* That's his favorite one. He spatters me with the others while I collect kindling or fish off the edge of the dock. *Algebra helping you with that?* I crack the ice on Gizmo's water bowl. Seal the cabin with old T-shirts. *Gonna eat a poem for lunch?* He smiles afterward, an attempt at shared laughter, but he doesn't know how bad the words sting.

He's not wrong. Two weeks here, and the questions still swirl around me, but I don't reach for them. They're not necessary to get the job done. The fire cools even if I don't know why it turns the wood black. School—a real education—was for a life I don't have. Alex talks about college. Moving to Seattle or another city out west. Becoming an engineer. A journalist. A guidance counselor. He'll need school for that future. A diploma, he says, a résumé.

For me, for this, all that work would be nothing more than paper.

The plants would still grow even if I didn't know about photosynthesis.

***

I spend an entire day guessing which school period I'd be in if I was still attending Willow Creek. Algebra just as it gets light. Hunger pains—Yo está hambre—hambro?

Dad says he can tell the time by looking at the sun. I never checked if he was right.

I build the second fire. Biology.

Me gusta la escuela.

The days go by faster when they're broken into even chunks.

A shout from over the hill. A low hum.

"What was that?"

Mom doesn't move under her blanket. I turn to Gizmo, whose dark eyes are ready to respond. "Dad?"

Gizmo barks, and I close the door behind me, racing to the motorcycle before heading toward the sound. The horizon is a blur, swirls of ice as the wind picks up the morning frost that never thawed. I'm calm as I climb the hill, though I sense I shouldn't be. Back and forth I scan the shades of brown, and then I see it, down the ravine to my left, hidden in the thicket. A flash of red. A boot. The wheel of his dirt bike twisted beneath the branches.

My bike drops feet from his body. His eyes are closed, his left arm draped across his chest like he's taking a nap across the cab seats. I search his face, too peaceful, my hands skimming the rest of his body. His Carhartt pants are torn. There's a red scrape along his temple. If his eyes were open, I wouldn't be so afraid.

Gizmo paces around me, his cold nose against Dad's cheek, but still he doesn't wake. I press my ear to his nose, but the wind's blowing too hard for me to tell what's coming from his lungs. Dad's eyes flicker open.

"Dad!"

"Larkie? Is my bike okay?"

Scuffed handlebars. The left brake lever dangles.

"It'll be fine. Can you get up?"

His eyes close, pulled back to sleep.

"Move!" I shout at Gizmo, pushing him with one hand as I press the other under Dad's chest. I heave him up and he groans, his eyes open but unseeing. His arms flop behind him, and I set him back down on the ground.

"Daddy, you've got to get up."

"Just let me lie here a minute." He retreats into his hood, like it's a summer day by the pond and he's going to nap while we wait for the fish to bite. "That old rig isn't worth shit."

"What? Dad?"

"Oil all over and we're gonna be late."

He's not making sense. On my knees, I roll him onto his side, then hug both arms tight around and pull him up.

"Larkie," he sighs as his legs tighten underneath him. He winces, pulling weight off his left foot. I don't see any blood. Or bone. But it could be hidden in his boot. I drape his arm over my shoulders, and his head tilts back. He smells of sweat and oil grease, and I'm grateful there isn't any blood. We almost fall when I lean to get the bike, but somehow, we're both on, Dad straddled behind me. I pull his arms tighter around my waist, hoping he doesn't slide off on the way back to the cabin. He moans each time the bike lurches, sucking his breath in quick pulls, and I don't know what will hurt him worse: the pain of the ride or not getting him there fast enough.

"Mom, get up!" I shout from the cabin door. She rolls over, her face hidden under the sheet. "Mom, now!"

Something in my voice triggers her, because she flaps the blanket back.

"Oh, god, Brett!" she screams, her voice small and afraid.

"Get out of the way. I need to set him down."

Mom moves as I drop him to the bed, his eyes closed again, his mouth gaping.

"What happened?"

"Crashed the bike. I don't know exactly, but we have to get him back to the house."

"But the first aid kit——" Mom reaches for the tub, and I stop her.

"I don't think it's enough for this."

"His face. Did he hit his head?"

"I don't know! We'll check him at the house, but we need to get the other bike. Come on."

"But he can't be by himself," Mom says.

"It's only for two minutes."

"He could have a concussion. He can't sleep . . . Brett." She brushes back his hair and I yank her arm.

"Come now!"

Again, another parent behind me, this time Mom's fingers tight around my stomach. Over the hill, following my tracks and we're at the bike. It looks mostly okay, but maybe it's like him, the broken parts hidden inside, not visible until we try to ride it. Together, Mom and I pull the bike out from under buckbrush, the branches tugging at the skin of my bare hands. In minutes, we're back at the cabin.

"Stay here and lock up. I'll start with Dad. I can't go that fast with him behind me. I'm not sure he'll be able to hang on the whole way."

Mom nods, alert now and ready. Inside, Dad has rolled into a ball on the bed. I sit beside him, rock his shoulder.

"Dad, it's time. You got to get up. We have to take you home. Dad?"

"Come on, Brett," Mom tries. "We gotta go, honey."

He slurs something in response.

"What?" Mom asks.

Again, the same mix of sounds.

"Help me get him up," I tell her, and together we haul him to his feet. He limps on his left ankle, tilting over toward Mom, who sinks under his weight.

"Is the bike okay?" Dad asks, and I'm relieved for clear words.

I assure him it's fine as we lead him to the motorcycle. I sit down, scooting toward the front of the seat so he has enough room.

"Move," Dad says. "I'll drive."

"No. Just get on."

"I'm fine!" he hollers, his arms grasping for the handle-bars. I swat him back.

"Brett, let her drive," Mom says, guiding him onto the seat behind me. "Hold on a sec!"

Mom races back toward the house.

"We don't have time!"

She comes back out with a wool stocking cap and pulls it over his head, her fingers pausing to hold his cheeks. She hands me a bungee cord. "In case he starts to fall off."

I doubt that will help, but it's all we have.

"Close up and then go," I say. "I'll see you at home."

Mom catches up to us at the end of the pasture, just as the

cow path turns into a worn dirt road. The bikes buzz side by side as we pass the Quonset. In a second, we'll see the house through the shelterbelt.

Alex.

His truck parked out front. I gasp, the cold burning my throat. He's here. How?

The sun is beginning to dip below the hills when we pull into the drive. Alex stands on the front step, the strands of his hair blowing underneath his cap.

"Alex, help me!" I scream, and he leaps down the stairs, stuttering on the ice. Together, we support Dad's shoulders and back him off the Honda. He's asking about his bike again. Mom rushes up the steps, disappearing into the house.

"What happened?"

"He crashed the dirt bike. He's barely talking. How . . . why are you here?"

Alex hoists Dad's arm over his shoulders, clutching Dad's hand in his to hold him steady. "Mike said the house had been dark for a while. I started driving by every evening to see when you got home. I spotted your bikes coming over the hill."

We hobble a few steps closer to the house. "Can you help me get him inside?"

"What? No. He needs to go to the hospital."

I've never been to a hospital. Dad says people go into hospitals but never come out. It looks like it's just his ankle, but his slurred words and the repeated questions—what if there's something else, something inside we can't see. Death pooled inside him waiting to seep out.

Like the babies.

"Are you sure? Maybe it's just—"

"He could have a concussion," Alex says. "Internal bleeding. Shock. That can kill him, too."

"Larkie," Dad coughs, his throat dry like my eyes.

"You're okay," I say, not knowing if he is. People die on farms. Tom Johnson down the road suffocated in the grain bin when I was six, the kernels of wheat covering his body and filling his lungs. A little girl in Wolf Point was run over by a tractor last summer.

People die on farms.

"You know how to get there?" I ask.

"The Wolf Point hospital is only forty-five minutes. I'll go ninety or a hundred."

I glance at Dad's face, but he doesn't register the word "hospital." I should feel a yes, but I don't.

"Lark! What's there to think about? He has to go the hospital."

I shake my head. I can't think. *Listen to Alex.* "Okay! Fine. Let's go."

We change our path, moving toward the truck. I open the back cab door, and then run around to the other side. Crawling onto the seat, I reach for him.

"Get in, Daddy."

He steadies himself on the doorframe, asking again about the bike, the oil, then crawls until his body is in the cab, his chest heaving with the effort. Alex bends his legs to rest on the dusty floorboards, before gently closing the door. I move the seat belt from under Dad's cheek.

"Is the bike okay?" he asks again.

"Yes, just rest, okay? You're going to be . . ." I don't finish because I don't want to lie.

"What are you doing?" Mom stands at the top of the steps, one hand on the door. The wind catches her open jacket and she pulls it closed. "Get him inside."

"We're going to take him to the hospital," I say, closing the door to the back seat. Alex is already behind the wheel. "Come with us."

"No. No hospitals," she argues.

"Get in, Lark," Alex says, his hands already on the wheel. We could go. Should go.

Mom races down the stairs, slipping on the final one and bracing herself on the railing.

"He has to go," I say. "He's barely awake. He could have a concussion . . . or" — *What's the word?* — "shock."

"He doesn't want to go to the hospital!" Mom says, yanking open the back door across from me. "Get him in the house. Alex, help us!"

Alex looks from her to me. He grabs the door handle, and I hold up a hand to stop him. Mom leans into the truck. "Get up, Brett, we gotta go."

Dad sits swaying, blinking too many times. He vomits out the open door.

"It's okay, honey," Mom says, wiping his chin with her hand. "Let's get you to bed."

"Mom! Stop! We have to go to the hospital."

I've never been to one. I don't know what lurks inside those walls, but I also don't know what will happen if we take him in the house.

The babies didn't die at the hospital. They died here.

"Please, Mom, Alex, we have to take him somewhere he can get help."

"No," Mom says, leading Dad up the stairs. "No hospitals. Your dad stays here. With me."

"But he could die!"

We could carry him, Alex and me, pull him out of her arms and back into the truck. We could take him to the hospital. But then they're inside, and I'm here by the truck waiting.

"Lark," Alex calls as I race up the stairs.

Inside, Dad sits on their unmade bed, the sheets still scattered and wrinkled, like Mom rolled out only minutes ago. She kneels on the floor, pulling off his jeans. Beside her, his boots lie in a pile, dried mud speckling the carpet. His left ankle is double the size of the right, the skin red, almost purple.

"Stop staring and help!" Mom says. "Start a fire so we can get some water boiling. Alex, can you do that?"

I didn't notice him behind me.

"Yes, ma'am."

Fear rushes in to fill his space.

"In my medicine cabinet, get my lavender essential oil, the tub of arnica salve, the bottle of fish oil. Bring those first. Once the water's boiling, make him turmeric tea. You remember how?"

My sprained ankle. When I was twelve. Lemon, honey, pepper, water. Turmeric, of course. "Yes."

"When you're finished, run to the shed and see if you can find some pieces of wood for a splint and maybe a few strips of cloth," Mom adds. "You can rip my dress in the laundry, the old blue one, if you can't find anything else."

Dad sinks back into the pillows, his face relaxing, and maybe Mom was right and it's better if he's here. He would have been terrified to realize he was in a hospital. The stress might have made it all worse.

"Oh, and bring a bowl of yogurt. Now!"

After I drop off the medicine with Mom, I head to the kitchen for the tea. Alex kneels over the wood stove, a pile of kindling at his feet.

"We can still take him to the hospital," Alex whispers as he strikes a match. "The two of us can carry him. It's not too late."

"He's in bed now." I grab a metal pot from the shelf and quickly run to the pantry to fill it with filtered water. We both stand over the stove and watch the water, willing the tiny bubbles to form at the base. Why does that happen? Why do they collect on the bottom before pushing to the top?

"You know that's not enough. Why are you listening to her?"

"He doesn't want to go to the hospital."

"I bet he wants to be alive," Alex says. "Besides, he's so in and out of it that we could easily get him there and looked at before he even realized what happened."

Arnica. Turmeric tea. Bandages. These will work.

Maybe.

I don't know.

"Your mom doesn't really know what she's doing. Tea isn't going to fix a severe concussion. Or whatever other internal injuries we're missing."

I ignore him. "I have to go to the shed."

I leave Alex at the stove and race outside where the sun has set behind the hills. I need to check on the chickens. And feed the cats.

I need my dad to stay alive.

It's hard to find anything in the shed, and my arm catches on a nail, tearing my skin. I finally find a few extra sticks we used for garden stakes and rush back to the pantry to grab Mom's blue dress, still draped across the basket waiting for me to wash and hang.

Inside the bedroom, Mom has cleaned Dad's legs, which stick out the bottom of the blanket she's folded up and over his chest.

"Hold these," she tells Alex, and he presses two sticks against the ankle. She wraps and wraps, tighter and tighter, Dad wincing at each pull.

"He needs to sleep now," Mom says, pulling the covers down. His chest rises slowly beneath Mom's palms.

"I thought you aren't supposed to sleep if you have a concussion," Alex says.

"No," Mom argues. "He can sleep. We just have to watch him."

In the kitchen, Alex leans against the counter while I make the turmeric tea. Yellow specks fall from the shaking spoon.

"I hope you know what you're doing," Alex says.

Boiling water sputters out of the kettle, splashing the counter, stinging my hands. Alex takes it, sets it down. His arms around me, squeezing tighter as I shake.

"I'm sorry," he whispers, his lips against my ear. On my forehead. Finding my mouth. "I shouldn't have said that."

I hold tighter, nestling into his neck.

"I'm really glad you're back. I came every day."

"I tried to leave a note."

"What happened? Was it Ms. Bearcub? She came?"

I nod, pulling back to wipe the drips on my face with my shirt. Mom's singing a lullaby in the bedroom, the one she made up for the babies.

"What if he gets worse?" I ask. What if I made the wrong choice?

"Then we'll take him to the hospital."

That's right. A no today can be a yes tomorrow. The beginning doesn't have to determine the ending.

I reach for Alex, grateful, for now, to be home.

Yogurt

Things It Cures	Things It Can't
Headache	A concussion
Cancer	Broken bones
Stomachache	Shock
Constipation	*Mental health issues*
Diarrhea	
Cuts, especially ones that smell	
Yeast infection (pain in private area)	
A cold	
High blood pressure	

CHAPTER 35

We're supposed to be taking shifts, one up while the other rests, but instead we both watch him sleep. Dad's body forms a V, his feet and head lifted by a stack of pillows. A hot water bottle tucked by his side. He was awake long enough for Mom to feed him a bowl of bone broth and some of the turmeric tea. We thought he might throw up again. He didn't.

Deep purple and red lines streak his left ankle, the color of my favorite sunsets. He flinches in his dreams, the pain not taking a rest or maybe he's remembering the crash. With the swelling, Mom says his ankle could be broken. They have names. I saw that on the internet. *Fibia*? *Tibia*? I don't know. *Bones*.

It's his head we're worried about. Every hour, Mom calls his name. *Brett. Wake up.* For a few seconds, I can't breathe while I wait to make sure he does. Mom checks his pupils to see if they're dilated, a message from his body that something's wrong. So far, they look the same.

Waiting and watching. For swelling, for dilated pupils, a fever from an infection, slurred words, memories he can't piece together. All signs of something I'll recognize but not understand.

I close my eyes and try to remember the pictures I saw of the body, the way the red and blue lines stretched across bones, organs with jobs I didn't know existed. If I could see inside, I would know the moment something goes wrong. A chance to catch it before it's too late.

Instead, we wait.

The chickens are dead.

A coyote, probably. Maybe a raccoon.

Dad would say it's collateral damage of a bug out. To be expected when we left without closing the coop.

I call it a waste.

"How's your dad?"

Alex shakes some Skittles into my hand, a collection of bright-colored sugar. He's been bringing me different treats to try every night after his practice when we sit together in the truck. The engine runs so we have heat, but Alex says he isn't worried about the gas. Doritos, chips in a tube, a tiny chocolate cake called a brownie, a Snickers, a Kit Kat, little sour kids that burned my tongue. I like Peanut M&M's the best so far.

A sweet and salty rebellion. Or it would have been a few months ago. Now it's just better-tasting food.

"His ankle any better?"

I shake my head. Nothing's better. He can't put weight on that leg, so he hobbles around the house using an old broom as a walking stick. His memory is fine and his scratches have hardened into scabs, but he's angry all the time. Yelling at Mom when she wraps his bandage wrong (too tight or too loose—she can never get it right). Tossing books across the room when his head hurts too much to read. I don't know why. Maybe the accident or ending the bug out early or even Ms.

Bearcub showing up a month ago. He's raw now, an exposed wire, and I have to work to avoid the shock.

He hasn't called me Larkie since the cabin.

"Not really," I say. "The swelling came down a little, but it might be broken. We'll never know."

Alex frowns. "You know you could, right?"

"Could what?"

"Know if it's broken."

I stare at him, imagining Dad's ankle like an engine I'd have to take apart to find the oil leak. "You can?"

"Yeah. At the hospital. They can do an X-ray. Even for his head, they could have run an MRI or a CT scan. See if he had a concussion." He digs his phone out of his pocket, pressing buttons before turning the screen toward me. Black-and-white photos with shapes like smoke or morning fog.

"See, that's a broken ankle on an X-ray. This one's really bad, obviously. Look how the broken piece has sort of curved up?"

I glance at my boots, wishing for bare feet so I could see the outlines of my own bones. "And what are those?"

"Pins. To hold the ankle together."

Tibia. It's printed over one of the pictures. I was right. I scroll through a few more photos, the same shadowy shapes with small differences. "They can do this for the brain, too?"

"It's a different machine because your brain isn't a bone, but yeah, here—"

He reaches out his phone, and suddenly I don't want to see. Not now, when it doesn't matter, when they'll only be pictures of someone else's problems. Problems they let a doctor solve. I try to swallow, my throat tight.

"Who do you play this weekend?" I ask, hoping he'll move away from the pictures with me. I sort the candy in my hand by color while I listen to Alex talk about the team who will crush them, his teammates who are still too young and inexperienced to hold up to a strong defense. Something about his shot percentage. My brain keeps traveling back to those pictures, wondering what we'd see if we had any of Dad's ankle, his brain.

I pop the rest of the red Skittles in my mouth.

CHAPTER 36

A thud. Then a grunt from the bedroom. I set the lantern I was rewiring down on the table. Dad's slumped against the bathroom door when I get to him, his face drained, white fingers clinging to the doorframe. He holds his hurt ankle out like he's balancing on a fence. I drape his arm over my shoulder.

"You're supposed to call me when you need something." Dad groans when his toes touch the carpet. He hops a step, his weight setting me off-balance. "I said I'd come if you needed me."

"I can take a shit without my daughter hovering over me."

No. He can't, not without me waiting outside the door. In case he faints again. Or like now, gets too tired to make it back. He can't do much on his own these days, as much as we both hate it. It's not helping him that I mind. It's his refusal to let me.

And the fear in seeing him like this and constantly wondering if it could still get worse.

Dad winces as I lay him back in bed. The sheets are crumpled, sweat hardening the folds. If it wasn't so damn cold outside, I'd open a window because it's starting to smell in here. I fluff the stack of pillows under his feet, then carefully move the ankle up. It's too big in my hands, the swelling forcing it into the size of small squash. The place around the bone is especially large, a perfectly round bulb. The color of the bruise has changed, too, a darkened purple like the winter afternoon.

Hidden under a blanket, his ankle looks fine. Probably why he thinks it is—the sheets concealing what he doesn't want to know, though he must feel it. The pain forces the truth. The scratches on his face have hardened into scabs. Dark circles under his eyes. Pale cheeks but otherwise he looks like himself, like normal.

But he's not.

"Do you need anything?" I ask. "I can bring you another book?"

He shakes his head, his brown hair flopping over his eyes. He needs a haircut. I might be able to get him to the kitchen. I've never done it before, but I've watched Mom enough times. And I know his hair.

When I was little, he loved to have me brush it. Evenings after he got back from chores, he'd sit on the living room floor, his head resting on the edge of my chair. Back and forth, I'd brush the thin brown strands, sometimes finding scraps of hay or revealing a mole or the scar he got from a boating accident with his cousin. He'd fall asleep, every time, and I'd stop, but the moment I set the brush down, he'd whisper, "Just a minute more, Larkie."

"I want you to check the bike again," Dad says, shifting under the sheets. "Really take a good look at the gas line."

There's nothing wrong with the gas line. No sand. No water. No cuts. The tires are bald and the chassis is cracked, but it's been that way for years.

"The line is fine."

"You're missing something."

"I'm not."

"I know she messed with that bike."

Ms. Bearcub didn't sabotage his motorcycle. She came to check on me, my education, not blow up his bike. I've thought about telling him the truth about why she came to the farm, but it wouldn't matter. She'd still be the government and the only reason he could possibly have crashed that day.

Dad rubs at his cracked lips. "Just look, okay. How hard is it to just look?"

"I'll check tomorrow. Let me see your ankle now."

I roll down the wool sock, and he sucks in a breath when I hit the biggest part. Every time I hear it—that quick intake of air, followed by the few seconds of silence as he holds his breath—I wish I had taken him to the hospital. Alex's worries have become mine: concussion, brain bleed, shock. One of the early nights while Mom and Dad were both sleeping, I tried to look up information on the computer. I wanted pictures, images of broken ankle bones so I could compare.

I didn't know his password, even though I guessed my name. Mom's. The babies'. Birthdates. *Justice. Freemen.* Nothing.

Maybe if we had just taken him, if Alex had driven away to the hospital in Wolf Point, he would be better. He could have been healed before he even woke up, before he realized where he was. He would have been mad, yes, but he wouldn't have been in pain. And even if he claimed the hospital was worthless and he would have been fine at home, I wouldn't have to watch him like this. I just needed to say yes. To not share his fears of places I've never known.

He was wrong about 9/11. He left things out about the Freemen. He's probably wrong about hospitals, but even if I didn't believe him, I wasn't brave enough to do anything about it. I didn't have the courage to stand up to either of them. I remove the once frozen rag and set it on the floor.

"Is it hurting right now? Do you want some more turmeric tea? I can rub some arnica cream on it?"

"It's fine," he huffs.

"It doesn't look like it's getting better."

"It takes time."

"But the swelling isn't going down. Mom said if it was a sprain the swelling would get better."

"It'll be fine. We're doing RICE."

"What?"

"Rest. Ice. Cooling. Evaluation." He shakes his head. "No, elevation. Whatever. It's what you're supposed to do for a sprained ankle."

"But what if it's not sprained, what if it's broken?"

"It's not."

"How do you know?"

"I would know if my ankle was broken, and it's not broken. It's just sprained."

The skin is cool and damp, the veins small creeks off the purple swell. My fingertips leave dents like hail on the truck hood.

"Damn! Don't touch it."

"Mom says we should try and stretch it."

She said that. A week ago. Back when she was whirling nonstop—cooking more food than we could eat, washing his sheets every day and bringing him fresh cups of tea. She never left his bedside. Never slept, even when I begged her to go lie down in my room. That light went out last week, and now she wakes from a nap only to come lie beside him, her body curled next to his as she falls into another sleep. Now I'm alone to guess what he needs, trying to remember directions she gave that might be right but maybe cause more harm than good. We might be putting gasoline in a diesel engine. It seems like he's going to survive this, but what about next time? He can't die, can't leave me here on this broken-down farm with a crumbling mom.

"Goddamn, that hurts like hell." Dad clenches the side of the mattress. The ankle barely moves in my hands, but I keep trying, tilting it back and forth, rotating it in small circles.

"If . . . if it doesn't get better, would you consider seeing someone?"

"Like who?"

His heel is heavy in my hand. "Like someone who knows about injuries like this."

"I don't need a doctor."

"You might."

"There is nothing that would make me trust one of those pompous assholes. I'd rather be dead."

Really? Would he truly rather die? Maybe.

They said the farm is the only reason I'm alive, but we lost other babies after we came here. Those weren't the doctors' fault.

Maybe it was theirs—Mom and Dad. Losing the babies didn't have to be an inevitability. Maybe they had a choice to make things different.

9/11. Racist Freemen. A sabotaged motorcycle. Is he really afraid of what would happen in the hospital or does he just not want to be wrong?

"What would happen, if you went to the hospital?"

"It won't help, Lark! Doctors just take your money. They don't care about making you better."

"So, if we went, they wouldn't do anything? They wouldn't even look at it?"

"They wouldn't do anything worthwhile."

"Maybe they could tell if it was broken. Maybe there's something else I should be doing." Anger burns in my throat, and I tilt my head to keep the tears from collecting. "I might be hurting you."

"No. We're doing what we need to. RICE."

"How do you even know RICE works? You don't! You're not a doctor! You drive a truck! One you can't even fix yourself."

"You need to get out of here, Lark, before you say something else you're gonna regret."

His gray eyes don't see me. I take his hand in mine.

"Please, Daddy, I can't do this. I don't know how to help you."

He pulls away, looking at me like I'm an outsider. "Then why don't you shut up and go check the damn bike."

Silently, I pull the sheet back over his foot, carefully tucking the edges beneath his heel. I grab the wet cloth from the floor and walk toward the door. I wish there was something I could say, a way to dig him out from under the grains of fear he's letting suffocate him. Truth could pull him out if only he'd grab on.

But he won't. He chooses this story of the world. He chooses this pain. Someday, maybe he'll even choose death.

Because of fear? Or pride? It doesn't matter, because Dad is not sure about some things and one hundred percent sure about everything else.

About this *I* am sure: I will not live my life by old answers to new questions. I won't ignore the things I know to be true simply because he's told me different.

And I can't do this anymore.

CHAPTER 37

It's so warm in Alex's truck that I don't have to wear my coat. Between us is chocolate that looks and smells like an orange. Alex whacked it against the dash, breaking it into the small slices we now share.

"Close your eyes," Alex says, and I shake my head.

"I don't want to do that."

No more surprises. Nothing good happens when I open my eyes again.

"That's okay," Alex says as he reaches behind the truck seat to pull out a rectangle wrapped in paper covered with holly. A big red bow is tied in the middle.

"What is this?"

Alex laughs. "It's your Christmas present. It's Christmas Eve tomorrow."

I didn't realize how much time had passed. Christmas changes every year depending on Dad's location and Mom's energy for decorations. This year, it would have come and gone without us noticing.

"You can save it for tomorrow if you want, or you can open it now." From his face, I can tell he wants me to open it with him.

I tug at the smooth bow, not sure what's it's made of. Not fabric. I've never had a present wrapped in anything other than pillowcases or just the cardboard box. I slide my hand under the seams so as not to tear it.

"I should have known you'd be one of those people," Alex says.

"What?"

"You can rip it. I'll bring you some fresh wrapping paper if you want it."

A few more slides of my finger, and I lift out a heavy white book. I flip it over.

The Human Body. Two bodies side by side: one of bones staring at one covered in muscles. Illustrations of parts of us I don't recognize. I flip a few pages—cells, skin, a few words I can't read—but always pictures. Pages and pages that will let me see inside.

"Alex . . . " I brush back the wetness on my cheek.

"I thought you'd like it."

"I didn't get you anything."

He smiles. "Watching you cry about a book is enough."

I skip deeper into the pages—heart disease, the immune system, purple lines like the highways on Dad's map. It's a few minutes before I realize the cab is silent and Alex is watching me. "How long are you going to do this, Lark?"

"Do what?"

"Stay home. Take care of your dad. Do all the chores by yourself. You're not eating enough. I can tell."

I finally got Mom to stop opening jars, cracking the lids on containers that were supposed to last us until summer. We didn't have that many to begin with. I've tried hunting on my own, but I'm still afraid to leave Dad for long hours now that Mom is sleeping again.

Mental health, Ms. Bearcub called it. Mom's problem. I like that I know its name, even if I can't do anything about it.

"As long as I need to," I say, closing the book.

Alex frowns. "So, what? You're done with the school thing?"

"I didn't say that."

"Fine. What are you saying?"

I think about it all the time. The order of my life. The story of me. The packets and Dad's speeches and the blurry words I couldn't put together and Willow Creek and Mavis Beacon Typing and the tiny cells on the computer screen. The government, the lies, Dad's invisible wounds. I rub a circle into the steam on the passenger window.

"They need me right now, but it won't be like this forever. Then I'll decide."

"Decide what? Are you going back to Ms. Bearcub?"

I shake my head. "No. Talking to her was too much. She's government. She's an outsider. I should have known this would have happened when I let her come here. She won't actually be able to help me, not with this."

"Then what?" Alex asks.

"I need to ask someone else."

CHAPTER 38

We pull into Grandma Betty's driveway, the tires of Alex's truck cutting lines in the smooth white snow.

"Someone should shovel that for her," Alex says as he turns off the engine. "Does she have one? I can do it."

"Probably in her garage. Or on the back porch."

"I'll do that instead of waiting in the truck. Unless you want me just to wait."

It doesn't matter, really, where he is, as long as he's nearby while Grandma Betty and I are alone. I need to have this conversation by myself.

Alex hangs by the truck door as I climb the stairs. A green wreath covered in tiny red bows is dusted with snow. The drapes on her picture window are closed, but I don't see her peering out. I ring the doorbell. Soon, the soft shuffle of her house slippers on the linoleum floor. The door creaks open.

"Look what the cat dragged in."

"Hi, Grandma."

She shoves a rumpled tissue into the front of her apron pocket, before looking over my shoulder. "Who's your friend?"

Alex waves, mimes shoveling the snow.

"That's Alex."

"What's he doing standing out in the snow?"

"He's gonna shovel your driveway for a minute while we talk."

Grandma raises an eyebrow, stepping back as she opens

the door wider. "That sounds serious. The shovel's on the back porch."

I gesture to Alex, who gives me a thumbs-up before disappearing around the side of the house. Without an answer, I follow her inside.

"And your mom? Where's she?" Grandma asks as she sets a pan of M&M bars—I recognize the letters and the colors—on the table.

"Home."

Grandma nods before grabbing the kettle and filling it with water at the sink. In the corner of the living room is a small silver tree with blue ornaments, three large socks hanging from the shelf, held down by Mom's high school pictures. Looking around this house, I wonder how Mom went from being a person who drank pop and ate grocery-store meat and watched movies and danced on the drill team to who she is now. Yes, the babies, I know the story, but with Dad, it seems like the wondering, the distrust has always been a part of him. He's someone who questions. Who disbelieves. He says he always was an outsider, even when he lived in town.

But not Mom. Once, she showed me pictures of her senior year scrapbook—sitting in the back of pickup trucks, painted jeans at a parade, a sparkly prom dress and a boy who wasn't Dad. Those moments were her life. Maybe once that ended, she had too much empty space, a mind without wondering, so Dad's ideas had room to grow. Squash vines that took over the carrots.

Me, I was even more empty, ready to be filled from the start. Each idea of Dad's latching onto the others, blooming and twisting until everything I knew, he had told me. What he believed, I never questioned.

And somehow, I cut them back. Snips here and there to make space for my ideas and my wonderings. My beliefs, my understanding haven't taken over, but they're present now. A comeback.

Which is why I'm here.

If I had a few years to wait, it's possible Grandma and I would come to love each other and this question would be easier to ask. But I'm out of time and out of choices.

Grandma fed me for a year, baked the Saturday dinner even if she wasn't sure we would come. She wanted me to go to school. Wanted a different life for me, maybe even the one I want for myself.

I need her to say yes.

Grandma sets a metal tin of packaged tea in front of me. She pulls out an I Love Lemon, setting the wrapper on a saucer she brought just for that. Hot Cinnamon. Earl Grey. Perfectly Mint. Constant Comment.

"They're all good," she says, and I grab the mint since it sounds the most familiar.

"How's your mom?"

Sleeping. Quiet. *Mental health issues.*

"She's okay."

"And your dad?"

Broken. Angry. *Mental health issues*, too?

"Not great. He wrecked his motorcycle a while back. His ankle isn't healing well."

Grandma grunts, sips her tea. "I bet he didn't go see a doctor."

"No."

I let the tea warm my hands, watching out the window as Alex scoops another path, tossing the snow onto the lawn. I wait for him to look up, hoping he'll see me, wave, but he jogs to the garage door and starts again.

"He your boyfriend?"

"I don't know." She laughs, but it doesn't really matter. He's my friend, the person I need. "We haven't really talked about it."

"Well, what do *you* want to talk about? You said you're not here to chitchat."

I've been practicing the words all week though I'm not confident that what I say really matters, if I even have the ability to influence her. Grandma Betty's tough—stubborn, Mom says, like Dad. I couldn't convince him. It might be the same way here, no matter what I say. But I'm hopeful there's a chance.

I dip my tea bag in the water, watching it bob, sending darker swirls throughout the murky water.

"I want to go to public school. Here, in Wolf Point." A small nod, maybe, I hope. I keep going, my eyes on my cup. "But if I do, I'll need to live in town. For three years."

I pause. No response. Not just yet.

"If I were to stay here, with you, I'd get a job to help pay for myself. Alex said I could get a waitress job or maybe even a CNA position at the hospital, like Mom did."

Grandma folds her hands in her lap. "Your parents okay with this?"

Without having asked them, I already know the answer. I take another sip of tea.

"I didn't think they could do it," Grandma says, her eyes on me. "Back when they had their wild idea to move out to the farm and live off the land. I didn't think some fresh tomatoes were going to change your mom and the babies, but then she had you."

Out the window, we watch skiffs of snow start to fall.

"Big ideas, that's what they had. Dreams. But you can't raise a baby on bright ideas."

She wraps her wrinkled fingers around her cup.

"Maybe I should have pushed her harder. Told her you needed better. I didn't think she'd listen. That girl never did." She takes a sip. Looks at me. Curls her wrinkled hand around mine. "I can make up the guest bedroom. It's full of boxes right now for the Knights of Columbus can drive. I'll move those."

A release through my chest, my stomach, down to my cold toes. A yes.

I have to tell Alex.

"When you thinking you'll move in?"

Soon. But first, I have to tell them.

"Do you want to be my boyfriend?" I ask later, on the drive home.

Alex looks down at our interlocked fingers. "I thought I already was."

That sounds right.

# CHAPTER 39

The first thing I ever fixed was a broken fishing rod. I'd do a better job now—use a welder, a new piece of metal—but it was easy to do. The steps laid out like a manual in my head. Twisted line, cracked rod, electrical tape and patience. As the machines got more complicated, the fixes still slid into my mind. Breaks were harder to spot, but always, I knew what came next. It was a problem with a solution I could see in my hands.

Dad sits on a chair in front of me, a fresh bath towel draped around his shoulders. He's hobbling around more now, the ankle puffy but less sore, especially if he keeps his weight off it. His brown hair sticks out at all sides, some pieces stuck together even though he washed it. I set the scissors back down on the counter, picking up the brush instead. I smooth his hair into place, wondering why I can't remember what it should look like. I didn't pay attention because it wasn't my job.

"Might as well get started," Dad says. "You can't screw it up much worse than it is."

Dad used to direct Mom through every cut, holding up a mirror to watch. Lots of arguing on haircut days. Lots of Mom's tears. He doesn't seem to care about his hair anymore.

Back to the scissors, I pull a few strands between my fingers, but this time I don't know what comes next. There's not a part to connect to another. I'm not clearing straight paths with a compact mower. Just a snip, hoping for empty spaces in the right spots.

The first strands fall to the floor.

"Tell me a story, Larkie."

That's the first time he's called me that in a while. "About what?"

Another piece lands on the towel.

"Whatever you want."

Gray hairs hide within the brown, patches by his hairline, lone strands scattered throughout. The rhythm relaxes me—slide, cut, fall, and I cup his ear with my hand, careful not to nick it.

"Alex wants me to teach him to fish," I say. "This summer. He's never been."

"Mike hates fishing."

"That's what he said."

"Where will you take him? You should drive up the back roads to Fort Peck. The dredges or even out on the lake if you can get someone to loan you their boat. But you decide."

He's quiet—no other suggested locations or tips for lures. I tell him about Alex's first time hunting—a disaster—and how he says he'll never fire a rifle again. Dad's head doesn't droop, but I wonder if he's sleeping. I almost wish he would.

I'm nervous to come around front and see what I've done, but surprisingly it doesn't look that bad. Dad watches me while I pull the ends on either side of his face, lining up the length like I've watched Mom do. His breath tickles my palms.

"Did you talk to that woman, Ms. Bearcub, about wanting to go to school? That's why she came?"

Frozen, my nose so close to his, and I can't meet his

eyes. Not today. Not yet. I steady my shaking fingers. A snip. Trimmings caught on the towel.

"I got you the books."

His voice is small. It'would be easier if he was loud. I planned for that—yelling, grabbing, his fist pounding the table.

"I know."

"I did a bad job when you were younger. I know that. I shouldn't have just let you learn it all yourself, but you're smart. You're quick. Always have been."

I don't know if I'm finished cutting because I can't look at him to check. I straighten up, grabbing the comb from the counter, combing back the already drying hair. Behind him again, I run through the parts I've already finished, looking for mistakes. My fingers shake, a thrum in my chest.

Now is the time to tell him.

Gutted, a blade between my bones, but maybe that's what needs to happen for him to really see me. I suck in a breath and tell him.

No, not because of Alex. Or the books. At least, not just them.

No, Ms. Bearcub didn't force me.

No. I won't. I won't change my mind.

Regret? Maybe. But I'm willing to risk it.

The towel falls to the floor as he stands, his feet scattering the hairs beneath us. The comb clutched in my hand.

Yes, I know what this means.

Yes, I will leave.

Yes, I understand. No daughter of his.

His eyes darken, the love I know he feels for me sinking

away, out of our reach. He could hold on to it, could listen to me, choose me.

But he doesn't.

"Don't you dare come crawling back when the shit hits the fan."

Earthquakes. Atom bomb. Total collapse of society. I won't come back—I could, I might want to—but I won't need to. I can look up and see the clouds and know it's just rain. I see it now.

The truth.

"Mom?"

No answer, but I know she's awake. Maybe even heard us. The room's brighter than I expected, especially with all the lights out, but the sun coming through the open shades fills the room, extra bursts of white as it reflects off the layers of snow outside. Mom's curled away from the door, a blanket falling off her shoulders. I say her name again, but she doesn't turn.

Dad's side is still made up, the covers rumpled but unslept in. I crawl onto the bed, resting beside Mom's curved back. In her hand, she's holding a small black-and-white picture, like the X-rays Alex showed me on his phone, but different. A hollow black space, with two rounded shapes inside it.

"We never got one of these for you," Mom says. "I knew there was no way since we weren't seeing the doctor anymore, but I always wanted one. For the others, too. Just in case."

Closer, and I see it: the curves of a very small human. A baby. Our baby.

"This is Augustine." She sets the picture on her nightstand.

Then rolls over, reaches up to twirl a strand of my hair around her finger.

"I knew you were gonna make it from the beginning. You were different. Stronger than them. Constantly flipping and that kick." She smiles. "I was sick the same—couldn't get a break from that—but I just knew you'd be okay. My Lark. You were always gonna be free."

She rubs my hand with her thumb, and I wish my words weren't going to break her.

"I'm going to go live with Grandma." I pause, give her a moment to hear me. "I want to go to school, and she says I can. If I stay with her."

Mom turns, shoving the pillow underneath her neck. "School isn't that great."

"You can come see me in town. It'll be just like when you and I did it. We can even go to real mass. Or do it at the house. Whichever you want."

I lean over to see a wet stream down her face.

"I'm not leaving you."

"Yes, you are."

"No."

"Just like them."

I wrap around her, curling her fingers in mine. "I'll come back."

"*You're likely never to have children.* That's what that doctor told me. And he was right, with the babies, but then I had you, and I wanted to drive into town and march into that doctor's office that smelled like chemicals with those office ladies who looked at me like I was so pathetic and hold you up and say, 'She is mine!'"

A tighter squeeze, a deep breath in her neck.

"Turns out he was right."

My throat burns, the pillow damp beneath my cheeks.

"It's just for a while. Three years while I finish school. I'll see you. I'll come back."

Mom turns, her red eyes cold. "You told him already?"

I nod.

"Course you did. You always were a daddy's girl." She flops back over, tugging her hands from mine and folding them under her chin. "He's not going to let you back. You're as good as dead to him."

A sob because I know she's right.

"No use crying. You did this to yourself. You wanted to be free. So go."

"But you could—"

"I am not turning against my husband. My family."

But that's me. I'm her family. A streak of sun in my eye, and I wish I could close the blinds, disappear into the dark. Instead, I pull out of her arms and off their bed.

"I'll be okay," she says, to her or to me. "Just one more baby gone."

On the step, the cold stings my eyes. How cold of a temperature would it have to be for my tears to freeze? My thick gloves muffle the sounds.

I was their miracle.

They said all of this was for me—the farm, the food, home-school. It was all to keep me safe.

But it wasn't.

It was for them.

To make them feel less afraid. Which is why they'd rather let me go than stop believing the lies they need to protect themselves.

My roots are shallower than I expected. Didn't know I could be so easily pulled out.

Gizmo barks at me as if he knows I no longer belong.

CHAPTER 40

Once-upon-a-time stories are the only kind Mom likes to tell. Her favorite: the story of a beautiful princess and a daring prince and the evil doctor who told them they would never have children. But the parents knew the doctor was wrapped up in Big Pharma's lies. They knew their dreams were possible, but they'd have to leave the kingdom to make them come true.

So off they went to a magical land of grassy fields and roaming deer, to a yellow farmhouse down a secondary road. Here, in this new place, there were no chemicals to poison their bloodstream, no government spies to corrupt their minds. No television, no phones, just the sound of the birds and two beating hearts.

Then, one day, three.

Mom stops there because that's when the fantasy ends. But it's my beginning, my once upon a time. For me, there once were two dreamers and their daughter and the babies who came but still went away. Together they survived on a farm that was not magic but work. Here there were chickens to pull from the coyote's mouth and bean plants that refused to grow. The dreams of a life away from it all shriveled with time, and the family's aching bellies told the truth their mouths wouldn't.

And now, I start telling my own truth.

He wasn't all wrong. Not about the vanilla and the gnats or jeans to prevent motorcycle burns. Freedom is life-giving, but I can't have wings in name only. His ideas are marks on a map, a path I could take if I choose.

His thoughts are not mine. His fears don't have to suffocate me, too. We are two minds, not one, a father and a daughter but no longer both patriots.

They gave me this name so I would have wings.

Now it's my turn to use them.

Things I Want to Learn

Everything

A YEAR AND A HALF LATER

Sunflowers in the fall when the petals have curled. Fresh reeds along the pond. The belt on Mike's old Ford tractor. Underneath the microscope, unexpected movement, and I keep trying to connect them to something I know since I can't quite accept what they are. Cilia, with their tiny hairs— flagella—whipping them through the drop of pond water. Circular clumps of algae bunched together, moving as one. They're not better off alone.

So much green.

That's chlorophyll.

Photosynthesis. I can see it now.

A buzz in my back pocket, and I pull out my phone to see a text from Alex: *Meet me in the library at lunch.* The clock says we have ten minutes left. Normally, Ms. Red Cloud lets me eat in here so I can have longer with the microscope. Pond water. Cheek cells. Sugar crystals. Yogurt. I doubt Mom would have eaten so much had she seen the rod-shaped bacteria swarming inside. *Lactobacillus bulgaricus.*

A timer buzzes at the front of the room, and I dash notes in my journal, not worrying about spelling, just hitting the sounds. Around me, classmates pack up their lab stations, wiping away the life on their slides. I hesitate before rinsing the glass plate in the sink. Feels different when I know they're alive.

A bell, a wave, no-I'm-not-staying-today, and into the hall with students whose names I finally know. Kyla waves as she passes, says she'll see me tonight. I send a quick text to Jessica, confirming that I'll meet her Saturday at the A&W. Even though we attend different schools, we still share chili fries and onion rings every couple of weeks.

"Lark! Can I get a ride with you and Alex today?" Alisha Tapaha asks. We sit together in choir. Her brother, Johnny, is Alex's friend from basketball. My friend, too.

"Just don't be late or Alex will leave you!"

Alisha laughs, shakes her head, because she knows.

The library is crowded when I arrive, seniors lined up at tables, others hugging and taking pictures of themselves. *Selfies.* One girl sobs into her friend's shoulder. I scan the crowd and find Alex talking to a teammate next to the computers.

"You're early," Alex says after he kisses me.

"I came when the bell rang."

Alex laughs. "I know, but weren't you doing the pond water lab today? I didn't expect you for another ten minutes."

"I came now."

"Here." Alex reaches behind him and grabs a maroon square. He pulls out tabs from the bottom and adjusts a string hanging from the side. He places it on my head, the strings tickling my nose. "And this."

He drapes a silver scarf over my shoulders, pausing to squeeze them before letting go.

"Perfect!"

I grab the square off my head. "What is this?"

"It's my cap and gown. For graduation. That's the National Honor Society stole."

I slide the smooth silver fabric between my fingers. Graduation, then summer, and then he's leaving. I can't think about it just yet.

"This will be you in a couple years," Alex says, twisting his fingers into mine. "I'll come back for your graduation. Shout your name when you cross the stage."

It'll just be him and Grandma Betty. Probably.

Grandma says to give them time. It might work for Mom. She broke rules before—to eat Saturday dinner with Grandma, to send me to Willow Creek. She might decide she wants to see me. Maybe she'll come to dinner again.

She might not.

I try not to have hope about her, but it's easier to keep alive. Not with Dad. He's not sure about some things, and one hundred percent sure that I'm no longer his daughter. He raised a patriot, and that's not me.

Sometimes my life feels like a microscope slide. I thought I could see all there was—all the possibility in my days, in me. What I had on the farm was what could be.

But I wasn't seeing it all. Couldn't. Not yet. I had to switch the slide. This life with school and Alex and friends and a graduation date and a college to choose was there, waiting nearby.

Now I can see it.

"Do you need me still?" I ask Alex, and he smiles.

"I always need you."

"I mean right now."

"Not if you have to go somewhere. I just wanted to show you my stuff."

I nod. "I'm going to go back to Ms. Red Cloud's room."

He squeezes my hand. "Go. I'll see you later."

Fifteen minutes left of lunch, and I rush toward the science wing. A few drops of water. A clear plastic slide. 40x. 100x. 400x.

There's so much left to see.

ACKNOWLEDGMENTS

This book is my love letter to education and Eastern Montana, and so I have to first thank the many people who filled up my childhood, both in the public schools I attended and the small towns in which I was raised. Despite living in a city a thousand miles away, I'm forever shaped by the people and places in the part of Montana that never makes it into the brochures (although it should).

I am especially grateful to the Flux team for taking on this quiet book. The question of how we determine the truth has become even more critical, and I'm grateful Lark's story will be available to teens who might be wondering the same thing. Thank you to Mari Kesselring for first loving this book and to Kelsy Thompson for shaping it with thoughtfulness and grace. I'm grateful for how much voice Meg Gaertner offered me throughout the design process and to Millie Liu for capturing the image that started this book with her cover illustration—it's perfection. I will forever marvel at the work of copy editors, and I am especially grateful to Jackie Dever for cleaning up this manuscript and pointing out my preference for the British English "towards" despite having grown up in rural Montana. Many thanks to Heather McDonough and Taylor Kohn for their hard work getting this book onto shelves.

As always, so much gratitude to my agent, Melissa Edwards, who pushes me with tough questions and supports me through the wild ride that is publishing. Here's to many more books together.

For the past decade I've worked with the WriteByNight team, and this book owes much to the notes of Erin M. Bertram and David Duhr. Erin, you supported the poetry of this book and cheered on Lark before she was fully formed. Thank you, David, for reminding me I'm a real writer even when I don't feel like it.

The research for this book was as frightening as it was fascinating, and I had specific help from Diana Hammond, a CPS worker in Sidney, Montana, who shared her experience with families that identify as sovereign citizens. Thank you also to Stacey Parshall Jensen for her authenticity read that helped me ensure a thoughtful representation of these characters.

To Anni Lindenberg, Ria Ferich, Beth Griesmer, and Natalie Neumann—thank you for your feedback on my drafts, title ideas, and cover designs. You provide me so much support as an author and a friend.

To my parents, the first people to encourage my many questions. Thank you, Mom, a forever farm kid, for reading multiple drafts and answering questions about tractors and chokecherry jelly (not jam). Dad: you've always encouraged me to think for myself, even when it meant we didn't agree. Together you have given me wings.

And to Shiva: earthquakes, atom bomb, total collapse of society—I could survive all of it with you.

AUTHOR BIO

Bridget Farr is an author and educator. Her recent novels include BookExpo Buzz Pick *Pavi Sharma's Guide to Going Home* (LBYR 2019) and *Margie Kelly Breaks the Dress Code* (LBYR 2021). She serves as a vice principal at a public elementary school. Originally from Montana, Bridget now lives in Austin, Texas, with her husband, Shiva, and the neighborhood cat, Sherman.